THE A

General E

R. B. Ker

Additional notes and editing
Mike Gould

MACBETH

William Shakespeare

COLLINS
CLASSICS

Harper Press
An imprint of HarperCollins*Publishers*
77–85 Fulham Palace Road
Hammersmith
London W6 8JB

This edition published 2010

A catalogue record for this book is available from the British Library

ISBN-13: 978–0–00–735098–8

Printed and bound in Great Britain by Clays Ltd, St Ives plc

FSC is a non-profit international organisation established to promote the
responsible management of the world's forests. Products carrying the FSC label
are independently certified to assure consumers that they come
from forests that are managed to meet the social, economic and
ecological needs of present and future generations.

Find out more about HarperCollins and the environment at
www.harpercollins.co.uk/green

Life & Times section © Gerard Cheshire
Classic Literature: Words and Phrases adapted from
Collins English Dictionary
Typesetting in Kalix by Palimpsest Book Production Limited,
Grangemouth, Stirlingshire

4

Prefatory Note

This Shakespeare play uses the full Alexander text. By keeping in mind the fact that the language has changed considerably in four hundred years, as have customs, jokes, and stage conventions, the editors have aimed at helping the modern reader – whether English is their mother tongue or not – to grasp the full significance of the play. The Notes, intended primarily for examination candidates, are presented in a simple, direct style. The needs of those unfamiliar with British culture have been specially considered.

Since quiet study of the printed word is unlikely to bring fully to life plays that were written directly for the public theatre, attention has been drawn to dramatic effects which are important in performance. The editors see Shakespeare's plays as living works of art which can be enjoyed today on stage, film and television in many parts of the world.

CONTENTS

An Elizabethan playhouse. Note the apron stage protruding into the auditorium, the space below it, the inner room at the rear of the stage, the gallery above the inner stage, the canopy over the main stage, and the absence of a roof over the audience.

The Theatre in Shakespeare's Day

On the face of it, the conditions in the Elizabethan theatre were not such as to encourage great writers. The public playhouse itself was not very different from an ordinary inn-yard; it was open to the weather; among the spectators were often louts, pickpockets and prostitutes; some of the actors played up to the rowdy elements in the audience by inserting their own jokes into the authors' lines, while others spoke their words loudly but unfeelingly; the presentation was often rough and noisy, with fireworks to represent storms and battles, and a table and a few chairs to represent a tavern; there were no actresses, so boys took the parts of women, even such subtle and mature ones as Cleopatra and Lady Macbeth; there was rarely any scenery at all in the modern sense. In fact, a quick inspection of the English theatre in the reign of Elizabeth I by a time-traveller from the twentieth century might well produce only one positive reaction: the costumes were often elaborate and beautiful.

Shakespeare himself makes frequent comments in his plays about the limitations of the playhouse and the actors of his time, often apologizing for them. At the beginning of *Henry V* the Prologue refers to the stage as 'this unworthy scaffold' and to the theatre building (the Globe, probably) as 'this wooden O, and emphasizes the urgent need for imagination in making up for all the deficiencies of presentation. In introducing Act IV the Chorus goes so far as to say:

> ...we shall much disgrace
> With four or five most vile and ragged foils,
> Right ill-dispos'd in brawl ridiculous,
> The name of Agincourt. (lines 49–52)

In *A Midsummer Night's Dream* (Act V, Scene i) he seems to dismiss actors with the words:

> The best in this kind are but shadows.

Yet Elizabeth's theatre, with all its faults, stimulated dramatists to a variety of achievement that has never been equalled and, in Shakespeare, produced one of the greatest writers in history. In spite of all his grumbles he seems to have been fascinated by the challenge that it presented him with. It is necessary to re-examine his theatre carefully in order to understand how he was able to achieve so much with the materials he chose to use. What sort of place was the Elizabethan playhouse in reality? What sort of people were these criticized actors? And what sort of audiences gave them their living.

The Development of the Theatre up to Shakespeare's Time

For centuries in England noblemen had employed groups of skilled people to entertain them when required. Under Tudor rule, as England became more secure and united, actors such as these were given more freedom, and they often performed in public, while still acknowledging their 'overlords' (in the 1570s, for example, when Shakespeare was still a schoolboy at Stratford, one famous company was called 'Lord Leicester's Men'). London was rapidly becoming larger and more important in the second half of the sixteenth century, and many of the companies of actors took the opportunities offered to establish themselves at inns on the main roads leading to the City (for example, the Boar's Head in Whitechapel and the Tabard in South-wark) or in the City itself. These groups of actors would come to an agreement with the inn-keeper which would give them the use of the yard for their performances after people had eaten and drunk well in the middle of the day. Before long, some inns were taken over completely by companies of players and thus became the first public theatres. In 1574 the officials of the City of London issued an order which shows clearly that these theatres were both popular and also offensive to some respectable people, because the order complains about 'the inordinate haunting of great multitudes of people, specially youth, to plays interludes and shows; namely occasion of frays and quarrels, evil practices of incontinency in great inns …' There is evidence that, on public holidays, the theatres on the banks of the Thames were crowded with noisy apprentices and tradesmen, but it would be wrong to think that audiences were always undiscriminating and loudmouthed. In spite of the disapproval of Puritans and the more staid members of society, by the 1590s, when Shakespeare's plays were beginning to be performed, audiences consisted of a good cross-section of English society, nobility as well as workers, intellectuals as well as simple people out for a laugh; also (and in this respect English theatres were unique in Europe), it was quite normal for respectable women to attend plays. So Shakespeare had to write plays which would appeal to people of widely different kinds. He had to provide 'something for everyone' but at the same time to take care to unify the material so that it would not seem to fall into separate pieces as they watched it. A speech like that of the drunken porter in *Macbeth* could provide the 'groundlings' with a belly-laugh, but also held a deeper significance for those who could appreciate it. The audience he wrote for was one of a number of apparent drawbacks which Shakespeare was able to turn to his and our advantage.

Shakespeare's Actors

Nor were all the actors of the time mere 'rogues, vagabonds and sturdy beggars' as some were described in a Statute of 1572. It is true that many of them had a hard life and earned very little money, but leading actors could become partners in the ownership of the theatres in which they acted: Shakespeare was a shareholder in the Globe and the Blackfriars theatres when he was an actor as well as a playwright. In any case, the attacks made on Elizabethan actors were usually directed at their morals and not at their acting ability; it is clear that many of them must have been good at their trade if they were able to interpret complex works like the great tragedies in such a way as to attract enthusiastic audiences. Undoubtedly some of the boys took the women's parts with skill and confidence, since a man called Coryate, visiting Venice in 1611, expressed surprise that women could act as well as they: 'I saw women act, a thing that I never saw before … and they performed it with as good a grace, action, gesture … as ever I saw any masculine actor.' The quality of most of the actors who first presented Shakespeare's plays is probably accurately summed up by Fynes Moryson, who wrote, '… as there be, in my opinion, more plays in London than in all the parts of the world I have seen, so do these players or comedians excel all other in the world.'

The Structure of the Public Theatre

Although the 'purpose-built' theatres were based on the inn-yards which had been used for play-acting, most of them were circular. The walls contained galleries on three storeys from which the wealthier patrons watched, they must have been something like the 'boxes' in a modern theatre, except that they held much larger numbers – as many as 1500. The 'groundlings' stood on the floor of the building, facing a raised stage which projected from the 'stage-wall', the main features of which were:

1 a small room opening on to the back of the main stage and on the same level as it (rear stage),
2 a gallery above this inner stage (upper stage),
3 a canopy projecting from above the gallery over the main stage, to protect the actors from the weather (the 700 or 800 members of the audience who occupied the yard, or 'pit' as we call it today, had the sky above them).

In addition to these features there were dressing-rooms behind the stage and a space underneath it from which entrances could be made through trap-doors. All the acting areas – main stage, rear stage, upper stage and under stage – could be entered by actors directly from their dressing rooms, and all of them were used in productions of Shakespeare's plays. For example, the inner stage, an almost cave-like structure, would have been where Ferdinand and Miranda are 'discovered' playing chess in the last act of *The Tempest*, while the upper stage was certainly the balcony from which Romeo climbs down in Act III of *Romeo and Juliet*.

It can be seen that such a building, simple but adaptable, was not really unsuited to the presentation of plays like Shakespeare's. On the contrary, its simplicity guaranteed the minimum of distraction, while its shape and construction must have produced a sense of involvement on the part of the audience that modern producers would envy.

Other Resources of the Elizabethan Theatre

Although there were few attempts at scenery in the public theatre (painted backcloths were occasionally used in court performances), Shakespeare and his fellow playwrights were able to make use of a fair variety of 'properties', lists of such articles have survived: they include beds, tables, thrones, and also trees, walls, a gallows, a Trojan horse and a 'Mouth of Hell'; in a list of properties belonging to the manager, Philip Henslowe, the curious item 'two mossy banks' appears. Possibly one of them was used for the

> bank whereon the wild thyme blows,
> Where oxlips and the nodding violet grows

in *A Midsummer Night's Dream* (Act II, Scene i). Once again, imagination must have been required of the audience.

Costumes were the one aspect of stage production in which trouble and expense were hardly ever spared to obtain a magnificent effect. Only occasionally did they attempt any historical accuracy (almost all Elizabethan productions were what we should call 'modern-dress' ones), but they were appropriate to the characters who wore them: kings were seen to be kings and beggars were similarly unmistakable. It is an odd fact that there was usually no attempt at illusion in the costuming: if a costume looked fine and rich it probably was. Indeed, some of the costumes were almost unbelievably expensive. Henslowe lent his company £19 to buy a cloak, and the Alleyn brothers, well-known actors, gave £20 for a 'black velvet cloak, with sleeves embroidered all with silver and gold, lined with black satin striped with gold'.

With the one exception of the costumes, the 'machinery' of the playhouse was economical and uncomplicated rather than crude and rough, as we can see from this second and more leisurely look at it. This meant that playwrights were stimulated to produce the imaginative effects that they wanted from the language that they used. In the case of a really great writer like Shakespeare, when he had learned his trade in the theatre as an actor, it seems that he received quite enough assistance of a mechanical and structural kind without having irksome restrictions and conventions imposed on him; it is interesting to try to guess what he would have done with the highly complex apparatus of a modern television studio. We can see when we look back to his time that he used his instrument, the Elizabethan theatre, to the full, but placed his ultimate reliance on the communication between his imagination and that of his audience through the medium of words. It is, above all, his rich and wonderful use of language that must have made play-going at that time a memorable experience for people of widely different kinds. Fortunately, the deep satisfaction of appreciating and enjoying Shakespeare's work can be ours also, if we are willing to overcome the language difficulty produced by the passing of time.

Shakespeare:
A Timeline

Very little indeed is known about Shakespeare's private life: the facts included here are almost the only indisputable ones. The dates of Shakespeare's plays are those on which they were first produced.

1558   Queen Elizabeth crowned.

1561   Francis Bacon born.

1564   Christopher Marlowe born.   William Shakespeare born, April
                                          23rd, baptized April 26th.

1566   Shakespeare's brother, Gilbert,
                                          born.
1567   Mary, Queen of Scots, de-
       posed.
       James VI (later James I of
       England) crowned King of
       Scotland.

1572   Ben Jonson born.
       Lord Leicester's Company (of
       players) licensed; later called
       Lord Strange's, then the Lord
       Chamberlain's and finally
       (under James) the King's
       Men.

1573   John Donne born.

1574   The Common Council of
       London directs that all plays
       and playhouses in London
       must be licensed.

1576   James Burbage builds the
       first public playhouse,
       The Theatre, at Shoreditch,
       outside the walls of the
       City.

1577   Francis Drake begins his
       voyage round the world
       (completed 1580).
       *Holinshed's Chronicles of
       England, Scotland and
       Ireland* published (which

Shakespeare later used extensively).

Year	Events	Shakespeare's life / Works
1582		Shakespeare married to Anne Hathaway.
1583	The Queen's Company founded by royal warrant.	Shakespeare's daughter, Susanna, born.
1585		Shakespeare's twins, Hamnet and Judith, born.
1586	Sir Philip Sidney, the Elizabethan ideal 'Christian knight', poet, patron, soldier, killed at Zutphen in the Low Countries.	
1587	Mary, Queen of Scots, beheaded. Marlowe's *Tamburlaine (Part I)* first staged.	
1588	Defeat of the Spanish Armada. Marlowe's *Tamburlaine (Part II)* first staged.	
1589	Marlowe's *Jew of Malta* and Kyd's *Spanish Tragedy* (a 'revenge tragedy' and one of the most popular plays of Elizabethan times).	
1590	Spenser's *Faerie Queene* (Books I–III) published.	
1592	Marlowe's *Doctor Faustus* and *Edward II* first staged. Witchcraft trials in Scotland. Robert Greene, a rival playwright, refers to Shakespeare as 'an upstart crow' and 'the only Shake-scene in a country'.	*Titus Andronicus* *Henry VI, Parts I, II and III* *Richard III*
1593	London theatres closed by the plague. Christopher Marlowe killed in a Deptford tavern.	*Two Gentlemen of Verona* *Comedy of Errors* *The Taming of the Shrew* *Love's Labour's Lost*
1594	Shakespeare's company becomes The Lord Chamberlain's Men.	*Romeo and Juliet*

1595	Raleigh's first expedition to Guiana. Last expedition of Drake and Hawkins (both died).	*Richard II* *A Midsummer Night's Dream*
1596	Spenser's *Faerie Queene* (Books IV–VI) published. James Burbage buys rooms at Blackfriars and begins to convert them into a theatre.	*King John* *The Merchant of Venice* Shakespeare's son Hamnet dies. Shakespeare's father is granted a coat of arms.
1597	James Burbage dies, his son Richard, a famous actor, turns the Blackfriars Theatre into a private playhouse.	*Henry IV (Part I)* Shakespeare buys and redecorates New Place at Stratford.
1598	Death of Philip II of Spain	*Henry IV (Part II)* *Much Ado About Nothing*
1599	Death of Edmund Spenser. The Globe Theatre completed at Bankside by Richard and Cuthbert Burbage.	*Henry V* *Julius Caesar* *As You Like It*
1600	Fortune Theatre built at Cripplegate. East India Company founded for the extension of English trade and influence in the East. The Children of the Chapel begin to use the hall at Blackfriars.	*Merry Wives of Windsor* *Troilus and Cressida*
1601		*Hamlet*
1602	Sir Thomas Bodley's library opened at Oxford.	*Twelfth Night*
1603	Death of Queen Elizabeth. James I comes to the throne. Shakespeare's company becomes The King's Men. Raleigh tried, condemned and sent to the Tower	
1604	Treaty of peace with Spain	*Measure for Measure* *Othello* *All's Well that Ends Well*
1605	The Gunpowder Plot: an attempt by a group of Catholics to blow up the Houses of Parliament.	

1606	Guy Fawkes and other plotters executed.	*Macbeth* *King Lear*
1607	Virginia, in America, colonized. A great frost in England.	*Antony and Cleopatra* *Timon of Athens* *Coriolanus* Shakespeare's daughter, Susanna, married to Dr. John Hall.
1608	The company of the Children of the Chapel Royal (who had performed at Blackfriars for ten years) is disbanded. John Milton born. Notorious pirates executed in London.	Richard Burbage leases the Blackfriars Theatre to six of his fellow actors, including Shakespeare. Pericles, Prince of Tyre
1609		Shakespeare's Sonnets published.
1610	A great drought in England	*Cymbeline*
1611	Chapman completes his great translation of the *Iliad*, the story of Troy. Authorized Version of the Bible published.	*A Winter's Tale* *The Tempest*
1612	Webster's *The White Devil* first staged.	Shakespeare's brother, Gilbert, dies.
1613	Globe theatre burnt down during a performance of *Henry VIII* (the firing of small cannon set fire to the thatched roof). Webster's *Duchess of Malfi* first staged.	*Henry VIII* *Two Noble Kinsmen* Shakespeare buys a house at Blackfriars.
1614	Globe Theatre rebuilt 'in 'far finer manner than before'.	
1616	Ben Jonson publishes his plays in one volume. Raleigh released from the Tower in order to prepare an expedition to the gold mines of Guiana.	Shakespeare's daughter, Judith, marries Thomas Quiney. Death of Shakespeare on his birthday, April 23rd.
1618	Raleigh returns to England and is executed on the charge for which he was imprisoned in 1603.	
1623	Publication of the Folio edition of Shakespeare's plays	Death of Anne Shakespeare (née Hathaway).

Life & Times

William Shakespeare the Playwright

There exists a curious paradox when it comes to the life of William Shakespeare. He easily has more words written about him than any other famous English writer, yet we know the least about him. This inevitably means that most of what is written about him is either fabrication or speculation. The reason why so little is known about Shakespeare is that he wasn't a novelist or a historian or a man of letters. He was a playwright, and playwrights were considered fairly low on the social pecking order in Elizabethan society. Writing plays was about providing entertainment for the masses – the great unwashed. It was the equivalent to being a journalist for a tabloid newspaper.

In fact, we only know of Shakespeare's work because two of his friends had the foresight to collect his plays together following his death and have them printed. The only reason they did so was apparently because they rated his talent and thought it would be a shame if his words were lost.

Consequently his body of work has ever since been assessed and reassessed as the greatest contribution to English literature. That is despite the fact that we know that different printers took it upon themselves to heavily edit the material they worked from. We also know that Elizabethan plays were worked and reworked frequently, so that they evolved over time until they were honed to perfection, which means that many different hands played their part in the active writing process. It would therefore be fair to say that any play attributed to Shakespeare is unlikely to contain a great deal of original input. Even the plots were based on well known historical events, so it would be hard to know what fragments of any Shakespeare play came from that single mind.

One might draw a comparison with the Christian bible, which remains such a compelling read because it came from the collaboration of many contributors and translators over centuries, who each adjusted the stories until they could no longer be improved. As virtually nothing is known of Shakespeare's life and even less about his method of working, we shall never know the truth about his plays. They certainly contain some very elegant phrasing, clever plot devices and plenty of words never before seen in print, but as to whether Shakespeare invented them from a unique imagination or whether he simply took them from others around him is anyone's guess.

The best bet seems to be that Shakespeare probably took the lead role in devising the original drafts of the plays, but was open to collaboration from any source when it came to developing them into workable scripts for effective performances. He would have had to work closely with his fellow actors in rehearsals, thereby finding out where to edit, abridge, alter, reword and so on.

In turn, similar adjustments would have occurred in his absence, so that definitive versions of his plays never really existed. In effect Shakespeare was only responsible for providing the framework of plays, upon which others took liberties over time. This wasn't helped by the fact that the English language itself was not definitive at that time either. The consequence was that people took it upon themselves to spell words however they pleased or to completely change words and phrasing to suit their own preferences.

It is easy to see then, that Shakespeare's plays were always going to have lives of their own, mutating and distorting in detail like Chinese whispers. The culture of creative preservation was simply not established in Elizabethan England. Creative ownership of Shakespeare's plays was lost to him as soon as he released them into the consciousness of others. They saw nothing wrong with taking his ideas and running with them, because no one had ever suggested that one shouldn't, and Shakespeare probably regarded his work in the same way. His plays weren't sacrosanct works of art, they were templates for theatre folk to make their livings from, so they had every right to mould them into productions that drew in the crowds as effectively as possible. Shakespeare was like the helmsman of a sailing ship, steering the vessel but wholly reliant on the team work of his crew to arrive at the desired destination.

It seems that Shakespeare certainly had a natural gift, but the genius of his plays may be attributable to the collective efforts of Shakespeare and others. It is a rather satisfying notion to think that *his* plays might actually be the creative outpourings of the Elizabethan milieu in which Shakespeare immersed himself. That makes them important social documents as well as seminal works of the English language.

Money in Shakespeare's Day

It is extremely difficult, if not impossible, to relate the value of money in our time to its value in another age and to compare prices of commodities today and in the past. Many items are simply not comparable on grounds of quality or serviceability.

There was a bewildering variety of coins in use in Elizabethan England. As nearly all English and European coins were gold or silver, they had intrinsic value apart from their official value. This meant that foreign coins circulated freely in England and were officially recognized, for example the French crown (écu) worth about 30p (72 cents), and the Spanish ducat worth about 33p (79 cents). The following table shows some of the coins mentioned by Shakespeare and their relation to one another.

GOLD	British	American	SILVER	British	American
sovereign (heavy type)	£1.50	$3.60	shilling	10p	24c
sovereign (light type)	66p–£l	$1.58–$2.40	groat	1.5p	4c
angel					
royal	33p–50p	79c–$1.20			
noble	50p	$1.20			
crown	25p	60c			

A comparison of the following prices in Shakespeare's time with the prices of the same items today will give some idea of the change in the value of money.

ITEM	PRICE British	American	ITEM	PRICE British	American
beef, per lb.	0.5p	1c	cherries (lb.)	1p	2c
mutton, leg	7.5p	18c	7 oranges	1p	2c
rabbit	3.5p	9c	1 lemon	1p	2c
chicken	3p	8c	cream (quart)	2.5p	6c
potatoes (lb)	10p	24c	sugar (lb.)	£1	$2.40
carrots (bunch)	1p	2c	sack (wine) (gallon)	14p	34c
8 artichokes	4p	9c	tobacco (oz.)	25p	60c
1 cucumber	1p	2c	biscuits (lb.)	12.5p	30c

INTRODUCTION

Macbeth is a simple play. That is to say, the plot is straightforward, the characters clearly presented, the opposition of good and evil perfectly plain. There is not even much doubt, at any stage, about the ultimate fate of Macbeth and his wife. In fact, a heavy sense of inevitability hangs over all their actions. Nevertheless, where so much is obvious, there is still a great deal of mystery. Why does this sturdy soldier become a mean killer and, worse, a hirer of thugs to do his killing for him, particularly when he knows, and says, that his plans are sure to bring retribution upon him? Why does Lady Macbeth, an apparently loving wife, see it almost as a duty to drive herself and her husband into evil ways? And why do so many quite good men allow this vicious couple to gain total power and ruin the state of Scotland?

Some aspects of the Macbeth story have become horribly familiar in the course of the history of our own century. Several modem dictators have begun as brave soldiers and ended as crazy destroyers, so that the line between legitimate warfare and power-hungry violence has become very blurred indeed. Psychologists have shown us that, behind seemingly straightforward human motives, good or bad, there are often extremely complicated emotions and intentions. For these and other reasons this play, now nearly four hundred years old, based on the life of a man who lived six hundred years before Shakespeare himself, still exerts a great fascination on audiences and readers all over the world. In the summing-up at the end of this book an attempt will be made to analyse the reasons for this continued interest, and to go more deeply into the questions raised in this introduction. In the meantime, those new to the play may care to consider some of the intriguing ingredients of the play they are about to study, particularly those that are likely to be evident on first seeing or reading it.

The witches These three sinister creatures introduce the play, in a very brief first scene. They intend to *meet with Macbeth*, and they immediately convey an impression of impending horror. There is no clue to the nature of this horror, but we are uneasily aware of limitless possibilities. These agents of evil are at hand, ready to be consulted, ready to influence for the worse, for much of the play.

The good king King Duncan of Scotland soon appears, and impresses us with his integrity and generosity, as well as with his determination to do all he can for his kingdom's welfare. He is, in the early stages, the representative of goodness, trust and benevolent order.

The 'decent' men We are introduced to a number of Scotsmen – *the bleeding Sergeant*, the king's sons, Malcolm and Donalbain, Lennox, Ross, Banquo and Angus – who serve their king and country as well as they can. Under good leadership they are faithful and useful. They react in various ways to the kingship of the ruthless Macbeth.

The strongholds Much of the action takes place in the Scottish castles of Inverness, Forres, Dunsinane and Fife. These grim, grey containers of human turmoil provide effective settings for the deeds done. We are frequently reminded of their walls, battlements and heavy gates. The principal murders take place in or near them. Such deeds are partly hidden by their walls, or by darkness, or by both.

The weather The play starts with thunder, lightning, *fog and filthy air*; there is a moment of serene summer (seen through Duncan's innocent eyes), followed by a brooding, overcast night, breaking into unprecedented tempest (the night of the first murder). The evening of the banquet is also calm, but with the prospect of rain. Banquo dies and, soon after, the Macduff family is destroyed. During the rest of the play there is no direct description of the weather. The disturbances seem to reflect not only Scotland's time of trial but also the upheaval in Macbeth's mind. For most of the last two acts he is settled in and almost resigned to his own evil.

Scotland and England Scotland, suffering under Macbeth's tyranny, and England, an idyllic country under the saintly King

Edward the Confessor, are vividly contrasted. But the essence of the contrast is not in any Scottish inferiority; rather, it is Scotland's sheer misfortune to have such an inexplicably evil ruler as Macbeth, and England's simple duty to help to destroy him.

Apparitions Apart from the witches themselves, there are several possibly supernatural elements in the play: the *air-drawn dagger* which Macbeth saw before he killed Duncan (though this might well have been the product of his own feverish imagination), the ghost of Banquo, and the things the witches conjure up for Macbeth's inspection at the beginning of Act IV. As a member of a modern audience, how would you explain these visions? Are they an embarrassment, or do they add to the horrible reality of the story?

The words of the play Finally, as you go through the play, it should be stimulating to notice how Shakespeare uses words to gain his effects. Unfortunately there are many words and phrases which require explanation to twentieth century readers (which is why notes are provided), but a little thought and imagination can make a great deal clear. The verse rhythms, the images, the descriptive words, even the punning and other forms of word-play, all add to the main impression: this is a tale of human evil and human goodness much of which appeals directly to us today.

After this brief outline of the main features of *Macbeth* we shall look more closely and intently at its constituent parts and examine the contribution each makes to the whole effect. After this analysis of the ingredients of the play, the 'Summing Up' (page 247) will attempt to put things together again and leave you better equipped to explore the play for yourself.

The Language of the Play

It has already been said that many Shakespearean words and phrases require explanation to twentieth century readers and play-goers. It is not at all surprising that a play written nearly four hundred years ago should present problems of understanding. Living languages are always changing and developing. Another difficulty is that playwrights have always interested and amused audiences by making topical references. An Elizabethan audience would have instantly recognized a mention of the Spanish Armada, or something relating to the contemporary troubles in Ireland, which people in a twentieth century theatre might not even notice. Although it must be said that much of what is most important 'gets across' quite readily, we can all gain more from a Shakespeare play by deepening our understanding of the text. But, however conscientiously readers follow any textual notes, they will only be adding to their comprehension of words and phrases. There is a broader strategy at work in Shakespeare's use of language that notes can only hint at. For example, the linguistic style often varies to suit the mood of the moment or the personality of the speaker. Macbeth begins with a heavy, menacing rhythm, a kind of incantation by the witches:

> *Fair is foul, and foul is fair:*
> *Hover through the fog and filthy air*
>
> (Act 1, Scene i, lines 12–13)

which breaks off suddenly and is replaced by a passage full of long, involved sentences of description and explanation. The wounded Sergeant tries to convey in detail to his king the reality of a terrible battle, and the almost superhuman impression that Macbeth's quality of fighting has made upon him. The Sergeant's account falters, he breaks off, exhausted, and the scene ends with a mixture of long, rolling lines and short, exclamatory ones. The news *seems* good: *The victory fell on us* (Act 1, Scene iii, line 59) says Ross, but the news of Cawdor's treachery is dismaying and the rhythms hint at confusion, not resolution. Ambiguous notes have been struck which condition our responses to what follows. As the play goes on, more doubts arise, and motives become obscure: these abstractions are reflected in the language. Macbeth and Lady Macbeth, when talking to themselves or to each other, are generally clear and direct in style:

Lady Macbeth:
> *Yet do I fear thy nature;*
> *It is too full o' th' milk of human kindness*
> *To catch the nearest way*

> (Act 1, Scene v, lines 15–17)

and

Macbeth:
> *He's here in double trust:'*
> *First, as I am his kinsman and his subject…*
> (Act 1, Scene vii, lines 12–13

Both of them, however, adopt a flamboyant, almost unctuous manner when they want to conceal their true feelings and intentions.

> *All our service*
> *In every point twice done, and then done double,*
> *Were poor and single business to contend*
> *Against those honours deep and broad wherewith*
> *Your Majesty loads our house;*
> (Act 1, Scene vi, lines 14–18)

says Lady Macbeth to Duncan, with murder in her mind, when welcoming him to the castle at Inverness. Her husband outdoes her in fulsome language, just after he has killed Duncan:

> *Here lay Duncan,*
> *His silver skin lac'd with his golden blood;*
> *And his gash'd stabs look'd like a breach in nature*
> *For ruin's wasteful entrance*
> (Act II, Scene iii, lines 111–14)

He goes on in such extravagant terms that (some critics suggest) Lady Macbeth has to pretend to faint in order to shut him up. Duncan and Banquo are almost the only characters whose true feelings are regularly reflected in their words. Even among some of those who represent the forces of goodness and truth, language is sometimes used to hide feelings rather than to express them. In the mysterious Act IV, Scene iii, Malcolm, who is to prove the saviour of Scotland, pours out hundreds of words of self-description, most of which he contradicts a little later on (*I…unspeak mine own detraction*).

By Act V, clarity and directness have returned. Lady Macbeth, in her madness, speaks the simple words of truth:

> *Yet who would have thought the old man to have had*
> *so much blood in him?*

(Act V, Scene i, lines 35–7)

Macbeth himself, face to face with ultimate reality, no longer has any need for words as disguises:

> *… that which should accompany old age,*
> *As honour, lover obedience, troops of friends,*
> *I must not look to have.*

(Act V, Scene in, lines 24–6)

So, although it is apparent that language in this play frequently reflects the moods and characters of the speakers, it often does so in subtle ways. In addition, deeper and wider impressions are being evoked, so that the language of the play throughout reflects its underlying ideas: the onset of evil fostered in human souls, doubt and insecurity (represented in ambiguous words) and finally the triumph of truth and justice. Some further suggestions are made in the Theme Index (page 214) about the use of particular words by which these wide-ranging impressions are conveyed.

Plot

The story of the play may be set down in the following matter-of-fact way:

ACT I

A note of doubt and confusion is struck by three witches in the first scene. They refer to a battle that is not yet concluded; they plan to meet Macbeth, one of the Scottish generals, in a deserted place, at the end of the day's fighting. This is followed by a scene in which Duncan, King of Scotland, hears an interim report on the battle between the rebels (Macdonwald and the Thane of Cawdor) together with an army of Norwegian invaders, and the loyal Scottish forces led by Macbeth and

Banquo. A wounded Sergeant describes a ferocious fight in which both Macbeth and Banquo are acquitting themselves with tremendous skill and determination. Ross, another Scottish lord, comes in to announce victory. King Duncan orders the execution of Cawdor and the honouring of Macbeth with the traitor's title.

The witches meet Macbeth as they had planned. Banquo, who is with him, addresses the witches with suspicion, seeing them as probably evil. Macbeth says little, but seems prepared to listen to them. They greet him as Thane of Glamis (his correct title), Thane of Cawdor (a title which, by now, is his, but he doesn't know it), and future king. Banquo notices that Macbeth reacts to what the witches say with apparent fear. He orders the witches to make some announcement about his future, too; they respond by telling his fortune in riddles. In particular, they say that he is to be the ancestor of kings, though not a king himself. The witches disappear, leaving the two men, bewildered, repeating the prophecies. Ross arrives to announce Macbeth's new title of Thane of Cawdor. Macbeth's thoughts turn at once to the possibility of being king, while Banquo shows again that he deeply distrusts the witches. (*What, can the devil speak true?*) Before the end of the scene Macbeth is already contemplating the murder of Duncan, though hoping that the final prophecy may come true without any action on his part.

In Scene iv, at the royal palace at Forres, King Duncan and Macbeth face each other. The former is warm, friendly, grateful for his general's services; the latter superficially responsive and dutiful Duncan proclaims his son Malcolm as his heir. This leaves Macbeth almost committed to the murder of Duncan, but well aware of the nature of what he contemplates (he refers to his *black and deep desires*). In Scene v, Lady Macbeth makes her first appearance. She is reading a letter she has just received from Macbeth in which he tells her about the witches' prophecies, and the speedy fulfilment of part of them. Lady Macbeth immediately determines that he shall be king, by whatever means may be necessary. She thinks he may be too good-natured to catch the nearest way (that is, to kill Duncan), but she feels confident that she can persuade him to do it. Fate seems to be on her side when a messenger enters to say that Duncan is on his way to honour them with a visit. In a speech in which she reveals much of her character (*The raven himself is hoarse...*, lines 38–54), she acknowledges her natural womanly feelings but appeals to the powers of darkness to make her cruelly resolute. Macbeth arrives and his wife makes it clear that she expects him to kill Duncan that night. He makes no clear response. Duncan and his court come to Inverness Castle and are greeted effusively by Lady Macbeth but, significantly, not by Macbeth himself.

In the final scene of the first Act, Macbeth struggles with his ambition and his conscience. He has left the banquet hall where the king is dining to try to work things out on his own. He knows that Duncan is a good king, and is clear that nothing but selfish ambition is pressing him towards a terrible crime. He has just concluded that the plan is a wicked one and that he will abandon it, when his wife appears and attacks him viciously and determinedly at his weakest point – his pride in his own courage and manliness. She accuses him of cowardice, and of not loving her. She follows this up with an appalling demonstration that she is willing to go to any lengths herself, declaring that she would dash her own baby to the ground rather than go back on her word. She outlines a plan of action. Macbeth is persuaded, though he is dreadfully aware of the wickedness of what they plan to do.

ACT II

Banquo, as well as Macbeth, seems to be plagued by disturbing thoughts and temptations, but when Macbeth suggests that they should meet to discuss the witches' prophecies Banquo stresses that he will do nothing dishonourable. Left alone, in another agonized soliloquy (*Is this a dagger which I see before me ...?*) Macbeth shows how deeply disturbed he is by the crime he is now committed to. He hears the bell, struck by Lady Macbeth, which is the signal for him to act; she has done her part by giving Duncan's servants drink, to make them sleepy. She hears Macbeth shout, and thinks that he has failed to kill the king, but he comes in saying that he has 'done the deed'.

He seems shattered, and she has to stop him thinking about the crime and his lost honour. As before, she uses the weapon of scorn against him, but this time it does not work. He cannot bring himself to return to the king's room with the bloody daggers which he should have left there. She goes instead and smears the servants with blood. A thunderous knocking is heard. Macbeth is obsessed with the horror of Duncan's blood on his hands; Lady Macbeth, on the contrary, whose hands are now also red, dismisses it as unimportant (*A little water clears us of this deed*).

The porter of the castle is roused at last from his drunken sleep by the knocking. He staggers to the door of the castle to let in Macduff and Lennox, who have come to wake the king. Macbeth comes to see them, pretending that he has only just been awakened himself, and escorts Macduff to the king's apartment. After Lennox has commented on the wild weather, Macduff re-enters, so appalled that he can hardly say what he has seen. All the thanes and and the two princes, Malcolm and Donalbain, are roused. Lennox, Ross and Macbeth go back to the king's room, where Macbeth kills the two servants who are covered in blood. Soon afterwards Lennox blames these servants for the murder, but Macduff seems to have some doubts, since he asks Macbeth why he killed them. Macbeth begins to explain in an elaborate, overwrought manner and Lady Macbeth either faints or pretends to do so. Malcolm and Donalbain, who have hardly had time to feel anything except fear, decide to go away. Malcolm's words suggest that he already suspects Macbeth.

The final scene in the Act presents a picture of total disorder in the natural world, reflecting the chaos in human society. An old man describes bizarre events. Macduff says that Malcolm and Donalbain, because they have fled, are suspected of paying the servants to kill Duncan, their father. He also says that Macbeth has been named as the new king; he is shortly to be crowned at Scone.

ACT III

Banquo clearly suspects that Macbeth has become king by foul means. Macbeth invites Banquo to a feast, and goes on to extract information from him about his planned movements in the afternoon. Because he is deeply concerned about the witches' prophecy that Banquo is to be the ancestor of kings, Macbeth is plotting to kill his comrade. As soon as he has said farewell to Banquo (*God be with you!*) he meets two murderers whom, with a strange mixture of lies, temptations, insults and compliments, he persuades to intercept Banquo as he returns towards the castle and kill him. Lady Macbeth tries to comfort her husband, who is full of gloom and fear but is not taking her into his confidence. He hints that he is arranging the removal of Banquo, the most obvious obstacle to his peace of mind. The murderers succeed in killing Banquo but, significantly, Fleance his son escapes.

While the banquet proceeds, the murderers tell Macbeth what has happened; he sinks again into gloom. Banquo's ghost enters and sits in Macbeth's seat. Macbeth, shaken with guilt and horror, creates a sensation among the guests and Lady Macbeth has to pretend that he often has such fits, which soon pass. The ghost disappears temporarily and Macbeth seems to recover, but when he proposes a toast to Banquo the ghost returns and Macbeth behaves like a madman. Lady Macbeth, worried that her husband will soon reveal his terrible secrets, ushers out the guests. Macbeth resolves to visit the witches and find out what his future holds. At the same time he contemplates even more frightful crimes (*Strange things I have in head that will to hand*).

After a brief and not very important scene in which Hecate, the witches' goddess, appears, two of the Scottish lords make it quite clear to each other that they strongly suspect Macbeth of the two murders. They reveal that Macduff has gone to the court of Edward the Confessor of England (where Malcolm, Duncan's son, is living) to beg his military assistance in opposing Macbeth.

ACT IV
Macbeth visits the witches who conjure up, first, a helmeted head; next, a bloody child; and then a crowned child with a

tree in his hand. The first apparition warns him to beware of Macduff; the second says that no man born of woman can harm him; and the third informs him that he will never be defeated until Birnam Wood moves towards his castle at Dusinane. Macbeth is encouraged by the second and third prophecies but insists on putting a question to the supernatural powers about Banquo's descendants: will they ever rule Scotland? In answer he is shown a line of eight kings, accompanied by Banquo, whom they all resemble; the last king holds a mirror in which still more Banquo-like kings are visible. Immediately after this, news comes that Macduff has fled to, England. Macbeth plans to attack his castle and slaughter his wife and entire family. In the next scene Lady Macduff has just been told by Ross that her husband has gone to England. She is angry and contemptuous of her husband and tells her small son that his father is dead. After a messenger has warned them that they are in danger, murderers sent by Macbeth enter and stab the son. We learn later that the whole family has been killed.

The scene switches to the English, court where Malcolm and Macduff have a long and strange conversation. Macduff is urging Malcolm to return to Scotland to attempt to destroy Macbeth, but Malcolm is suspicious: he thinks Macduff (on Macbeth's behalf) may be trying to lure him back to Scotland. He tests Macduff by describing himself as a thoroughly wicked man, totally unsuited to be king in Macbeth's place. He wants to see if Macduff will go on encouraging him beyond all reasonable limits, in which case he will know that he is being deceived. Up to a point Macduff accepts Malcolm's supposed vices, but eventually he despairs, says Malcolm is not even fit to live, let alone govern Scotland, and prepares to leave. This convinces Malcolm that Macduff is honest. When a doctor suddenly appears to tell them that King Edward is about to cure sick people by the laying on of hands, a new note of hope is introduced (the implication is that he will help Malcolm cure the social and political sickness in Scotland). Malcolm and Macduff are reconciled. Ross comes from Scotland with the appalling news of the destruction of Macduff's family and, after cursing himself for neglecting them, Macduff determines to seek revenge. The English army under Siward is ready and Malcolm, Macduff and Ross prepare to march northward.

ACT V

The last Act begins with talk between a doctor and a gentlewoman about the serious illness of Lady Macbeth. We are told that she is in the habit of sleepwalking in a state of great agitation. She says things that seem to incriminate herself and her husband. Then Lady Macbeth herself enters with a lighted taper and the doctor prepares to record what she says. She appears to be washing her hands, and, in a fragmentary way, gives details of the murder of Duncan. She also refers to the killing of Lady Macduff and of Banquo. The watchers express their horror at the significance of what she has said.

A Scottish army is about to combine with the English forces under Malcolm and Siward, and attack Macbeth at Dunsinane. In Scene iii, Macbeth declares his desperate trust in the statements of the witches' apparitions: Birnam Wood cannot possibly move, and all men are born of women. Soon after this he is brought news of the approach of an army of ten thousand men; he sinks temporarily into a state of despair, seeing his own life as near its end. The doctor tells him that there is no change in Lady Macbeth's state. Macbeth rouses himself and prepares for battle.

The combined army halts near Birnam Wood and Malcolm gives orders for the soldiers to camouflage themselves with leafy boughs cut from the trees. In Dusinane Castle Lady Macbeth's death is announced and Macbeth reacts by commenting on the meaninglessness of life. A messenger tells him that Birnam Wood is moving towards them. Macbeth flies into an almost insane rage, then lapses into weary resignation, and finally determines to die fighting. Two brief scenes follow (vii and viii) in which the battle is presented. Macbeth is still half-depending on the statement that he cannot be killed by any man 'of woman born' and, when he kills young Siward, is re-encouraged. He encounters the angry Macduff, who tells him that he was born by Caesarian section (i.e. cut from his mother's body). The last of the supernatural assurances is shown to be a deception. Macbeth refuses to fight Macduff and then, after all, decides to rely on his own strength and courage. They go off fighting. Soon afterwards Macduff returns with Macbeth's severed head. Malcolm ends the play by heralding a new era for his kingdom of Scotland.

Characterization

Even in such a prosaic summary of the plot, attitudes and relationships in the war between good and evil have to be presented and to some extent explained. In the process, certain characters stand out. It has often been said that Shakespeare's supreme achievement is in the depth and range of the characters he creates – that he constantly presents us with totally credible *individuals*. In most of his plays, certainly, the characters 'ring true'. Some of them are profound and convincing portraits, 'psychologically accurate', to use a familiar modern phrase. Shakespeare seems to have succeeded in creating people. He is assisted, of course, by the fact that we usually meet these characters as they are embodied by skilful actors and actresses. We watch a human being in the part, speaking the lines, frowning, moving, gesticulating. Gradually the illusion takes a grip upon us, our imaginations take over (guided by the imagination of the playwright) and we react for a time as though we are watching and listening to real people living their own real lives. In Macbeth there are certainly two characters who are presented skilfully, imaginatively and fully enough to have this effect upon us from the stage and, indeed, even from the pages of a book: Macbeth and Lady Macbeth. A good deal has been said about them in this introduction already, but it may be helpful to say a little more. It has been pointed out that the play is one battle in the universal war of good and evil, and that the battle is not between thoroughly bad people and thoroughly good ones. Notwithstanding, by the middle of the play, Macbeth and his wife epitomize the evil which is feared and hated by almost everyone else and, by the end, it is virtually Macbeth versus the rest. The battle also goes on within the two chief characters. There is some danger of seeing them as figures in a sensational horror, story, but close attention dispels this tendency. We have to believe Lady Macbeth when she says that her husband is *full o' th' milk of human kindness* when we listen to what he says. No-one expresses the positive side of human nature more truly, from Macbeth's early comments on Duncan:

> this Duncan
> Hath borne his faculties so meek, hath been
> So clear in his great office, that his virtues
> Will plead like angels...
>
> (Act I, Scene vii, lines 16–19)

to his poignant regrets at the end of his life:

> My way of life
> is fall'n into the sear, the yellow leaf...
>
> (Act V, Scene iii, lines 22–3)

How does a man who knows what human goodness is, and respects it, decline so rapidly into a murderous tyrant? Essentially, he chooses to do so, and *knows* that it is his choice, because of his ambition, the influence of a beloved wife, and the value he attaches to being thought a brave man. None of these aspects of his character is, in itself, evil, but he allows himself to be led by them into evil Ambition becomes an insatiable hunger, his love for his wife leads him to agree to frightful deeds, and his fighting quality degenerates into bloodlust. Accordingly, he alienates all our respect, yet evokes genuine pity at the last. We recognize a human being.

Lady Macbeth seems to alienate respect in playgoers and readers even more completely, and may not evoke pity, even at the end of her life. Yet she is, potentially, a 'partner in greatness' who, like Macbeth, takes it for granted that greatness is all that matters. Like so many other words in the play, this word is interpreted in various ways by various people. Lady Macbeth is a woman who will 'do anything' for her husband, just as he will 'do anything' for her. She is even willing, and able, to deny her own deepest feelings as a woman and a human being: it is at the moment when she declares that she would kill her own child rather than go back on her word that she inspires most repugnance; and it is at this moment that they are at one. It is the moment of commitment for both of them, and the signal for the train of events which plunges the whole of their society into tragic suffering. She is broken by it, and before long becomes a pathetic, deranged creature, as much a prey to guilt as Macbeth is.

No other character in the play is nearly as fully drawn as Macbeth and Lady Macbeth. Duncan is a good old man, reluctant to see evil in anyone. Malcolm is a tougher version of his father, and his personality seems at one point to veer towards interesting complexity (in the long conversation with Macduff at the English court). Banquo acts as a foil to Macbeth, as a man similarly tempted but too staunchly honourable to fall into evil ways himself – though he appears to do nothing to follow up his suspicions of Macbeth. Even Macduff, although he becomes the tyrant's executioner, does not develop into a particularly subtle personality, perhaps because we are not allowed to see him agonizing over the decision to leave his family and go to England. All these supporting characters revolve around Macbeth and Lady Macbeth, however. After Macbeth has died, we just feel confident that those who have survived will lead Scotland wisely and well.

Dramatic Structure and the Thematic Pattern

The first comment in this introduction was 'Macbeth is a simple play'. This is particularly true of its dramatic structure and thematic pattern, both of which depend on the central issue of a struggle between good and evil. The play begins with a clear-cut physical conflict with, seemingly, no ambiguities. Scotland is a 'good' society ruled by a good man: the enemies are traitors, vicious invaders and contemptible mercenaries. Macbeth emerges as the champion of goodness and is immediately transformed into the enemy of goodness. Evil power proliferates, good men are destroyed, other good men run away. By Act IV, Scene iii, evil seems triumphant. Then Malcolm and Macduff reach agreement and the good King Edward lends his holy power. Faith and hope return and fortune swings away from evil. Act V shows the final battle. Scotland is cleansed and the new king acknowledges the need for supernatural goodness (*the grace of Grace*) to support human striving.

LIST OF CHARACTERS

Duncan	King of Scotland
Malcolm *Donalbain*	} sons Macbeth
Banquo *Macduff*	} Generals of the King's army
Lennox *Ross* *Menteith* *Angus* *Caithness*	} Noblemen of Scotland
Fleance	son to Banquo
Siward	Earl of Northumberland, General of the English forces
Young Siward	his son
Seyton	an officer attending on Macbeth
Boy	son to Macduff
A sergeant	
A porter	
An Old Man	
An English Doctor	
A Scots Doctor	
Lady Macbeth	
Lady Macduff	
Gentlewoman	attending on Lady Macbeth
The Weird Sisters	
Hecate	
The Ghost Of Banquo	
Apparitions	

Lords, Gentlemen, Officers, Soldiers, Murderers, Attendants and Messengers

The Scene: Scotland and England

ACT I SCENE I

This short opening scene gives an immediate impression of mystery, horror and uncertainty. These witches would have been truly frightening to an audience in Shakespeare's day, many of whom would have seen, or at the very least known about, women burnt at the stake for selling themselves to the Devil. Macbeth is introduced by name by the Third Witch, and this raises questions in the audience's mind – who is he? And what can these disgusting hags want with him?

3. *hurlyburly* the confused noise of storm and battle. Thunder was produced for the Elizabethan stage by rolling cannon-balls. Nowadays the same effect is produced by shaking sheets of metal, or through electronic and digital sound equipment.

4. *lost and won* the first of many apparent contradictions and confusions (see line 12 of this scene). The words can mean 'decided one way or the other'.

9. *Graymalkin* a name for a grey cat, which was a common 'familiar' of witches. A familiar was a demon which attended and assisted a witch; these spirits usually took some rather sinister form.

10. *Paddock* a toad. This is the Second Witch's familiar. Sounds were probably made off-stage to represent the calls of these familiar spirits, though it is difficult to imagine what sound a toad was supposed to make.

11. *Anon!* I am coming at once.

12. This line is a kind of motto for the witches. They delight in a reversal of all the normal values. Macbeth seems to involve himself with them by echoing the phrase in Act I, Scene iii, line 39.

13. *fog and filthy air* this may have been produced by burning resin under the stage; again, in today's theatre if an effect is required it is more likely to be produced by smoke machine, dry ice or something similar.

ACT ONE
Scene I

An open place

[Thunder and lightning. Enter three WITCHES.]

First Witch
  When shall we three meet again?
  In thunder, lightning, or in rain?
Second Witch
  When the hurlyburly's done,
  When the battle's lost and won.
Third Witch
  That will be ere the set of sun.   5
First Witch
  Where the place?
Second Witch
  Upon the heath.
Third Witch
  There to meet with Macbeth.
First Witch
  I come, Graymalkin.
Second Witch
  Paddock calls.   10
Third Witch
  Anon!
All
  Fair is foul, and foul is fair:
  Hover through the fog and filthy air.

[WITCHES vanish.]

SCENE II

The second scene deals mainly with the report of the battle in which the 'Macbeth' we have already heard about, and another man, Banquo, have excelled. However, the feeling of uncertainty is maintained, because the outcome of the battle is left in doubt by the Sergeant. He nevertheless presents Macbeth as the decisive factor, and Ross gives the same impression from his point of view when he provides the final news that the battle has been won. We get a remarkable picture of Macbeth as a kind of superman, a fearless, ferocious, almost untouchable champion of right against treachery.

1–3. *He can report … state* He looks as though he has come, wounded, straight from the battle, and will be able to give us an up-to-date report.

5. *'Gainst my captivity* to save me from being captured.

6. *knowledge of the broil* news of the battle.

9. *choke their art* (the two exhausted swimmers) prevent each other from using their swimming skill.

10. *to that* to that end, i.e. to show that he is without doubt a traitor.

12. *swarm upon him* like lice.

12. *Western Isles* islands to the west, including Ireland and the Hebrides.

13. *kerns and gallowglasses* lightly-armed foot-soldiers and horsemen armed with axes.

14–15. *Fortune* the Roman goddess Fortuna, regarded as highly unreliable. Macbeth ignores her *(Disdaining Fortune,* line 17) and takes his fate into his own hands, a trait we are to see repeated later in the play.

17–18. *brandished steel … execution* His sword steamed with the hot blood of those he had just killed.

19. *valour's minion* the favourite of Valour (personified in much the same way as Fortune).

carv'd out his passage cut his way through the men on the battlefield.

22–3. *Till he unseam'd …* he thrust his sword in at the navel (nave), ripped him open up to the jaws (chaps), then cut his head off and stuck it on the battlements.

Scene II

A camp near Forres

[Alarum within. Enter KING DUNCAN, MALCOLM,
DONALBAIN, LENNOX *with* ATTENDANTS, *meeting a
bleeding* SERGEANT.]

Duncan
    What bloody man is that? He can report,
    As seemeth by his plight, of the revolt
    The newest state.
Malcolm   oldest son
                This is the sergeant
    Who like a good and hardy soldier fought
    'Gainst my captivity. Hail, brave friend!   5
    Say to the King the knowledge of the broil
    As thou didst leave it.
Sergeant
                Doubtful it stood,
    As two spent swimmers that do cling together
    And choke their art. The merciless Macdonwald –
    Worthy to be a rebel, for to that   10
    The multiplying villainies of nature
    Do swarm upon him – from the Western Isles
    Of kerns and gallowglasses is supplied;
    And Fortune, on his damned quarrel smiling,
    Show'd like a rebel's whore. But all's too weak;   15
    For brave Macbeth – well he deserves that name –
    Disdaining Fortune, with his brandish'd steel
    Which smok'd with bloody execution,
    Like valour's minion, carv'd out his passage
    Till he fac'd the slave;   20
    Which ne'er shook hands, nor bade farewell to him,
    Till he unseam'd him from the nave to th' chaps,
    And fix'd his head upon our battlements.

24. *cousin* Macbeth and Duncan were both grandsons of King Malcolm, but in any case the word cousin was often used by sovereigns of their noblemen.

24. *worthy gentleman!* What Macbeth has just done seems hardly gentlemanly, but there is no irony in Duncan's remark. Such actions in defence of king and country would have been regarded as truly to be admired.

25–8. *As whence ... Discomfort swells* 'Just as storms fatal to ships can burst out of the east, where the sun first shines, so danger springs from the place where everything seems well.' Note the irony here, even if the Sergeant doesn't realize it. These words could be a warning to Duncan about Macbeth, who seems fair.

30. *Compell'd ... heels* Forced these unreliable soldiers to rely on running away.

31. *Norweyan* an old form of Norwegian.

31. *surveying vantage* seeing his chance. No doubt Duncan's troops had relaxed on seeing the kerns run away.

32. *With furbished arms* 'having repaired their weapons' (or perhaps taken up new ones).

34–5. *Yes ... the lion* The Sergeant is being very sarcastic. 'Yes, they were about as dismayed as an eagle is by a sparrow, or a lion by a hare,' he says.

36. *sooth* truth.

37. *as cannons ... cracks* Like cannons with double charges of gunpowder.

39–40. *Except they meant ... Golgotha* Unless they intended to bathe in the steaming wounds (of their enemies) or make the battle as grimly memorable a scene as the crucifixion of Christ.

43–4. *So well ... both* Your words and your wounds do you equal honour.

44. *smack* taste.

45. *Thane* a Scottish nobleman and landowner, often the chief of a clan

47. *So should he ... strange* His appearance suggests that he has strange news to tell.

Duncan
O valiant cousin! worthy gentleman!
Sergeant
As whence the sun gins his reflection 25
Shipwrecking storms and direful thunders break,
So from that spring whence comfort seem'd to come
Discomfort swells. Mark, King of Scotland, mark:
No sooner justice had, with valour arm'd,
Compell'd these skipping kerns to trust their heels, 30
But the Norweyan lord, surveying vantage,
With furbish'd arms and new supplies of men,
Began a fresh assault.
Duncan
                    Dismay'd not this
Our captains, Macbeth and Banquo?
Sergeant
                                    Yes;
As sparrows eagles, or the hare the lion. 35
If I say sooth, I must report they were
As cannons overcharg'd with double cracks;
So they doubly redoubled strokes upon the foe.
Except they meant to bathe in reeking wounds,
Or memorize another Golgotha, 40
I cannot tell –
But I am faint; my gashes cry for help.
Duncan
So well thy words become thee as thy wounds;
They smack of honour both. – Go get him surgeons.

[Exit SERGEANT, *attended. Enter* ROSS.*]*

Who comes here?
Malcolm
                    The worthy Thane of Ross. 45
Lennox
What a haste looks through his eyes!
So should he look that seems to speak things strange.

50–1. *Where ... cold* Where the Norwegian banners mock the (Scottish) sky and, as they wave, freeze our men with fear.
52. *Norway himself* King Sweno of Norway.

54. *a dismal conflict* one which filled the Scottish forces with foreboding.
55. *Bellona's bridegroom* the bridegroom of Bellona, the Roman goddess of war. Macbeth is being compared with Mars, the god of war himself.
55. *lapp'd in proof* wearing tried and tested armour.
56. *Confronted ... self-comparisons* Gave him something (i.e. a model of a fighting man) to compare himself with.
58. *Curbing his lavish spirit* overcoming his insolent courage.

61. *craves composition* begs for peace terms.
62. *Nor would we ... men* We would not allow him to bury his dead soldiers.
63. *disbursed* paid.
63. *Saint Colme's Inch* a small island in the Firth of Forth, now called Inchcolm. (St. Colme is another form of St. Columba.)
64. *dollars* These coins were in fact not minted until the early sixteenth century, 500 years after the time of the real Duncan and Macbeth. Does it matter that Shakespeare that Shakespeare isn't worried about such inaccuracy? Could it have had a deliberate purpose?
65–6. *deceive ... interest* treacherously attack our dearest interests.
pronounce his present death order his immediate execution.

Ross
   God save the King!
Duncan
   Whence cam'st thou, worthy thane?
Ross
                     From Fife, great King
   Where the Norweyan banners flout the sky   50
   And fan our people cold.
   Norway himself, with terrible numbers,
   Assisted by that most disloyal traitor
   The Thane of Cawdor, began a dismal conflict,
   Till that Bellona's bridegroom, lapp'd in proof,   55
   Confronted him with self-comparisons,
   Point against point rebellious, arm 'gainst arm,
   Curbing his lavish spirit; and to conclude,
   The victory fell on us.
Duncan
               Great happiness!
Ross
   That now   60
   Sweno, the Norways' king, craves composition;
   Nor would we deign him burial of his men
   Till he disbursed, at Saint Colme's Inch,
   Ten thousand dollars to our general use.
Duncan
   No more that Thane of Cawdor shall deceive   65
   Our bosom interest. Go pronounce his present death,
   And with his former title greet Macbeth.
Ross
   I'll see it done.
Duncan
   What be hath lost, noble Macbeth hath won.

          [Exeunt.]

SCENE III

The meeting of Macbeth and the witches, which we heard them predict in Act I, Scene i, is about to take place. However, before Macbeth arrives on the heath, unaware of what he will find, the witches plan to torment a sea-captain whose wife has annoyed them.

2. *Killing swine* Witches were said to kill farm animals, often in revenge for some supposed insult.

7. *Aroint thee ... !* Get out!

7. *rump-fed* this probably means 'fed on rump-steak', therefore sleek and plump. The gaunt witches would envy her.

7. *ronyon* worthless woman.

8. *Tiger* a common name for a ship in Shakespeare's time.

9. There are records of criminal trials in which so-called witches confessed that they went to sea in a sieve.

10. Another special ability witches were belived to have was to turn themselves into animals, but when they did this they became tailless and could be identified.

11. She seems almost fuming with rage and malice. What do you think she intends to do?

15–18. *I myself have ... card* 'I have control of all the other winds and (I know) the exact harbours from which they blow, from all points of the compass.' The main point is that she wants to prevent the *Tiger* from entering any port, and leave the poor ship miserably tossing on the waves.

19. Because the *Tiger* will not be able to refill her water-supply.

20–1. This is an ominous suggestion of Macbeth's later insomnia (see, for example, Act III, Scene iv, line 141).

21. *pent-house lid* An eyelid slopes something like the roof of a penthouse. (A penthouse is a small structure built against a larger one, therefore having only one roof-slope).

22. *forbid* cursed.

23. *sev'nights* weeks. Compare the similar word fortnight (fourteen nights) which is still in regular use. The witch is going to manipulate the winds to keep the ship at sea for 81 weeks.

Scene III

A blasted heath

[Thunder. Enter the three WITCHES.*]*

First Witch
  Where hast thou been, sister?
Second Witch
  Killing swine.
Third Witch
  Sister, where thou?
First Witch
  A sailor's wife had chestnuts in her lap,
  And mounch'd, and mounch'd, and mounch'd.   5
  'Give me' quoth I.
  'Aroint thee, witch!' the rump-fed ronyon cries.
  Her husband's to Aleppo gone, master o' th' Tiger;
  But in a sieve I'll thither sail
  And, like a rat without a tail,   10
  I'll do, I'll do, and I'll do.
Second Witch
  I'll give thee a wind,
First Witch
  Th'art kind.
Third Witch
  And I another.
First Witch
  I myself have all the other;   15
  And the very ports they blow,
  All the quarters that they know
  I' th' shipman's card.
  I'll drain him dry as hay:
  Sleep shall neither night nor day   20
  Hang upon his pent-house lid;
  He shall live a man forbid;
  Weary sev'nights, nine times nine,

24. *dwindle, peak* become thin.

25. *bark* ship. It is important to note that the power of the witches is limited. At crucial points in the play Macbeth excuses or explains his past actions or what he is about to do by assuming that they have absolute power and knowledge, but this is not so.

29. *a pilot's thumb*. Bits of dead bodies were valued ingredients in making spells.

31. Is this perhaps a supernatural drum? There is no indication that Macbeth and Banquo have an escort, but they may have.

32. *Weird* This coms from an Old English word 'wyrd' which means fate.

33. *Posters* creatures which travel quickly.

35-6. Three and multiples of three have always been regarded as magic numbers. At this point they also indicate roughly the steps of their dance: 'three paces your way, three paces my way, and three more paces (in the direction of the Third Witch).'

37. *wound up* 'set, and ready for action'. At this very moment Macbeth and Banquo enter, as though brought there by the charm.

38. *So foul and fair* Macbeth's unconscious echo of the witches' words in Act I, Scene i, confirms the impression that he is already under their influence.

39. *How far is't called ... ?* How far do they reckon it is ...?

39-61. Banquo's reaction to the first sight of the witches is a suspicious one. Macbeth says little, but seems far more prepared than Banquo to accept the witches' words.

42-3. *aught that man may question?* beings with whom one is allowed to communicate?

44. *choppy* chapped. The fact that the witches put their fingers on their lips in answer to Banquo seems to suggest that they want to speak, not to him, but to Macbeth.

Shall he dwindle, peak, and pine.
Though his bark cannot be lost,   25
Yet it shall be tempest-tost.
Look what I have.
Second Witch
Show me, show me.
First Witch
Here I have a pilot's thumb,
Wreck'd as homeward he did come.   30

[Drum within.]

Third Witch
A drum, a drum! Macbeth doth come.
All
The Weird Sisters, hand in hand,
Posters of the sea and land,
Thus do go about, about;
Thrice to thine, and thrice to mine,   35
And thrice again, to make up nine.
Peace! The charm's wound up.

[Enter MACBETH *and* BANQUO.*]*

Macbeth
So foul and fair a day I have not seen.
Banquo
How far is't call'd to Forres? What are these,
So withered, and so wild in their attire,   40
That look not like th' inhabitants o' th' earth,
And yet are on't? Live you, or are you aught
That man may question? You seem to understand me,
By each at once her choppy finger laying
Upon her skinny lips. You should be women,   45
And yet your beards forbid me to interpret
That you are so.
Macbeth
                    Speak, if you can. What are you?

50. *hereafter* in the future. They have just addressed him as the present Thane of Cawdor, as well as Glamis.

51. Banquo notices that Macbeth jumps when he hears the witches' greetings. Is this just normal surprise and wonder, or has Macbeth already considered the possibility of becoming king, by foul means if necessary?

53. *fantastical* imaginary.

53–4. *or that ... ye show?* or are you what you appear to be?

55–6. *present grace* being Thane of Glamis.
great prediction Of noble having becoming Thane of Cawdor.
royal hope becoming king.

57. *rapt withal* entranced by them (the witches' mysterious greetings).

58. *look into the seeds of time* Banquo is prepared to accept the witches' power to see into the future, but he goes on to show (lines 60–1) that he will not put himself in their power. Their response is to speak to him in riddles, whereas they gave Macbeth plain statements.

67. *get kings*: be the ancestor of kings.

70. *imperfect speakers* Macbeth says this because he wants to know more. He has come out of his trance and now demands further information.

71. *Sinel* Macbeth's father, from whom he had inherited the title of Thane of Glamis.

73–4. Neither Macbeth nor Banquo seems to have heard of Cawdor's treachery.

First Witch
All hail, Macbeth! Hail to thee. Thane of Glamis!
Second Witch
All hall, Macbeth! Hail to thee. Thane of Cawdor!
Third Witch
All hail, Macbeth, that shalt be King hereafter! 50
Banquo
Good sir, why do you start, and seem to fear
Things that do sound so fair? I' th' name of truth,
Are ye fantastical, or that indeed
Which outwardly ye show? My noble partner
You greet with present grace and great prediction 55
Of noble having and of royal hope,
That he seems rapt withal. To me you speak not.
If you can look into the seeds of time
And say which grain will grow and which will not,
Speak then to me, who neither beg nor fear 60
Your favours nor your hate.
First Witch
Hail!
Second Witch
Hail!
Third Witch
Hail!
First Witch
Lesser than Macbeth, and greater. 65
Second Witch
Not so happy, yet much happier.
Third Witch
Thou shalt get kings, though thou be none.
So, all hail, Macbeth and Banquo!
First Witch
Banquo and Macbeth, all hail!
Macbeth
Stay, you imperfect speakers, tell me more. 70
By Sinel's death I know I am Thane of Glamis;
But how of Cawdor? The Thane of Cawdor lives,

74. *Stands not ... belief* Is so unlikely as to be unbelievable.

76. *owe* own, possess.
intelligence information.

78. Having asked for information twice, Macbeth becomes bolder and orders the witches to answer him.

79–80. The witches have vanished like burst bubbles. Although they had seemed very real, physical, living creatures, it now appears that they belong to the supernatural.

81. *corporal* made of flesh and blood.

84–5. *the insane root ... prisoner* the root (of the hemlock or some other plant) which causes madness when eaten.

86. Is Macbeth envious and annoyed because no mention was made of his own heirs?

91. *Thy personal ... fight* Your individual contribution in putting down the rebellion of Macdonwald.

95. Ross goes on to mention the other phase of the battle, against the Norwegian forces.

95. *stout* bold, tough.

A prosperous gentleman; and to be King
Stands not within the prospect of belief,
No more than to be Cawdor. Say from whence   75
You owe this strange intelligence, or why
Upon this blasted heath you stop our way
With such prophetic greeting? Speak, I charge you.

[WITCHES vanish.]

Banquo
   The earth hath bubbles, as the water has,
   And these are of them. Whither are they vanish'd?   80
Macbeth
   Into the air; and what seem'd corporal melted
   As breath into the wind. Would they had stay'd!
Banquo
   Were such things here as we do speak about?
   Or have we eaten on the insane root
   That takes the reason prisoner?   85
Macbeth
   Your children shall be kings.
Banquo
                      You shall be King.
Macbeth
   And Thane of Cawdor too; went it not so?
Banquo
   To th' self-same tune and words. Who's here?

[Enter ROSS and ANGUS.]

Ross
   The King hath happily receiv'd, Macbeth,
   The news of thy success; and when he reads   90
   Thy personal venture in the rebels' fight,
   His wonders and his praises do contend
   Which should be thine or his. Silenc'd with that,
   In viewing o'er the rest o' th' self-same day,
   He finds thee in the stout Norweyan ranks,   95

96–7. *Nothing afeard ... death* Ross comments that Macbeth is not frightened by the sight of the mangled bodies of those he has killed. We will see a different reaction later.

97–100. Macbeth's great achievement was acclaimed in all the messages which piled up in front of Duncan. It is especially ironic that just when the audience is beginning to suspect Macbeth's intentions, everyone else on stage is praising him.

98. *post with post* message after message.

102. *herald ... sight* escort you into the king's presence.

104. *for an earnest* as a first instalment.

105–6. The words are close enough to those of the Second Witch to underline the rapid fulfilment of the prophecy.

106. *addition* title.

106. Banquo has clearly decided that the witches are evil.

108–9. The play contains many examples of imagery related to clothes, particularly those that do not fit. This creates a picture of Macbeth wearing clothes that were not meant for him. Keep this in mind as the play develops.

110–11. The ex-thane of Cawdor is under sentence of death (see Act 1, Scene ii, line 66).

111. *was combin'd* allied himself.

112. *line the rebel* assist Macdonwald.

113. *hidden help and vantage* secret aid.

114. *labour'd ... wreck* worked to ruin his country.

115. *treasons capital* acts of treason worthy of the death penalty.

117. *The greatest is behind* the fulfilment of the Third Witch's prophecy, the Kingship, will follow after this stage, in the future (hence the word 'behind').

118. Macbeth again refers to the prophecy about Banquo's children becoming kings.

Nothing afeard of what thyself didst make,
Strange images of death. As thick as tale
Came post with post, and every one did bear
Thy praises in his kingdom's great defence,
And pour'd them down before him.

Angus

                            We are sent   100
To give thee, from our royal master, thanks;
Only to herald thee into his sight,
Not pay thee.

Ross

And, for an earnest of a greater honour,
He bade me, from him, call thee Thane of Cawdor;   105
In which addition, hail, most worthy Thane!
For it is thine.

Banquo

               What, can the devil speak true?

Macbeth

The Thane of Cawdor lives; why do you dress me
In borrowed robes?

Angus

               Who was the Thane lives yet;
But under heavy judgment bears that life   110
Which he deserves to lose. Whether he was combin'd
With those of Norway, or did line the rebel
With hidden help and vantage, or that with both
He labour'd in his country's wreck, I know not;
But treasons capital, confess'd and prov'd,   115
Have overthrown him.

Macbeth

  [aside]   Glamis, and Thane of Cawdor!
The greatest is behind. – Thanks for your pains.
[Aside to BANQUO*]* Do you not hope your children
        shall be kings,
When those that gave the Thane of Cawdor to me
Promis'd no less to them?

120. *trusted home* believed in fully.

122–6. Banquo reveals his own deep distrust of the witches and their words, saying 'The Devil's helpers often impress us and win our confidence by telling us some small truths about our lives so that, once we are in their power, they can deceive us in really important matters (and thus destroy us).'

128–9. *the swelling act ... theme* Macbeth sees himself as king at the climax of a great drama.

130. *soliciting* prompting, egging on.

131–3. What Banquo suspected and dismissed (a small truth leading to betrayal *In deepest consequence)* Macbeth also suspects but will not dismiss.

134–7. *If good ... nature?* Already Macbeth is contradicting Ross's remark in lines 97–8. Here is an image of death of which he is clearly afraid. Is it one of his own creation or not? He is certainly considering murder (see line 140).

135. *unfix my hair* make my hair stand on end.

136. *seated* firmly fixed.

137. *Against the use of nature* in an unnatural way.

137–8. *Present fears ... imaginings* A real cause of fear (e.g. a fierce enemy in the recent battle) is less frightening than something horrible which you imagine.

139–42. Macbeth is obsessed by the idea of murder and is incapable of normal action. Nothing seems real to him except what he is creating in his mind.

143. *rapt* lost in his own thoughts.

144–5. At first, in order to escape his horrible imaginings, Macbeth adopts the attitude of saying to himself: 'There is no need for me to take any action; if it is my fate to be king, it will just happen that way.'

145–6. *New honours ... use* The honours which have just come to him (Macbeth) are like new clothes which take time to shape themselves comfortably to the body. Note the reference to clothing imagery again.

Banquo
  [aside to MACBETH*]*   That, trusted home,   120
  Might yet enkindle you unto the crown,
  Besides the Thane of Cawdor. But 'tis strange;
  And oftentimes to win us to our harm,
  The Instruments of darkness tell us truths,
  Win us with honest trifles, to betray's   125
  In deepest consequence. –
  Cousins, a word, I pray you.
Macbeth
  [aside]   Two truths are told,
  As happy prologues to the swelling act
  Of the imperial theme. – I thank you, gentlemen.
  [Aside] This supernatural soliciting   130
  Cannot be ill; cannot be good. If ill,
  Why hath it given me earnest of success,
  Commencing in a truth I am Thane of Cawdor.
  If good, why do I yield to that suggestion
  Whose horrid image doth unfix my hair   135
  And make my seated heart knock at my ribs
  Against the use of nature? Present fears
  Are less than horrible imaginings.
  My thought, whose murder yet is but fantastical,
  Shakes so my single state of man   140
  That function is smothered in surmise,
  And nothing is but what is not.
Banquo
  Look how our partner's rapt.
Macbeth
  [aside] If chance will have me King, why, chance
          may crown me,
  Without my stir.
Banquo
                  New honours come upon him,   145
  Like our strange garments, cleave not to their mould
  But with the aid of use.

147–8. *Come what ... roughest day* Macbeth continues to shrug off his troubled thoughts: 'I suppose I shall live through it. Even the most troubled day has to come to an end.' The words give him something to hang on to.

149. Banquo indicates politely that they are waiting until Macbeth is ready to go.

150–1. 'Do forgive me. My over–tired brain was disturbed by things that I can't even remember now'. This may not seem a big lie, but it is a lie nevertheless.

151. *your pains* your services to me.

152–3. *where every day ... read them* i.e. in his mind.

155. *The interim having weigh'd it* the interval having given us a chance to consider it.

156. *Our free hearts* Can either of their hearts be described as free?

Macbeth [aside]
                            Come what come may,
    Time and the hour runs through the roughest day.
Banquo
    Worthy Macbeth, we stay upon your leisure.
Macbeth
    Give me your favour. My dull brain was wrought   150
    With things forgotten. Kind gentlemen, your pains
    Are register'd where every day I turn
    The leaf to read them. Let us toward the King.
    [Aside to BANQUO*]* Think upon what hath chanc'd;
            and, at more time,
    The interim having weigh'd it, let us speak   155
    Our free hearts each to other.
Banquo
    [aside to MACBETH*]*   Very gladly.
Macbeth
    [aside to BANQUO*]* Till then, enough. – Come, friends.

                    [Exeunt.]

SCENE IV

The rebels and the foreign invaders have been defeated. King Duncan
wants to celebrate his country's safety by making Malcolm, his eldest
son, the official heir to the throne. It is a formal occasion, which
would have been vividly presented by Shakespeare's company, the
King's Men, with rich costume and all the symbols of majesty. The
scene appears to stress happy, natural relationships between those
present with Duncan as the warm-hearted father-king. Macbeth's
apparently unexpected arrival gives Duncan further opportunity for
rejoicing.

2. *Those in commission* 'the officials charged with the duty' (Ross
was sent to deal with it. Act 1, Scene ii, lines 66–7).

9. *As one ... death* Like an actor perfectly trained in a death-scene.
9. *studied* learnt by heart.
10. *the dearest thing he ow'd* his life.
10. *ow'd;* owned.
11. *careless* not worth any care.
11–12. *There's no art ... face* 'There's no way of telling, from a man's
face, what's going on in his mind'. At this moment Macbeth enters.
Duncan has no idea that his own words could be accurately applied
to his new Thane of Cawdor. This is a good example of dramatic
irony.

16–18. *Thou art ... overtake thee* You are so far ahead in worth and
ability that it's difficult for admiration and reward to catch up with
you.
19–20. *That the proportion ... mine!* So that I could have thanked
you and rewarded you according to your merit.

Scene IV

Forres. The palace

[Flourish. Enter DUNCAN, MALCOLM, DONALBAIN, LENNOX
and ATTENDANTS.*]*

Duncan
Is execution done on Cawdor? Are not
Those in commission yet return'd?
Malcolm
My liege,
They are not yet come back. But I have spoke
With one that saw him die; who did report
That very frankly he confess'd his treasons, 5
Implor'd your Highness' pardon, and set forth
A deep repentance. Nothing in his life
Became him like the leaving it: he died
As one that had been studied in his death
To throw away the dearest thing he ow'd 10
As 'twere a careless trifle.
Duncan
There's no art
To find the mind's construction in the face.
He was a gentleman on whom I built
An absolute trust.

[Enter MACBETH, BANQUO, ROSS *and* ANGUS.*]*

O worthiest cousin!
The sin of my ingratitude even now 15
Was heavy on me. Thou art so far before
That swiftest wing of recompense is slow
To overtake thee. Would thou hadst less deserv'd,
That the proportion both of thanks and payment
Might have been mine! Only I have left to say, 20
More is thy due than more than all can pay.

41

22–3. *The service ... itself* Macbeth is just saying 'I was only doing my duty'. Do you think this is a sign of guilt or embarrassment?

24–7. *our duties ... honour* Macbeth's comments indicate an awareness of the value of stable relationships in family and state – relationships which he is soon to shatter brutally.

27. *Safe toward ... honour* with a sure respect to you, in love and honour.

28–9. *I have ... growing* Duncan uses natural imagery to express his spontaneous, warm personality and, in lines 32–3, Banquo's response is in similar terms. Macbeth, on the other hand, is already considering highly unnatural courses.

34. *Wanton* not held back, unlimited.

34–5. *Seek ... sorrow* (my joyful feelings) disguise themselves in tears, which usually express sorrow.

37. *We* Duncan now speaks formally, as king (the royal 'we')

37–9. The throne of Scotland was not hereditary. The king was allowed to appoint his successor from among his relatives (Macbeth was eligible, among others) and usually made him Prince of Cumberland at the same time. This was the recognized title of the heir to the throne, just as Prince of Wales is of the heir to the throne of Great Britain today.

39–42. *which honour ... deservers* My son's new title will not be the only honour to be given out; everyone who deserves recognition will receive it.

42. *From hence to Inverness* Duncan turns to Macbeth, who is to be his host at Inverness.

43. *bind us further to you* Duncan indicates again that he is already deeply in Macbeth's debt for his bravery and success in battle; now he is to be indebted to him as his guest.

44. *The rest ... you;* A rather strained piece of politeness; 'any time or trouble not spent in serving you is hard work'.

45. *harbinger* a man who rode ahead to make arrangements for accommodation for an army or a royal company.

Macbeth

    The service and the loyalty I owe,
    In doing it, pays itself. Your Highness' part
    Is to receive our duties; and our duties
    Are to your throne and state children and servants,   25
    Which do but what they should by doing everything
    Safe toward your love and honour.

Duncan

                          Welcome hither.
    I have begun to plant thee, and will labour
    To make thee full of growing. Noble Banquo,
    That hast no less deserv'd, nor must be known   30
    No less to have done so, let me infold thee
    And hold thee to my heart.

Banquo

                  There if I grow,
    The harvest is your own.

Duncan

                My plenteous joys,
    Wanton in fulness, seek to hide themselves
    In drops of sorrow. Sons, kinsmen, thanes,   35
    And you whose places are the nearest, know
    We will establish our estate upon
    Our eldest, Malcolm, whom we name hereafter
    The Prince of Cumberland; which honour must
    Not unaccompanied invest him only,   40
    But signs of nobleness, like stars, shall shine
    On all deservers. From hence to Inverness,
    And bind us further to you.

Macbeth

    The rest is labour, which is not us'd for you.
    I'll be myself the harbinger, and make joyful   45
    The hearing of my wife with your approach;
    So, humbly take my leave.

Duncan

                My worthy Cawdor!

48–53. Macbeth realises that Duncan making Malcolm the heir to the throne is a serious obstacle if he wishes to be king. So, he commits himself to evil action. His words show he knows only too well how evil his desires are. They are black and deep and fit only for the darkest night.

52–3. *The eye ... to see* Macbeth tries to distance himself from what he is about to do, saying, 'Let my eye be blind to what my hand does, but let the deed be done, even though the murdered body is too horrible to look at.'

54. While Macbeth has been soliloquizing (speaking alone, probably at the front of the stage), Banquo has been praising him to Duncan.

55–6. *And in ... to me* Hearing him praised gives me as much satisfaction as a fine meal eaten with ceremony and in good company.

58. *peerless* unequalled. Some critics have called Duncan a weak king. Is there any evidence for this from what you have read so far?

Macbeth
  [aside] The Prince of Cumberland! That is a step,
  On which I must fall down, or else o'er-leap,
  For in my way it lies. Stars, hide your fires;   50
  Let not light see my black and deep desires.
  The eye wink at the hand; yet let that be
  Which the eye fears, when it is done, to see.

                        [Exit.]

Duncan
  True, worthy Banquo: he is full so valiant;
  And in his commendations I am fed;   55
  It is a banquet to me. Let's after him,
  Whose care is gone before to bid us welcome.
  It is a peerless kinsman.

                   [Flourish Exeunt.]

SCENE V

Macbeth's last words in the previous scene expressed his firm commitment, if horrified, to carry out what needed to be done, and his letter to his wife seems confident. Her reaction to it is one of fierce passion and eagerness. But, she worries that Macbeth's better feelings (human kindness) will stand in the way of ambition, so she plans to overcome them. First she has to cope with the gentler side of her own nature, and does so in a terrible appeal to the forces of evil. When Macbeth finally enters he is guarded in what he says, and does not commit himself one way or the other about the murder.

1. When Lady Macbeth begins to speak she is halfway through the reading of the letter. There is no mention of the witches' promises to Banquo in the part we hear.

2–3. *by the perfects'st report ... knowledge* It sounds as though Macbeth is referring to way the Cawdor prophecy came true.

6. *missives* messengers.

10. *to deliver thee* to pass on to you.

11–12. *the dues of rejoicing* your fair share of joy.

13. *Lay it to thy heart* 'consider well what I have written'. But she probably also takes the words literally by hiding the letter in her bosom.

14–15. *shalt be ... promised* Lady Macbeth begins with a direct statement that her husband shall become king.

17. *To catch the nearest way* to take the shortest route (to what you want).

19. *The illness should attend it* the evil which must go alongside Macbeth's ambition.

19–20. *What thou ... holily* You would like to attain your great ambition without doing anything wrong.

21. *wrongly win* gain what you are not entitled to.

22. *Thou'dst have* You want.

22–3. *that which cries ... have it* the thing (i.e. the crown) which cries 'You must do the murder' if you want it.

24–5. Lady Macbeth knows that Macbeth wishes Duncan to be murdered but that he himself will hesitate to do it.

25. *Hie thee hither* hurry here.

25–30. The crime which Macbeth is considering, has already begun to destroy his character, and is having an equally powerful effect on his wife. All her aggressive, unfeminine instincts are being encouraged, and in lines 40–54 she makes a conscious request that her tender, womanly qualities should be taken away.

Scene V

Inverness. Macbeth's castle

[Enter LADY MACBETH, *reading a letter.]*

Lady Macbeth
'They met me in the day of success; and I have
learn'd by the perfect'st report they have more in
them than mortal knowledge. When I burn'd in desire
to question them further, they made themselves air,
into which they vanish'd. Whiles I stood rapt in the   5
wonder of it, came missives from the King, who all-
hail'd me "Thane of Cawdor"; by which title, before,
these weird sisters saluted me, and referr'd me to the
coming on of time, with "Hail, king that shalt be!"
This have I thought good to deliver thee, my dearest   10
partner of greatness, that thou mightst not lose the
dues of rejoicing by being ignorant of what greatness
is promis'd thee. Lay it to thy heart, and farewell.'
Glamis thou art, and Cawdor; and shalt be
What thou art promis'd. Yet do I fear thy nature;   15
It is too full o' th' milk of human kindness
To catch the nearest way. Thou wouldst be great;
Art not without ambition, but without
The illness should attend it. What thou wouldst highly
That wouldst thou holily; wouldst not play false,   20
And yet wouldst wrongly win.
Thou'dst have, great Glamis, that which cries
'Thus thou must do' if thou have it;
And that which rather thou dost fear to do
Than wishest should be undone. Hie thee hither,   25
That I may pour my spirits in thine ear,
And chastise with the valour of my tongue

28. *the golden round* the crown.

29. *fate and metaphysical aid* Both powers (fate and the supernatural) are combined in the witches (see note to Act I, Scene iii, line 33).

31. Lady Macbeth is so astonished by the way fate has placed the king in her hands due to the news that he will shortly arrive that she is taken off her guard.

33. *Would ... preparation* Would have let me know so that I could get things ready.

35. *had the speed of him* was able to ride faster.

36–7. *had scarcely more ... message* gave his news with what was almost his last breath.

37. *Give him tending* Look after him (i.e. get him refreshment, etc.).

38–40. *The raven ... battlements* The raven, an ominous bird, with a harsh croaking cry, is even more hoarse than usual. Lady Macbeth, unlike her husband, does not hesitate for a moment with regard to the crime that is planned. Notice that she says *my battlements*. She has taken over from her husband, in some respects, already.

40–1. *spirits ... thoughts* the spirits which deal with murderous and destructive ideas in human minds.

41. *unsex me here* She appeals to the powers of evil to take away her feminine qualities and to replace them with *direst cruelty.* This is certainly horrible, but note that it implies that she begins by being feminine and having tender feelings. Later, we will find out that she was unable to completely repress her womanly nature (see Act V, Scene i). Her tortured sleep-walking suggest she is very much a broken woman, and not an evil monster.

43–4. *Make thick ... remorse* thicken my blood so that pity and sorrow cannot flow through my veins (and soften my heart).

45. *compunctious visitings of nature* pangs of conscience.

46. *fell* deadly.

46–7. *keep peace ... and it* restrain me from putting my purpose into effect.

48. *take my milk for gall* 'change my milk into gall' (an intensely bitter substance).

49. *sightless* invisible.

50. *You wait ... mischief* (wherever) you direct your evil influences in the sphere of nature.

50–4. There is a remarkable similarity between this part of her 'prayer' and Macbeth's *Stars, hide your fires* (Act 1, Scene iv, lines 50–3). However, she welcomes night and darkness with much more

All that Impedes thee from the golden round
Which fate and metaphysical aid doth seem
To have thee crown'd withal.

[Enter a MESSENGER.*]*

                          What is your tidings?   30

Messenger
The King comes here to-night.
Lady Macbeth
                        Thou'rt mad to say it.
Is not thy master with him? who, were't so,
Would have inform'd for preparation.
Messenger
So please you, it is true. Our Thane is coming.
One of my fellows had the speed of him,   35
Who, almost dead for breath, had scarcely more
Than would make up his message.
Lady Macbeth
                      Give him tending:
He brings great news.

[Exit MESSENGER.*]*

               The raven himself is hoarse
That croaks the fatal entrance of Duncan
Under my battlements. Come, you spirits   40
That tend on mortal thoughts, <u>unsex me here;</u>
And fill me, from the crown to the toe, top-full
Of direst cruelty. Make thick my blood,
Stop up th' access and passage to remorse,
That no compunctious visitings of nature   45
Shake my fell purpose nor keep peace between
Th' effect and it. Come to my woman's breasts,
And take my milk for gall, you murd'ring ministers,
Wherever in your sightless substances
You wait on nature's mischief. Come, thick night,   50

[handwritten margin notes: "gender confusion", "forces of hell", "weak man must kill Duncan"]

determination than her husband. In her attempt to block out Heaven, note that she again uses the word *my*; this time it is *my keen knife*, as though she intends to commit the murder herself.

51. *pall thee* shroud yourself.

51. *dunnest* darkest.

54. *Hold* Stop.

55. *the all-hail hereafter* these words are very close to those of the Third Witch's

57. *This ignorant present* the present which knows nothing of the future.

57–8. *I feel now ... instant* She stresses that the deed is as good as done, the crown virtually gained already. Macbeth does not respond to this, although he must understand it. Note the contrast between Lady Macbeth's eager confidence and Macbeth's reluctance.

60–1. *O, never Shall ... morrow see* She says emphatically that the next morning will not *see* Duncan departing. There is also a hint of god-like power about the words, as though she and Macbeth between them could stop the sun rising. Ross's account of the wild weather of the following morning (Act II, Scene iv, lines 5–10) shows that there is something unintentionally prophetic in her words.

63. *beguile the time* 'deceive everyone' (i.e. those present on the occasion).

64. *Look like the time* put on an expression which suits the occasion.

66–8. These dreadful euphemisms (phrases that hide the reality) such as *provided for* and *This night's great business* may be signs that Lady Macbeth is not as ruthless as she would wish.

68. *into my dispatch* 'Leave it all to me' she says, but she also puns on the word *dispatch*, which means both 'management' and 'killing'.

69–70. (Tonight's events) will give us absolute power for the rest of our lives.

71. Macbeth does not share her confidence in the outcome, and cannot look her in the eye, as her next remark shows.

72. To change one's expression always reveals fear (and suspicion is aroused).

And pall thee in the dunnest smoke of hell
That my keen knife see not the wound it makes,
Nor heaven peep through the blanket of the dark
To cry 'Hold, hold'.

      [Enter MACBETH.*]*

               Great Glamis! Worthy Cawdor!
Greater than both, by the all-hail hereafter!   55
Thy letters have transported me beyond
This ignorant present, <u>and I feel now</u>
<u>The future in the instant.</u>

King ✹

Macbeth
              My dearest love,
Duncan comes here to-night.
Lady Macbeth

              And when goes hence?

Macbeth
To-morrow – as he purposes.
Lady Macbeth

            O, never   60
<u>Shall sun that morrow see!</u>
Your face, my thane, is as a book where men
May read strange matters. To beguile the tune,
Look like the time; bear welcome in your eye,
Your hand, your tongue; look like th' innocent
    flower,
But be the serpent under't. He that's coming
Must be provided for; and you shall put   65
This night's great business into my dispatch;
Which shall to all our nights and days to come
Give solely sovereign sway and masterdom.   70

Pretend innocent

Macbeth scared

Macbeth
We will speak further.
Lady Macbeth

          Only look up clear.
To alter favour ever is to fear.
Leave all the rest to me.

      [Exeunt.]

SCENE VI

There is a dreadful irony about this scene, with the innocent king delighting in the appearance of the Macbeths' castle. He also comments on the generous hospitality of the Macbeths themselves. Lady Macbeth seems almost to overdo her humble greeting (lines 14–20) but the king suspects nothing. Do you see him as naive or even senile in his innocence?

Stage Direction *Hautboys* oboes.

1. *seat* situation.
3. *gentle senses* Perhaps Duncan means that his senses have become less acute with age; in any case the word helps to build up our impression of him.
3. *guest of summer* migrant bird
4. *martlet* This is almost certainly the house-martin, and not the swift (which is its modem meaning). Banquo suggests that it prefers to build its nest on church walls (again, very ironic, given what is about to happen!)
4. *approve* show.
5. *By his lov'd mansionry* by the fact that it chooses the castle for its home-building.
5–6. *the heaven's breath ... here* the breezes are soft and attractive here.
6. *jutty* projecting part of the building.
8. *pendent bed and procreant cradle* the hanging nests in which the birds produce their young.
10. *delicate* soft and sweet.
11–14. Duncan seems to be saying something like this: 'I am sometimes bothered by the love my attendants show me (perhaps because he is such a modest man) but I always acknowledge it. You should pray God to reward me for the trouble I am causing you'.

14–20. Lady Macbeth returns Duncan's compliment in perfecr politeness. We know she is insincere, but we also recognize her skill here. Briefly, she is saying that, even if her efforts were quadrupled, they would not measure up to the honour of having the king as a visitor.

20. *We rest your hermits* 'We will always pray for you' (like a religious recluse).

Scene VI

Inverness. Before Macbeth's castle

[Hautboys and torches. Enter DUNCAN, MALCOLM,
DONALBAIN, BANQUO, LENNOX, MACDUFF, ROSS, ANGUS
and ATTENDANTS.*]*

Duncan
> This castle hath a pleasant seat; the air
> Nimbly and sweetly recommends itself
> Unto our gentle senses.

Banquo
>   This guest of summer,
> The temple-haunting martlet, does approve
> By his lov'd mansionry that the heaven's breath   5
> Smells wooingly here; no jutty, frieze,
> Buttress, nor coign of vantage, but this bird
> Hath made her pendent bed and procreant cradle.
> Where they most breed and haunt, I have observed
> The air is delicate.

[Enter LADY MACBETH.*]*

> sweet older   acts innocent kind   thanks lady for late notice

Duncan
>   See, see, our honour'd hostess!   10
> The love that follows us sometime is our trouble,
> Which still we thank as love. Herein I teach you
> How you shall bid God 'ield us for your pains,
> And thank us for your trouble.

Lady Macbeth
>   All our service
> In every point twice done, and then done double,   15
> Were poor and single business to contend
> Against those honours deep and broad wherewith
> Your Majesty loads our house; for those of old,
> And the late dignities heap'd up to them,
> We rest your hermits.

22. *purveyor* one who went on ahead of a king to prepare accommodation for him.
23. *holp* helped.

25–8. Your servants always have their servants, themselves and everything that belongs to them ready to please your Highness, and to offer to him what is really his already.

31. *By your leave* He is really repeating that he wants to take her hand, or else he kisses her on the cheek.

Duncan

                                    Where's the Thane of Cawdor?   20
We cours'd him at the heels and had a purpose
To be his purveyor; but he rides well,
And his great love, sharp as his spur, hath holp him
To his home before us. Fair and noble hostess,
We are your guest to-night.

Lady Macbeth

                                    Your servants ever   25
Have theirs, themselves, and what is theirs, in compt,
To make their audit at your Highness' pleasure,
Still to return your own.

Duncan

                                    Give me your hand;
Conduct me to mine host. We love him highly,
And shall continue our graces towards him.   30
By your leave, hostess.

                        [Exeunt.]

SCENE VII

In this scene Macbeth argues a convincing case against murdering Duncan, and decides against it. However, the force of Lady Macbeth's scorn and eloquence changes his mind; her determination and confidence brush aside his fears and scruples.

Stage Direction *Sewer* This word originally meant the servant who tasted the food of a prominent person to make sure that it was not poisoned. Here it seems to refer to the man who superintends the laying of the banquet table.

1–28. This speech, like most Shakespeare soliloquies, provides an opportunity for the speaker to reveal how he really feels. In this case, Macbeth begins uneasily arguing with himself, perhaps almost muttering, but later he becomes deeply moved and eloquent.

1. The first *done* means 'over and done with'.

2–3. *If th'assassination ... consequence* if the murder could be completely decisive and without unpleasant results.

3. *trammel* entangle in a net

4. *surcease* death.

5. *here* on earth.

6. *this bank and shoal of time* Macbeth seems to view human life as a sandbank in eternity, as if he were in a shipwreck, stuck and unable to go forward or back.

7. *We'd jump the life to come* I'd risk what comes after death.

8–10. Macbeth is worried that a bloody act often provokes bloody retaliation.

10–12. *This even-handed justice ... lips*: Justice rules that we should drink the poison we give to others.

12–28. Macbeth now speaks with real emotion, and in doing so reveals a genuine respect for Duncan's goodness, and also a respect for decent human values. He fully understands how evil the act of murder is.

12–16. The *double trust* is that he is both a relative and a subject of the king, and is also the king's host!

17. *Hath borne ... meek* Has used his authority as king with such genuine humility.

18. *clear* innocent.

20. *taking-off* murder.

21–5. Cherubs were not chubby babies (as we think of them today) but senior angels. But both baby and angels are riding the winds (*blast* and *sightless couriers or* invisible runners) and they are all, in Macbeth's vivid imagination, going to make the crime known everyone (*blow the horrid deed in every eye*).

Scene VII

Inverness. Macbeth's castle

[Hautboys, torches. Enter a SEWER, and divers SERVANTS
with dishes and service over the stage. Then enter
MACBETH.]

Macbeth
If it were done when 'tis done, then 'twere well
It were done quickly. If th' assassination
Could trammel up the consequence, and catch,
With his surcease, success; that but this blow
Might be the be-all and the end-all here –   5
But here upon this bank and shoal of time –
We'd jump the life to come. But in these cases
We still have judgment here, that we but teach
Bloody instructions, which being taught return
To plague th' inventor. This even-handed justice   10
Commends th' ingredience of our poison'd chalice
To our own lips. He's here in double trust:
First, as I am his kinsman and his subject –
Strong both against the deed; then, as his host,
Who should against his murderer shut the door,   15
Not bear the knife myself. Besides, this Duncan
Hath borne his faculties so meek, hath been
So clear in his great office, that his virtues
Will plead like angels, trumpet-tongu'd, against
The deep damnation of his taking-off;   20
And pity, like a naked new-born babe,
Striding the blast, or heaven's cherubin hors'd
Upon the sightless couriers of the air,
Shall blow the horrid deed in every eye,
That tears shall drown the wind. I have no spur   25
To prick the sides of my intent, but only

27–8. Jumping directly into one's saddle was a young man's way of showing-off. Possibly Shakespeare means 'overshoots and falls to the ground on the other side' by the last few words. Or it could mean simply that the rider, having cleared an obstacle, falls off his horse on the other side of it.

29. This is the first of several occasions when Lady Macbeth sharply questions her husband on his actions.

31. Macbeth's statement sounds decisive, and it certainly follows on logically from his recent argument with himself, but it does not take Lady Macbeth very long to make him retreat.

32–5. It is interesting that Macbeth does not mention to his wife the objections to the murder that appear to carry most weight with him – the moral and ethical objections. To her he merely talks about ruining his reputation *(Golden opinions)*.

34. *in their newest gloss* like fresh, new clothes, perfectly clean.

35–7. Lady Macbeth takes up Macbeth's metaphor from clothing and mixes it with one from drunkenness. She goes on to suggest that Macbeth is like someone waking up with a hangover *(green and pale)* who forgets or ignores what he had decided to do when he was drunk.

39–41. *Art thou afeard … in desire ?* Are you afraid to put firmly into practice what you really want to do?

39–45. She uses two very powerful (and unfair) weapons here. She says 'I see you don't really love me' *(From this time Such I account thy love)* and accuses him of being a coward. Macbeth has no defence against such tactics.

45. *th' adage* the proverb. Lady Macbeth is referring to 'The cat who would like to catch fish, but isn't prepared to get her feet wet…'. The ridiculousness of the comparison between Macbeth and the cat seems to affect him deeply because he asks her to be quiet.

47–8. *What beast was't then … to me?* Does this reference to an *enterprise* that Macbeth has discussed with his wife suggest that they have talked about the murder 'off-stage', i.e. in a scene that Shakespeare has not written for us? Or was Macbeth't letter to his wife a clear enough reference to the plan ?

Vaulting ambition, which o'er-leaps itself,
And falls on th' other.

[Enter LADY MACBETH.*]*

How now! What news?
Lady Macbeth
He has almost supp'd. Why have you left the chamber?
Macbeth
Hath he ask'd for me?
Lady Macbeth
Know you not he has?   30
Macbeth
We will proceed no further in this business.
He hath honour'd me of late; and I have bought
Golden opinions from all sorts of people,
Which would be worn now in their newest gloss,
Not cast aside so soon.
Lady Macbeth
Was the hope drunk   35
Wherein you dress'd yourself? Hath it slept since,
And wakes it now to look so green and pale
At what it did so freely? From this time
Such I account thy love. Art thou afeard
To be the same in thine own act and valour   40
As thou art in desire? Wouldst thou have that
Which thou esteem'st the ornament of life,
And live a coward in thine own esteem,
Letting 'I dare not' wait upon 'I would',
Like the poor cat i' th' adage?
Macbeth
Prithee, peace;   45
I dare do all that may become a man;
Who dares do more is none.
Lady Macbeth
What beast was't then
That made you break this enterprise to me?

50–1. *And to be more ... the man* You would be even more brave and manly if you made yourself king, rather than just a thane.

51–4. *Nor ... you* When there was no opportunity, you wished to create one; now when the opportunity presents itself, you are afraid to take it.

54–9. Lady Macbeth has seen the effect of her taunts on her husband and now comes out with the most outrageous and shocking statement of all. It sounds as though the *murd'ring ministers* she appealed to (Act I, Scene v, lines 47–8) have done as she asked; yet the force of these words depends on her and her husband's awareness that they are horrible and unnatural. In reply all Macbeth can say is, feebly, *If we should fail?*

60. *We fail!* How do you think she says these words – realistically ('Well, then, we fail') or scornfully ('How could we possibly fail?')?

64. *chamberlains* officials of the royal bedchamber.

65. *wine and wassail* drink and partying. It almost sounds as though Lady Macbeth intends personally to spend time with them, urging them to enjoy themselves, but probably she proposes simply to leave them plenty of drink, and encourage them to have a good time after she has left.

66–8. *That memory ... only* Memory, the keeper of one part of the brain, will be turned into smoke by the drink, which will smother the rest of the brain, where the rational part is.

68. *limbec* alembic, a kind of reply.

69. *drenched* drowned – but a 'drench' is animal medicine (e.g. poured down a horse's throat from a bottle) so perhaps this hints at the way Lady Macbeth views these puppets in her dreadful game – as animals?

72. *spongy* drunken.

73. *quell* murder (the word comes from the same origin as 'kill').

74. *mettle* spirit, temperament.

75. *receiv'd* accepted.

When you durst do it, then you were a man;
And to be more than what you were, you would   50
Be so much more the man. Nor time nor place
Did then adhere, and yet you would make both;
They have made themselves, and that their fitness now
Does unmake you. I have given suck, and know
How tender 'tis to love the babe that milks me –   55
I would, while it was smiling in my face,
Have pluck'd my nipple from his boneless gums,
And dash'd the brains out, had I so sworn
As you have done to this.

Macbeth

                If we should fail?

Lady Macbeth

We fail!   60
But screw your courage to the sticking place,
And we'll not fail. When Duncan is asleep –
Whereto the rather shall his day's hard journey
Soundly invite him – his two chamberlains
Will I with wine and wassail so convince   65
That memory, the warder of the brain,
Shall be a fume, and the receipt of reason
A limbec only. When in swinish sleep
Their drenched natures lie as in a death,
What cannot you and I perform upon   70
Th' unguarded Duncan? what not put upon
His spongy officers, who shall bear the guilt
Of our great quell?

Macbeth

                Bring forth men-children only;
For thy undaunted mettle should compose
Nothing but males. Will it not be receiv'd,   75
When we have mark'd with blood those sleepy two
Of his own chamber, and us'd their very daggers,
That they have done't?

80. *bend up* i.e. like a man preparing a crossbow for firing.

81. *Each corporal agent* All my physical powers.

82–3. Although now *settled*, Macbeth remains fully aware of the deceit and wickedness involved, whereas, at times, his wife seems to be able to delude herself that there is glory in the deed (e.g. line 73, *great quell*. Macbeth calls it a *deep damnation* in line 20, and a *terrible feat* in line 81).

Lady Macbeth

                    Who dares receive it other,
As we shall make our griefs and clamour roar
Upon his death?

Macbeth

                  I am settled, and bend up   80
Each corporal agent to this terrible feat.
Away, and mock the time with fairest show;
False face must hide what the false heart doth know.

[Exeunt.]

ACT II SCENE I

Apart from developing the story, and creating the atmosphere of horror before the murder, this scene also shows the difference between Banquo and Macbeth. Banquo and his son Fleance are good companions, and Banquo, suffering from *cursed thoughts,* appeals to the *Merciful powers of* goodness for help in fighting them. He also makes it fairly clear just afterwards that he is not happy about Macbeth's association with the witches.

1–5. As usual in the daylight of the Elizabethan theatre, it is necessary for Shakespeare to convey the time of day with words.

4. *There's husbandry in heaven* 'They are being thrifty up in heaven' (they have put their candles – stars – out).
5. *that* Having given Fleance his sword Banquo probably hands him his shield or cloak or dagger. Then, when Macbeth enters (line 9) his first instinct is to ask for his sword back, quickly.
6. *A heavy summons* i.e. to sleep.

13. *unusual pleasure* Probably because he is so appreciative of Macbeth's recent services and so confident of his thane's support and loyalty.
14. *largess* generous gifts.
14. *offices* servants' quarters.
15. *withal* with.
16–17. *shut up In measureless content* Duncan's day has ended in unlimited happiness.

ACT TWO

Scene I

Inverness. Court of Macbeth's castle

[Enter BANQUO, and FLEANCE with a torch before him.]

Banquo
How goes the night, boy?
Fleance
The moon is down; I have not heard the clock.
Banquo
And she goes down at twelve.
Fleance
                                          I tak't, 'tis later, sir.
Banquo
Hold, take my sword. There's husbandry in heaven;
Their candles are all out. Take thee that too.   5
A heavy summons lies like lead upon me,
And yet I would not sleep. Merciful powers
Restrain in me the cursed thoughts that nature
Gives way to in repose!

[Enter MACBETH and a SERVANT with a torch.]

                                          Give me my sword.
Who's there?   10
Macbeth
A friend.
Banquo
What, sir, not yet at rest? The king's a-bed.
He hath been in unusual pleasure, and
Sent forth great largess to your offices.
This diamond he greets your wife withal,   15
By the name of most kind hostess; and shut up
In measureless content.

17–19. *Being unprepar'd ... have wrought* Because we were not prepared, our wish to provide the king with generous hospitality could not be fulfilled.

22–4. *Yet, when ... the time* When we can find a convenient time, let us talk about the witches – if you are willing to do so.

25–6. These words of Macbeth's are deliberately vague. They could mean 'If you will follow my advice at the appropriate time' or 'If you will join my group of supporters *(consent)* when we emerge'.

26–29. Banquo's reply, refusing to commit himself to anyone, could be seen as equally unclear, and mean that either he is waiting to see what lies in store for him (after all, the witches have said his heirs will be king) or that he is rejecting the path Macbeth wishes to take. Either way, it is clear to Macbeth that Banquo is suspicious of him, and that he can't count on him for absolute support.

27. *augment* increase.

28. *bosom franchise and allegiance clear* my conscience free from guilt and my allegiance innocent.

29. *I shall be counselled* I will accept your advice.

33–49. In the first part of this soliloquy Macbeth is revealed even more deeply than usual in such speeches, for the illusion of the bloody dagger shows us what we would now call his subconscious mind. Like Lady Macbeth he is denying his own true nature in preparing to commit the murder, and one of the penalties is a *heat-oppressed brain.*

66

Macbeth
>>> Being unprepar'd,
Our will became the servant to defect;
Which else should free have wrought.

Banquo
>>> All's well.
I dreamt last night of the three Weird Sisters,   20
To you they have show'd some truth.

Macbeth
>>> I think not of them;
Yet, when we can entreat an hour to serve,
We would spend it in some words upon that business,
If you would grant the time.

Banquo
>>> At your kind'st leisure.

Macbeth
If you shall cleave to my consent, when 'tis,   25
It shall make honour for you.

Banquo
>>> So I lose none
In seeking to augment it, but still keep
My bosom franchis'd and allegiance clear,
I shall be counsell'd.

Macbeth
>>> Good repose the while!

Banquo
Thanks, air; the like to you!   30

[Exeunt BANQUO and FLEANCE.]

Macbeth
Go bid thy mistress, when my drink is ready,
She strike upon the bell. Get thee to bed.

[Exit SERVANT.]

Is this a dagger which I see before me,
The handle toward my hand? Come, let me clutch thee.

36–7. *sensible To feeling as to sight?* (something that can be) touched as well as seen?

39. *heat-oppressed* feverish.
40. *palpable* touchable.

42. The dagger is probably moving towards Duncan's bedroom, as though it is encouraging Macbeth to go and do the deed.
44–5. *Mine eyes ... the rest* Either my eyes are deceived (my other senses tell me there is no dagger) or else they are worth all my other senses put together (what I see really is a dagger).
46. *dudgeon* handle.
46. *gouts* drops.
48. *the bloody business* the murder plan playing on his imagination.
49. *the one half–world* the darkened northern hemisphere.
51. *curtain'd sleep* sleep behind closed eyelids, or behind the curtains of a four-poster bed.
52. *Pale Hecate's offerings* The goddess of witchcraft's rituals
52–6. *and wither'd murder...* Murder, personified as an aged, perhaps skeleton-like man, is awakened by the howl of a wolf, which keeps the time for him, and he moves stealthily, ghost-like (or in the same way that Tarquin went to rape Lucretia), to do his killing. Tarquin was an infamous King of Ancient Rome who raped the very virtuous Lucretia.
58. *prate* talk.
60. *threat* threaten.
61. He is telling himself to stop talking and get on with it.
62. The sound of the bell comes before the murder; the sound of knocking on the gate follows it.

63. *knell* a funeral bell

I have thee not, and yet I see thee still.   35
Art thou not, fatal vision, sensible
To feeling as to sight? or art thou but
A dagger of the mind, a false creation,
Proceeding from the heat-oppressed brain?
I see thee yet, in form as palpable   40
As this which now I draw.
Thou marshall'st me the way that I was going;
And such an instrument I was to use.
Mine eyes are made the fools o' th' other senses,
Or else worth all the rest. I see thee still;   45
And on thy blade and dudgeon gouts of blood,
Which was not so before. There's no such thing:
It is the bloody business which informs
Thus to mine eyes. Now o'er the one half-world
Nature seems dead, and wicked dreams abuse   50
The curtain'd sleep; now witchcraft celebrates
Pale Hecate's offerings; and wither'd murder,
Alarum'd by his sentinel the wolf,
Whose howl's his watch, thus with his stealthy pace,
With Tarquln's ravishing strides, towards his design   55
Moves like a ghost. Thou sure and firm-set earth,
Hear not my steps which way they walk, for fear
Thy very stones prate of my whereabout
And take the present horror from the time,
Which now suits with it. Whiles I threat, he lives;   60
Words to the heat of deeds too cold breath gives.

[A bell rings.]

I go, and it is done; the bell invites me.
Hear it not, Duncan, for it is a knell
That summons thee to heaven or to hell.

[Exit.]

SCENE II

Lady Macbeth now reveals that she, too, like the chamberlains she mentioned earlier, has been drinking, but in her case the effect has been to give her an artificial courage. Is this perhaps another sign that she is not quite as tough as she seems?

2. *quench'd* put them out (like extinguished candles); in contrast. Lady Macbeth has been 'set alight' by the drink.

2. *Hark!* in spite of everything she is still capable of being frightened, in this case by an owl's cry.

3. The cry of an owl was thought to indicate that someone was about to die.

3–4. *the fatal bellman ... good-night* the night before a man was to be executed an official used to ring a bell outside the door of his cell.

4. *stern'st good-night* the final, most serious farewell, when a man is about to die.

4. *He is about it* Macbeth is now murdering the king.

5. *surfeited* having had too much of something, in this case strong drink. The word *groom* was applied to any low-grade servant. These grooms are attendants on the king who act as bodyguards.

6. *mock their charge with snores* they show how hopelessly they have failed by snoring while on duty.

6. *drugged their possets* a posset was a nightcap containing milk, egg and some alcoholic drink, with other ingredients. Lady Macbeth had made quite sure that the men would be put out of action by adding a drug to the drink.

7. *nature* life. Life and death are here thought of as two persons each of whom argues that the grooms belong to him.

8. Like his wife, Macbeth is startled by a sound. The effect of his frightened shout is all the greater because it comes from off-stage.

10–11. *Th' attempt ... Confounds us* if, as I fear, he has tried to kill the king but failed, we shall be ruined.

11. *I laid their daggers ready* Lady Macbeth has taken the grooms' daggers out of their scabbards and left them ready for Macbeth to do the stabbing. In his absent-minded horror Macbeth comes in with these daggers. How do you think he is carrying them?

13. *My husband!* what emotions do you think are packed into these words? Surprise? Admiration? Any others?

15. Both owls and crickets were thought to foretell death.

Scene II

Inverness. Macbeth's castle

[Enter LADY MACBETH.*]*

Lady Macbeth
That which hath made them drunk hath made me bold
What hath quench'd them hath given me fire.
    Hark! Peace!
It was the owl that shriek'd, the fatal bellman,
Which gives the stern'st good-night. He is about it.
The doors are open; and the surfeited grooms   5
Do mock their charge with snores. I have drugg'd
    their possets,
That death and nature do contend about them,
Whether they live or die.

Macbeth
[within]   Who's there! What, ho!

Lady Macbeth
Alack! I am afraid they have awak'd,
And 'tis not done. Th' attempt, and not the deed,   10
Confounds us. Hark! I laid their daggers ready;
He could not miss 'em. Had he not resembled
My father as he slept, I had done't.

[Enter MACBETH.*]*

                    My husband!

Macbeth
I have done the deed. Didst thou not hear a noise?

Lady Macbeth
I heard the owl scream and the crickets cry.   15
Did not you speak?

Macbeth
            When?

Lady Macbeth
                Now.

16–20. The jerky conversation obviously adds to the tension in the audience and also shows how jumpy Macbeth and his wife are.

19. Why does Lady Macbeth mention only Donalbain, when Malcolm too seems to be sleeping in the *second chamber* (next room) ?

20. *sorry* wretched, miserable.

22. Who are these two men? It's not absolutely clear, but it is perhaps more likely they are the king's sons rather than the grooms, given that they say 'their prayers.'

25. *There are two lodg'd together* Lady Macbeth is pointing out that, as the two princes – if it is them – are sharing a room, the disturbance may be confined to them.

27. *hangman's hands* the word *hangman* was used for an executioner, whatever method he used; but since he usually 'drew' and 'quartered' the body (disembowelled it and cut it into pieces) even when the man had been hanged, a hangman's hands would often have been covered with blood.

28. *List'ning their fear* listening to

35–9. In this speech Macbeth expresses his horror at the fact that he has killed a man in the helpless innocence of sleep; in his imagination he condemns himself to a fitting punishment – never to sleep again.

Macbeth
                                            As I descended?
Lady Macbeth
  Ay.
Macbeth
    Hark!
  Who lies i' th' second chamber?
Lady Macbeth
                                            Donalbain.
Macbeth
  [looking on his hands] This is a sorry sight.   20
Lady Macbeth
  A foolish thought to say a sorry sight.
Macbeth
  There's one did laugh in's sleep, and one cried 'Murder!'
  That they did wake each other. I stood and heard them
  But they did say their prayers, and address'd them
  Again to sleep.
Lady Macbeth
                          There are two lodg'd together.   25
Macbeth
  One cried 'God bless us,' and 'Amen' the other,
  As they had seen me with these hangman's hands.
  List'ning their fear, I could not say 'Amen'
  When they did say 'God bless us!'
Lady Macbeth
                                    Consider it not so deeply.   30
Macbeth
  But wherefore could not I pronounce 'Amen'?
  I had most need of blessing, and 'Amen'
  Stuck in my throat.
Lady Macbeth
                        These deeds must not be thought
  After these ways: so, it will make us mad.
Macbeth
  Methought I heard a voice cry 'Sleep no more;   35
  Macbeth does murder sleep' – the innocent sleep,

37. *knits up the ravell'd sleave* probably *sleave* means a piece of coarse silk; it has become (as we say) unravelled or frayed, but can be restored by knitting or stitching. In modern terms, sleep helps to soothe frayed nerves.

38. *sore labour's bath* like a refreshing bath after a hard day's work

39–40. *great nature's second course. Chief nourisher in life's feast* a pudding or sweet used to be the first course at dinner; the main meat dish came after it.

44. Lady Macbeth, always more practical than her husband, is puzzled to know who could have been making the frightening comments about sleep.

45–6. She shows a familiar reaction to evidence of his mental instability; 'Pull yourself together and don't be silly (brainsick)!'

46. *Go, get some water* ... an apparently sensible, realistic way of dealing with the situation, but later it will prove completely inadequate as she tries to rid herself of the memory of the crime (See Act V, Scene i, line 40: *What, will these hands ne'er be clean?*)

47. *witness* evidence.

52. *Infirm of purpose!* Lady Macbeth's most effective way of bullying her husband is to comment scornfully on his weak will.

53–5. *The sleeping* ... she sounds strong and confident now, in contrast with Macbeth, yet earlier in this very scene (lines 12–13) she saw Duncan with *the eye of childhood* herself, and could not kill him.

55. *A painted devil* a mere picture of a devil.

56–7. *gild the faces* paint with blood. Her use of the word *guilt* is a pun on 'gilt', a layer of gold (although of course here the layer will be red). Do you find such punning out of place at such a terrible moment? For the Elizabethans they often conveyed tension and irony, not just rather obvious humour.

57. *Whence is that knocking?* Macbeth takes the knocking at first to be a supernatural thing. In the next scene we find out that Macduff and Lennox have been knocking at the castle gate in order to come in and wake the king.

59. Macbeth is becoming so obsessed with the sight of his own bloody hands that they almost blind him.

60. Neptune was the Roman god of the sea.

Sleep that knits up the ravell'd sleave of care,
The death of each day's life, sore labour's bath,
Balm of hurt minds, great nature's second course,
Chief nourisher in life's feast.
Lady Macbeth

                     What do you mean?   40

Macbeth
Still it cried 'Sleep no more' to all the house;
'Glamis hath murder'd sleep; and therefore Cawdor
Shall sleep no more – Macbeth shall sleep no more'.
Lady Macbeth
Who was it that thus cried? Why, worthy Thane,
You do unbend your noble strength to think   45
So brainsickly of things. Go get some water
And wash this filthy witness from your hand.
Why did you bring these daggers from the place?
They must lie there. Go carry them, and smear
The sleepy grooms with blood.
Macbeth

                       I'll go no more: 50
I am afraid to think what I have done;
Look on't again I dare not.
Lady Macbeth

                  Infirm of purpose!
Give me the daggers. The sleeping and the dead
Are but as pictures; 'tis the eye of childhood
That fears a painted devil. If he do bleed,   55
I'll gild the faces of the grooms withal,
For it must seem their guilt.

             [Exit. Knocking within.]

Macbeth

                Whence is that knocking?
How is't with me, when every noise appals me?
What hands are here? Ha! they pluck out mine eyes.
Will all great Neptune's ocean wash this blood   60

61–3. Macbeth says that if he tries to wash his hands in the sea there is so much blood it will make the whole ocean red.

62. *multitudinous* vast.

62. *incarnadine* turn red (literally flesh-coloured). After putting this wildly imaginative idea in long words derived from Latin, Shakespeare almost repeats it in short Anglo-Saxon words.

63. *one red* entirely red;

65. *a heart so white* accusations of cowardice are another of Lady Macbeth's weapons against her husband.

67. She sounds confident but she too is later obsessed with the impossibility of washing the blood away (Act V, Scene i).

70. They have not changed into their night-clothes so far. She reminds him to do so, otherwise those who are knocking will think it strange that she and Macbeth are up and about, fully-clothed, in the middle of the night.

73. Macbeth knows that he cannot face fully the deed he has done, and take responsibility for it.

Clean from my hand? No; this my hand will rather
The multitudinous seas incarnadine,
Making the green one red.

[Re-enter LADY MACBETH.]

Lady Macbeth
  My hands are of your colour; but I shame
  To wear a heart so white. *[Knock]* I hear a knocking   65
  At the south entry; retire we to our chamber.
  A little water clears us of this deed.
  How easy is it then! Your constancy
  Hath left you unattended. *[Knock]* Hark! more knocking,
  Get on your nightgown, lest occasion call us   70
  And show us to be watchers. Be not lost
  So poorly in your thoughts.
Macbeth
  To know my deed, 'twere best not know myself. *[Knock]*
  Wake Duncan with thy knocking! I would thou couldst!

[Exeunt.]

SCENE III

It may seem strange that the Porter's speech and conversation with Macduff and Lennox comes here, and some critics have even claimed that Shakespeare didn't write this opening. However, the audience do need *some* relief after the tension of the previous scene; it is certainly ironically appropriate that the Porter compares himself with the *porter of hell gate*, and this is almost what he is given what has just happened. The unlocking of the gate also brings in the decent, outside world and introduces us to the central figure of Macduff.

2. The word *old* was often used in the sense of much, a lot of.

4. *Beelzebub* Satan's lieutenant – but the name is often used of the Devil himself.

4–5. *Here's a farmer ... plenty* The Porter imagines himself to be a kind of guide showing us round Hell. The first of the damned he sees is a farmer who has committed suicide because the good harvest will put the price of corn down.

5–6. *Come in time ... sweat for't* Come early, then you can enjoy the bonfire of Hell and sweat freely, so you'll need cloths to wipe yourself.

7. *i'th'other devil's name?* It sounds as though the Porter cannot remember the name of any other devil.

8. *equivocator* Probably a Jesuit priest, because the Jesuits were then believed to use words deceptively (to equivocate) in their defence against charges of treason.

9. *the scales* Justice, personified as a woman, held scales in which to balance the evidence.

10–11. *could not equivocate to heaven* A well-known Jesuit called Garnet was hanged and that ended all his equivocation ... perhaps Shakespeare is referring to him.

12–13. *an English tailor ... French hose* Tailors had a reputation for making clothes their customers ordered with the minimum of material and keeping the rest themselves. French hose had been very full and loose, and this gave the thieving tailors plenty of scope. But the French fashion had recently changed and tight hose made it obvious when they got up to their cloth-stealing tricks.

14. *roast your goose* A goose was a tailor's smoothing-iron, but the phrase probably also meant something like 'kill the goose that laid the golden eggs', i.e. the tailor has tried his trick once too often and will profit no more from stealing customers' material.

18. *the primrose way ... bonfire* the pleasant, easy path to Hell.

19–20. *remember the porter* He is suggesting that they should tip him (even though he has taken so long to open the gate).

Scene III

Inverness. Macbeth's castle

[Knocking within. Enter a PORTER.]

Porter

Here's a knocking indeed! If a man were porter of
hell-gate, he should have old turning the key. *[Knock]*
Knock, knock, knock! Who's there, i' th' name of
Beelzebub? Here's a farmer that hang'd himself on
th' expectation of plenty. Come in time; have napkins   5
enow about you; here you'll sweat for't. *[Knock]*
Knock, knock! Who's there, i' th' other devil's name?
Faith, here's an equivocator, that could swear in both
the scales against either scale; who committed treason
enough for God's sake, yet could not equivocate to   10
heaven. O, come in, equivocator. *[Knock]* Knock,
knock! Who's there? Faith, here's an English tailor
come hither for stealing out of a French hose. Come
in, tailor, here you may roast your goose. *[Knock]*
Knock, knock; never at quiet! What are you? But this   15
place is too cold for hell. I'll devil-porter it no further.
I had thought to have let in some of all professions
that go the primrose way to th' everlasting bonfire.
[Knock] Anon, anon! *[Opens the gate]* I pray you
remember the porter.   20

[Enter MACDUFF and LENNOX.]

Macduff

Was it so late, friend, ere you went to bed, that you
do lie so late?

23. *carousing* drinking riotously.

23. *second cock* This was a way of saying 'three o'clock in the morning'.

23–40. In this conversation the Porter plays the part of a typical Elizabethan working-man as shown on stage, making rude jokes and relishing playing with words, while Macduff is the upper-class listener, willing to go along with the joke for a while.

26. *nose-painting* getting yourself a red nose (from too much alcohol)

Lechery lust.

29. *equivocatar* deceiver.

33. *equivocates him in a sleep* sends him to sleep and gives him lustful dreams (but no satisfaction for his lust).

33–4 & 35. *giving him the lie ... gave thee the lie* These could mean 'to lay out', as in wrestling or boxing.

36–9. The Porter plays with the wrestling metaphor and the idea of relieving himself.

36. *requited him* paid him back.

38–9. *made a shift* managed.

42. *Good morrow* Good morning.

44. *timely* early.

Porter

Faith, sir, we were carousing till the second cock; and
drink, sir, is a great provoker of three things.

Macduff

What three things does drink especially provoke?   25

Porter

Marry, sir, nose-painting, sleep, and urine. Lechery,
sir, it provokes and unprovokes; it provokes the
desire, but it takes away the performance. Therefore
much drink may be said to be an equivocator with
lechery: it makes him, and it mars him; it sets him on,   30
and it takes him off; it persuades him, and disheartens
him; makes him stand to, and not stand to; in conclusion, equivocates him in a sleep, and, giving nun the
lie, leaves him.

Macduff

I believe drink gave thee the lie last night.   35

Porter

That it did, sir, i' the very throat on me; but I requited
him for his lie; and, I think, being too strong for him,
though he took up my legs sometime, yet I made a
shift to cast him.

Macduff

Is thy master stirring?   40

[Enter MACBETH.]

Our knocking has awak'd him; here he comes.

Lennox

Good morrow, noble sir!

Macbeth

                    Good morrow, both!

Macduff

Is the King stirring, worthy Thane?

Macbeth

                              Not yet.

Macduff

He did command me to call timely on him;

45. *slipped the hour* missed my appointment.

46–7. 'I know this is a duty that you take pleasure in. but still it is an inconvenience'. Macbeth replies in the elaborately polite style that he seems to use at times of strain.
48. *physics pain* acts as medicine to the pain (in this case the inconvenience) and removes it.

50. *limited* appointed. Macduff has already explained that the King had instructed him to wake him early.

53–60. Lennox's description of the wild weather clearly suggests a supernatural origin for it. Nature, in Shakespeare's work, often reflects tragic or horrible events in human life.

57–8. *Of dire combustion ... woeful time* Terrible confusion developing out of this dreadful time.
58–9. *the obscure bird ... night* the owl screamed right through the night.
59–60. *the earth Was feverous* the earth trembled (in an earthquake) like a man in a fever.

61–2. There has never been such a night in my comparatively short life.

63–4. Strictly speaking Macduff has the two subjects the wrong way round; what he means is 'The imagination cannot conceive such a horror and the tongue cannot express it'.

I have almost slipp'd the hour.   45

Macbeth

                                    I'll bring you to him.

Macduff

I know this is a joyful trouble to you;
But yet 'tis one.

Macbeth

The labour we delight in physics pain.
This is the door.

Macduff

                    I'll make so bold to call,
For 'tis my limited service.   50

[Exit MACDUFF.]

Lennox

Goes the King hence to-day?

Macbeth

He does; he did appoint so.

Lennox

The night has been unruly. Where we lay,
Our chimneys were blown down; and, as they say,
Lamentings heard i' th' air, strange screams of death,   55
And prophesying, with accents terrible,
Of dire combustion and confus'd events
New hatch'd to th' woeful time; the obscure bird
Clamour'd the livelong night. Some say the earth
Was feverous and did shake.

Macbeth

                            'Twas a rough night.   60

Lennox

My young remembrance cannot parallel
A fellow to it.

[Re-enter MACDUFF.]

Macduff

O horror, horror, horror! Tongue nor heart
Cannot conceive nor name thee.

65. *Confusion* This was a very strong word, meaning something like utter chaos. This speech of Macduff's expresses the view of kingship as a powerful symbol of all order, linked to God, who created order in the first place.

67. *The Lord's anointed temple* Duncan, who like many kings, right down to the present day, was anointed with holy oil at his coronation.

71. *a new Gorgon* In the classical legend Medusa and her two sisters, all known as Gorgons, are represented as hideous women with snakes for hair who could turn to stone those who looked at them.

75. *downy sleep ... counterfeit* soft sleep, a gentle image of death.

77. *The great doom's image!* Macduff sees the murder of the King as comparable with the Day of Judgment at the end of the world.

78. *sprites* ghosts

81–2. That such a harsh trumpet calls those sleeping in the castle to a discussion (like opposing troops at a truce during war).

83–6. For the audience, there is a terrible irony in the idea of Lady Macbeth being too gentle and feminine to stand the awful news.

85. *repetition* report.

Macbeth and Lennox

What's the matter?

Macduff
　Confusion now hath made his masterpiece.
　Most sacrilegious murder hath broke ope 65
　The Lord's anointed temple, and stole thence
　The life o' th' building.

Kings are sacred
murder is sacreligious

Macbeth

What is't you say – the life?

Lennox
　Mean you his Majesty?

Macduff
　Approach the chamber, and destroy your sight 70
　With a new Gorgon. Do not bid me speak;
　See, and then speak yourselves.

[Exeunt MACBETH *and* LENNOX.*]*

Awake, awake!
　Ring the alarum bell. Murder and treason!
　Banquo and Donalbain! Malcolm! awake!
　Shake off this downy sleep, death's counterfeit, 75
　And look on death itself. Up, up, and see
　The great doom's image! Malcolm! Banquo!
　As from your graves rise up and walk like sprites
　To countenance this horror! Ring the bell.

[Bell rings. Enter LADY MACBETH.*]*

Lady Macbeth
　What's the business, 80
　That such a hideous trumpet calls to parley
　The sleepers of the house? Speak, speak!

Macduff
　O gentle lady,
　'Tis not for you to hear what I can speak!
　The repetition in a woman's ear 85
　Would murder as it fell.

[Enter BANQUO.*]*

85

89. *What, in our house?* Does Lady Macbeth slip up in saying these words, or are they natural enough in the mouth of a supposedly horrified hostess?

91–6. Here is Macbeth's elaborate style again-as though he had prepared the speech beforehand to prove how he feels.

91. *before this chance* before what has happened.

93. There's nothing worth attention in the whole of human activity.

94. *toys* triviality.

95–6. 'All the wine of life has been drawn from the cask and there is nothing but the dregs left', *(this vault* presumably the earth). The whole of this speech of Macbeth's has a dreadful irony about it. He is striving to act the part of a loyal, sorrowful subject but perhaps his words reveal his true feelings about what he's done and how it has changed him.

97. When Macbeth says the two young men are *amiss* he means they are ruined by their father's death.

98–9. *spring, head, fountain, source* all describe the place at which a river or stream commences. Macbeth is using four words which mean the same thing.

101–5. The Macbeths must be pleased that Lennox puts the blame on the grooms, but later it appears that this explanation doesn't satisfy everyone.

102. *badg'd* splotched (as though with red badges).

                    O Banquo, Banquo,
Our royal master's murder'd!
Lady Macbeth

                       Woe, alas!
What, in our house?
Banquo

                 Too cruel anywhere.
Dear Duff, I prithee contradict thyself,
And say it is not so.   90

      [Re-enter MACBETH, LENNOX, *with* ROSS.*]*

Macbeth
Had I but died an hour before this chance,
I had liv'd a blessed time; for, from this instant,
There's nothing serious in mortality –
All is but toys; renown and grace is dead;
The wine of life is drawn, and the mere lees   95
Is left this vault to brag of.

      [Enter MALCOLM *and* DONALBAIN.*]*

Donalbain
What is amiss?
Macbeth

               You are, and do not know't.
The spring, the head, the fountain of your blood,
Is stopp'd; the very source of it is stopp'd.
Macduff
Your royal father's murder'd.
Malcolm

               O, by whom?   100
Lennox
Those of his chamber, as it seem'd, had done't.
Their hands and faces were all badg'd with blood;
So were their daggers, which unwip'd we found
Upon their pillows. They star'd and were distracted;
No man's life was to be trusted with them.   105

107. Macduff seems to express particular puzzlement about Macbeth's killing the grooms. Perhaps his doubts about Macbeth's character start here.

108–18. Questioned so directly Macbeth makes great verbal efforts to sound convincing, but produces a string of very forced metaphors, and possibly only succeeds in convincing his wife that she must do something to draw attention away from him.

110. *expedition* rush.

111. *the pauser reason* reason, which causes a person to delay before acting.

116. *Unmannerly breech'd with gore* Macbeth is referring, in rather exaggerated language, to the daggers as though they had trousers of blood on them right up to the hilts. This is one of a large number of images from clothing in the play (see the Theme Index at the end).

116. *refrain* hold himself back (i.e. refrain from killing the grooms in righteous indignation).

118. Some think that Lady Macbeth's fainting-fit is put it on in order to draw attention from her husband's over-acting; others regard it as the emotion and pressure having got to her – showing she is not as tough as she seems – and the beginning of her decline into madness.

120–1. Why are we keeping quiet, since we (Duncan's sons) have the best reason to express grief?

122. *auger-hole* an auger is the tool a carpenter uses for boring small holes. Donalbain is suggesting that their fate may be hidden nearby, ready to spring out and overwhelm them without warning (i.e. the murderer of their father may be prepared to kill them too). The expression also conveys the idea of the kind of hole made in a human body by a dagger.

124. People in the first shock of bereavement often find that they can't express their feelings freely by weeping. Donalbain is contrasting his own and his brother's reluctance to show their feelings with Macbeth's noisy display.

125. *Upon the foot of motion* ready to be expressed.

Macbeth
  O, yet I do repent me of my fury
  That I did kill them.
Macduff
                          Wherefore did you so?
Macbeth
  Who can be wise, amaz'd, temp'rate, and furious,
  Loyal and neutral, in a moment? No man.
  The expedition of my violent love   110
  Outrun the pauser reason. Here lay Duncan,
  His silver skin lac'd with his golden blood;
  And his gash'd stabs look'd like a breach in nature
  For ruin's wasteful entrance: there, the murderers,
  Steep'd in the colours of their trade, their daggers   115
  Unmannerly breech'd with gore. Who could refrain,
  That had a heart to love, and in that heart
  Courage to make's love known?
Lady Macbeth
                                    Help me hence, ho!
Macduff
  Look to the lady.
Malcolm
  [*aside to* DONALBAIN] Why do we hold our tongues
      that most may claim   120
  This argument for ours?
Donalbain
  [*aside to* MALCOLM]   What should be spoken
  Here, where our fate, hid in an auger-hole,
  May rush and seize us? Let's away.
  Our tears are not yet brew'd.
Malcolm
  [*aside to* DONALBAIN]   Nor our strong sorrow
  Upon the foot of motion.
Banquo
                              Look to the lady.   125

  [LADY MACBETH *is carried out.*]

126. *naked frailties* unclothed, weak bodies

129. *scruples* doubts.

130–2. Banquo makes it clear that he is committed to an honest, open way of life, and he loathes the deceit *(undivulg'd pretence)* and hate *(malice)* that have killed Duncan. (Some critics think that Banquo is already fearful that Malcolm may soon be killed also, and that the *undivulg'd pretence* is the intention to destroy him.)

133. *manly readiness* either simply men's clothes (men may still be in their night-clothes) *or* masculine qualities such as courage and determination.

135. *consort* mix, associate.

136. *unfelt sorrow* This does not imply that Malcolm is unaffected by his father's death. The brothers have already agreed in lines 124–5 that they had not had time yet to be clear about their feelings and to express them.

136. *office* duty.

137. It is pretty clear that *the false man* is Macbeth, and that Malcolm and Donalbain know who their enemy is. *easy* easily.

138–9. *our separated fortune ... safer* 'we'll be safer if we stay apart'. But why?

139–40. *Where we are ... smiles* 'Here in Scotland those who smile at us (i.e. Macbeth) are really our deadly enemies'. Does this suggest that Macbeth has gone out of his way in this scene to appear friendly? If you were producing the play and wanted to make this point, where would you instruct Macbeth to smile?

140–1. *the near in blood ... bloody* those closest to us (Macbeth is a relative) may be the ones who are most murderous

141–2. *This murderous shaft ... lighted* An odd statement, because it has certainly *lighted* (fallen) once already, on Duncan. Malcolm means that it will hurt others before it has finished its flight.

144. *dainty of leave-taking* leave without ceremony.

145. *shift away* slip away secretly *(shift* here has the meaning of planning or contriving to do something).

145–6. *There's warrant ... left* Malcolm is a little uneasy about running away, but justifies it on the grounds that their enemy is ruthless. *steals* 'goes stealthily away' as well as 'robs'.

And when we have our naked frailties hid,
That suffer in exposure, let us meet,
And question this most bloody piece of work,
To know it further. Fears and scruples shake us.
In the great hand of God I stand, and thence   130
Against the undivulg'd pretence I fight
Of treasonous malice.

Macduff
           And so do I.

All
               So all.

Macbeth
Let's briefly put on manly readiness
And meet i' th' hall together.

All
           Well contented.

[Exeunt all but MALCOLM *and* DONALBAIN.*]*

Malcolm
What will you do? Let's not consort with them.   135
To show an unfelt sorrow is an office
Which the false man does easy. I'll to England.

Donalbain
To Ireland I; our separated fortune
Shall keep us both the safer. Where we are,
There's daggers in men's smiles; the near in blood,   140
The nearer bloody.

Malcolm
          This murderous shaft that's shot
Hath not yet lighted; and our safest way
Is to avoid the aim. Therefore to horse;
And let us not be dainty of leave-taking,
But shift away. There's warrant in that theft   145
Which steals itself, when there's no mercy left.

[Exeunt.]

SCENE IV

Shakespeare frequently shows scenes in which strange and sinister events in Nature reflect human horrors and disasters. The disturbing things that Ross and the Old Man tell us about emphasize the unnaturalness of Macbeth's crime. Another purpose of the scene is to present Macduff as a decent man (he is referred to as *the good Macduff*) who strongly suspects Macbeth and is unwilling go to Scone for Macbeth's coronation (line 36).

Stage Direction *Without* outside. When Macduff enters be comes straight from the castle with the latest news.

1. *Threescore and ten* the traditional life-span of a man is 70 years, so this Old Man, who must be nearly 80, looks back with particular authority; even he can recall nothing like the night that has just passed.

3–4. *this sore night ... knowings* this terrible night has made all previous experiences seem trivial.

6. *his bloody stage* the stage on which man carries out his bloody deeds – that is, the earth.

7. *strangles the travelling lamp* obscures the sun.

12–13. *tow'ring* and *place* terms from falconry, *towering* means spiralling upwards to the place or 'pitch', which was the height from which a hawk 'stooped' or swooped down on to its prey. For an owl to attack and kill a falcon would have been unusual

13. *mousing* hunting mice.

15. *minions* favourites – that is, the best of their kind.

16. *Turned wild in nature* went back to being wild - no longer domestic animals.

17. *as* as if.

18. *eat* the past tense, now spelt 'ate'.

Scene IV

Inverness. Without Macbeth's castle

[Enter ROSS *with an* OLD MAN.*]*

Old Man
    Threescore and ten I can remember well;
    Within the volume of which time I have seen
    Hours dreadful and things strange; but this sore night
    Hath trifled former knowings.
Ross
                Ah, good father,
    Thou seest, the heavens, as troubled with man's act,   5
    Threatens his bloody stage. By th' clock 'tis day,
    And yet dark night strangles the travelling lamp.
    Is't night's predominance, or the day's shame,
    That darkness does the face of earth entomb,
    When living light should kiss it?
Old Man
                    'Tis unnatural,   10
    Even like the deed that's done. On Tuesday last,
    A falcon, tow'ring in her pride of place,
    Was by a mousing owl hawk'd at and kill'd.
Ross
    And Duncan's horses – a thing most strange and
        certain –
    Beauteous and swift, the minions of their race,   15
    Turn'd wild in nature, broke their stalls, flung out,
    Contending 'gainst obedience, as they would make
    War with mankind.
Old Man
              'Tis said they eat each other.
Ross
    They did so; to the amazement of mine eyes,
    That look'd upon't.

23. Macduff is careful at first to only say what is being said officially, but before the end of the scene it becomes evident that he has, privately, other ideas.
24. *pretend* intend.
24. *suborn'd* paid to do the deed.

27. *'Gainst nature still* Yet another unnatural event!
28. *Thriftless* unprofitable.
28. *ravin up* 'wolf down', swallow greedily.
29. *Thine own life's means* the source of their own life, i.e. their father.
29. *like* likely.
30. New kings of Scotland were appointed by a form of election.
31. *Scone* the ancient royal city; kings were crowned on the Stone of Destiny, which was supposed to be Jacob's pillow (see *Genesis* 28, verse 11). In 1296 Edward I of England took the stone to Westminster Abbey and, since then, all British sovereigns have been crowned on it.
32. *To be invested* to go through the coronation ceremony.
33. *Colmekill* The name means Colm's, or St Columba's, cell, on the island of Iona; this was where Scottish kings were buried.
34. *The sacred ... predecessors* the place where previous kings had been buried.

36. *Fife* the home of Macduff, Thane of Fife.

[Enter MACDUFF.]

     Here comes the good Macduff. 20
How goes the world, sir, now?
Macduff
        Why, see you not?
Ross
Is't known who did this more than bloody deed?
Macduff
Those that Macbeth hath slain.
Ross
       Alas, the day!
What good could they pretend?
Macduff
       They were suborn'd
Malcolm and Donalbain, the King's two sons, 25
Are stol'n away and fled; which puts upon them
Suspicion of the deed.
Ross
      'Gainst nature still.
Thriftless ambition, that wilt ravin up
Thine own life's means! Then 'tis most like
The sovereignty will fall upon Macbeth. 30
Macduff
He is already nam'd, and gone to Scone
To be invested.
Ross
    Where is Duncan's body?
Macduff
Carried to Colmekill,
The sacred storehouse of his predecessors
And guardian of their bones.
Ross
      Will you to Scone? 35
Macduff
No, cousin, I'll to Fife.

37. *Well* Macduff repeats, probably sarcastically, Ross's neutral-sounding '*Well*'

40. *benison* blessing.
40–1. The Old Man's hopes are the first suggestion of a possible reversal of fortunes in the future. So far only those who have turned good into bad have been successful.

Ross

Well, I will thither.

Macduff

Well, may you see things well done there! Adieu,
Lest our old robes sit easier than our new.

Ross

Farewell, father.

Old Man

God's benison go with you, and with those   40
That would make good of bad, and friends of foes.

[Exeunt.]

ACT III SCENE I

Banquo is now almost certain that Macbeth became king by foul means. He, too, would like to have the witches' prophecies about him fulfilled, but apparently has no intention of using Macbeth's methods. Do you think he should have been more actively anti-Macbeth? Does Banquo strike you as someone with the right ideas, but without the determination to go through with them? Or is he, in his own way as ambitious as Macbeth?

4. *It should ... posterity* Your descendants would not become kings.
6. *them* the witches.
7. *their speeches shine*: their words come gloriously true
8. *verities* truths.
9. *oracles* An oracle, among the Greeks and Romans, was a person who acted as a mouthpiece of the gods. Banquo wonders whether the witches do perhaps tell the truth, and whether what they said about him may prove reliable.
10. *But, hush, no more* Banquo dismisses his own ambitious thoughts.

Stage Direction *Sennet sounded* a sennet was a series of notes on a trumpet, announcing an important arrival, such as that of a king.

11–13. Macbeth begins by deliberately flattering Banquo, and Lady Macbeth joins in with even more flowery language (there is an ominous echo of the Macbeths' invitation to Duncan).

13. *all-thing unbecoming* totally unfitting.
14. *solemn* formal (the word usually means this in Shakespeare).

15–18. The style of Banquo's response seems as artificial as the invitation. Do you blame him for this? (It is possible that, when he says *Let your Highness Command upon me*, he means 'If you, as King, order me, I haven't much alternative'. At least this may be what he implies.)

ACT THREE

Scene I

Forres. The palace

[Enter BANQUO.*]*

Banquo
    Thou hast it now – King, Cawdor, Glamis, all
    As the weird women promis'd; and I fear
    Thou play'dst most foully fort; yet it was said
    It should not stand in thy posterity;
    But that myself should be the root and father   5
    Of many kings. If there come truth from them –
    As upon thee, Macbeth, their speeches shine –
    Why, by the verities on thee made good,
    May they not be my oracles as well
    And set me up in hope? But, hush, no more.   10

  [Sennet sounded. Enter MACBETH *as King,* LADY MACBETH
as Queen; LENNOX, ROSS, LORDS, LADIES *and* ATTENDANTS.*]*

Macbeth
    Here's our chief guest.
Lady Macbeth
                 If he had been forgotten,
    It had been as a gap in our great feast,
    And all-thing unbecoming.
Macbeth
    To-night we hold a solemn supper, sir,
    And I'll request your presence.
Banquo
                 Let your Highness   15
    Command upon me; to the which my duties
    Are with a most indissoluble tie
    For ever knit.

19. The reason for this question, and the ones in lines 23 and 35, will soon become obvious. They are put privately to Banquo; the rest of the court should not hear them.

21. *which still ... prosperous* Which has always been well-considered and productive.

22. *but we'll take to-morrow* I, the King, will have to hear your advice tomorrow instead.

25. *this* now.

25–7. *Go not my horse ... twain* Unless my horse goes faster (than usual), it will have been dark for an hour by the time I get back.

29. *are bestow'd* have settled.

31. *parricide* killing a father.

32. The *strange invention* is the idea ('invented' according to Macbeth) by Malcolm and Donalbain that Macbeth was the murderer of their father. Some time has now gone by and the sons have no doubt been trying to gain support abroad by giving their version of what had happened.

33. *therewithal* besides that.

33–4. *cause of state ... jointly* state affairs which will require our combined attention.

34. *Hie you* Hurry.

36. *our time does call upon's* we should be going.

40–3. You're all free to do as you wish until seven o'clock this evening; I will remain unattended until supper-time, so that human company will be all the pleasanter then.

43. *While* Until.

Macbeth
Ride you this afternoon?
Banquo
                                    Ay, my good lord.
Macbeth
We should have else desir'd your good advice –   20
Which still hath been both grave and prosperous –
In this day's council; but we'll take to-morrow.
Is't far you ride?
Banquo
As far, my lord, as will fill up the time
Twixt this and supper. Go not my horse the better,   25
I must become a borrower of the night
For a dark hour or twain.
Macbeth
                                    Fail not our feast.
Banquo
My lord, I will not.
Macbeth
We hear our bloody cousins are bestow'd
In England and in Ireland, not confessing   30
Their cruel parricide, filling their hearers
With strange invention; but of that to-morrow,
When therewithal we shall have cause of state
Craving us jointly. Hie you to horse; adieu,
Till you return at night. Goes Fleance with you?   35
Banquo
Ay, my good lord; our time does call upon's.
Macbeth
I wish your horses swift and sure of foot,
And so I do commend you to their backs.
Farewell. *[Exit* BANQUO*]*
Let every man be master of his time   40
Till seven at night; to make society
The sweeter welcome, we will keep ourself
Till supper-time alone. While then. God be with you!

44. *Attend those men our pleasure?* 'Are those men waiting for me?' (Macbeth must already have mentioned them to his servant.)

45. *without* outside.

46–7. *To be thus ... safely thus* Just being king is nothing; to be safely established on the throne is what's important.

48. *Stick deep* Are like thorns (or daggers) sticking in my flesh.

48. *royalty of nature* Banquo was the ancestor of later Scottish (and English) kings, but the word *royalty* also suggests Macbeth envies Banquo's noble and firm character, qualities he lacks.

50. *to* in addition to.

51–2. *He hath a wisdom ... in safety* We have seen this prudent side of Banquo earlier in the scene. Can you recall an occasion when he showed his *dauntless temper?*

53–5. *under him ... by Caesar* This refers to an old belief that one man's 'guardian angel' might be overcome by another's, resulting in the first man's destruction. The Caesar referred to is Octavius Caesar who, although a younger man, defeated Mark Antony.

55. *chid* literally 'scolded', but 'spoke sternly to' might be better.

59. *fruitless crown* 'a crown that I would not be able to pass on'; **60. *barren sceptre*** in the next line is an exactly parallel phrase. *Crown* and *sceptre* were the two main symbols of kingship.

61. *with an unlineal hand* 'by the hand of someone unrelated to me'. Macbeth hates the idea of someone else's son becoming king after him.

63. *fil'd* defiled.

65. *rancours* bitterness and hatred.

65–8. The *vessel* Macbeth has in mind may be the communion cup, because he goes on in religious terms.

66. *eternal jewel* his immortal soul.

67. *the common enemy of man* the Devil. What he can't bear is that he has thrown away his own hope of salvation in order to put Banquo's descendants *(seeds)* on the Scottish throne.

69–70. Roughly, Macbeth is saying, 'I'd rather fight Fate itself to the bitter end' as if in a medieval tournament. The *list* was the enclosure in which such tournaments were held, to *champion* was to challenge, and 'a l'outrance' *(to th' utterance)* meant 'until one of the contestants died'.

[Exeunt all but MACBETH *and a* SERVANT.*]*

Sirrah, a word with you. Attend those men our pleasure?

Servant
    They are, my lord, without the palace gate.   45
Macbeth
    Bring them before us. *[Exit* SERVANT*]* To be thus is nothing,
    But to be safely thus. Our fears in Banquo
    Stick deep; and in his royalty of nature
    Reigns that which would be fear'd. 'Tis much he dares,
    And to that dauntless temper of his mind   50
    He hath a wisdom that doth guide his valour
    To act in safety. There is none but he
    Whose being I do fear; and under him
    My Genius is rebuk'd, as it is said
    Mark Antony's was by Caesar. He chid the Sisters   55
    When first they put the name of King upon me,
    And bade them speak to him; then prophet-like,
    They hail'd him father to a line of kings.
    Upon my head they plac'd a fruitless crown
    And put a barren sceptre in my gripe,   60
    Thence to be wrench'd with an unlineal hand,
    No son of mine succeeding. If't be so,
    For Banquo's issue have I fil'd my mind;
    For them the gracious Duncan have I murder'd;
    Put rancours in the vessel of my peace   65
    Only for them, and mine eternal jewel
    Given to the common enemy of man
    To make them kings – the seeds of Banquo kings!
    Rather than so, come. Fate, into the list,
    And champion me to th' utterance! Who's there?   70

[Re-enter SERVANT *and two* MURDERERS.*]*

Now go to the door and stay there till we call.

[Exit SERVANT.*]*

72–140. Macbeth goes to great lengths to persuade the murderers to kill Banquo. It seems (see lines 73–82) that he has previously told them that Banquo is responsible for their lack of success, not himself as they had believed. In fact, they grudgingly accept that Banquo had persecuted them personally. (*You made it known to us,* line 82). Macbeth then goes on to bully them verbally, as his wife bullied him not long before (Act I, Scene vii, lines 35–59) by questioning their manhood and eventually they give in to the pressure.

75–6. *which held you So under fortune* who held you down lower than you deserve.

77–8. *I made good to you … pass'd in probation with you* Both phrases mean 'I proved to you'.

79. *How you were borne in hand* What tricks of deceit were practised on you.

79. *how cross'd* how you were frustrated.

79. *the instruments* what means were used.

80. *Who wrought with them* who used those means.

84–9. *Do you find … for ever?* Patience and Christian forgiveness are presented as contemptible weaknesses. Note that the thing which is now bothering Macbeth most is mentioned here; Banquo's *issue* (children).

91–106. In this astonishing tirade about dogs of various kinds Macbeth argues that all kinds of dogs have their special functions in Nature's orderly arrangement, yet he is using the argument to persuade the men to destroy the human order by becoming murderers.

92. *Shoughs* shaggy northern dogs.

92. *water-rugs* rough water-dogs.

92. *demi-wolves* the offspring of dogs and wolves – perhaps something like huskies

92. *clept* called.

93. *The valued file* The list in which their various qualities are set down.

95. *The house-keeper* what we would call 'a good house-dog', one that can be relied upon to keep intruders away.

96–7. *the gift … in him closed* the particular ability which generous Nature has enclosed in him (or endued him with).

97–9. *whereby he does receive … all alike* by which be receives a special quality that distinguishes him in the general category 'dog'.

Was it not yesterday we spoke together?
First Murderer
It was, so please your Highness.
Macbeth

Well then, now
Have you consider' d of my speeches? Know
That it was he, in the times past, which held you   75
So under fortune; which you thought had been
Our innocent self. This I made good to you
In our last conference, pass'd in probation with you,
How you were borne in hand, how cross'd, the
          instruments,
Who wrought with them, and all things else that
          might   80
To half a soul and to a notion craz'd
Say 'Thus did Banquo.'
First Murderer

You made it known to us.
Macbeth
I did so; and went further, which is now
Our point of second meeting. Do you find
Your patience so predominant in your nature   85
That you can let this go? Are you so gospell'd,
To pray for this good man and for his issue,
Whose heavy hand hath bow'd you to the grave
And beggar'd yours for ever?
First Murderer

We are men, my liege.
Macbeth
Ay, in the catalogue ye go for men;   90
As hounds, and greyhounds, mongrels, spaniels, curs,
Shoughs, water-rugs, and demi-wolves, are clept
All by the name of dogs. The valued file
Distinguishes the swift, the slow, the subtle,
The house-keeper, the hunter, every one   95
According to the gift which bounteous nature
Hath in him clos'd; whereby he does receive

102–4. *And I will ... us* I will reveal the secret details of the plan the execution of which will destroy your enemy and make me your ally.

105–6. Macbeth declares that, as long as Banquo is alive, he cannot enjoy life like a healthy man. He is also suggesting that he is in constant danger from Banquo.

110. *tugg'd with fortune* 'pushed around by fortune', as in a wrestling match.

112. *To mend it or be rid on't* To improve my life or to put an end to it

114. *in such bloody distance* in such deadly rivalry

115–16. *every minute ... new'st of life* 'every minute that he's alive I'm in desperate danger' *(thrusts Against my near'st of life* suggests a sword about to enter a vital part of the body).

117. *bare-fac'd power* naked force.

118. *bid my will avouch it* say that he is being destroyed simply because I feel like it

119. *For* Because of.

120. *Whose loves ... drop* Whose respect and affection I don't want to lose.

120–1. *but wail ... struck down* but I must instead mourn the death of the man I myself destroyed.

122. That I make such strong appeals for your assistance.

Particular addition, from the bill
That writes them all alike; and so of men,
Now, if you have a station in the file,   100
Not i' th' worst rank of manhood, sayt;
And I will put that business in your bosoms
Whose execution takes your enemy off,
Grapples you to the heart and love of us,
Who wear our health but sickly in his life,   105
Which in his death were perfect.

Second Murderer

                   I am one, my liege,
Whom the vile blows and buffets of the world
Hath so incens'd that I am reckless what
I do to spite the world.

First Murderer

               And I another,
So weary with disasters, tugg'd with fortune,   110
That I would set my life on any chance,
To mend it or be rid on't.

Macbeth

              Both of you
Know Banquo was your enemy.

Both Murderers

                True, my lord.

Macbeth

So is he mine; and in such bloody distance
That every minute of his being thrusts   115
Against my near'st of life; and though I could
With bare-fac'd power sweep him from my sight,
And bid my will avouch it, yet I must not,
For certain friends that are both his and mine,
Whose loves I may not drop, but wail his fall   120
Who I myself struck down. And thence it is
That I to your assistance do make love,
Masking the business from the common eye
For sundry weighty reasons.

128. This is a puzzle. Some people think the mysterious Third Murderer who joins the other two at the beginning of Act III, Scene iii is this *perfect spy o' th' time* . But it's more likely that the phrase means 'the exact, or best guess of the time you will be needed'.

130. *something from the palace* a certain distance from the palace.

130–1. *always thought ... a clearness* you must fully understand that I cannot be linked to the crime in any way.

131. *him* Banquo.

132. *no rubs nor botches* 'no imperfections or errors' (they must make a completely successful job of it).

134. *material* important.

136. *Resolve yourselves apart* Go away and make up your minds.

138. *I'll call upon you straight* I shall require your services very soon.

Second Murderer

                         We shall, my lord,
Perform what you command us.

First Murderer

                               Though our lives –   125

Macbeth

    Your spirits shine through you. Within this hour at most,
    I will advise you where to plant yourselves,
    Acquaint you with the perfect spy o' th' time,
    The moment on't; for 't must be done to-night,
    And something from the palace; always thought   130
    That I require a clearness; and with him,
    To leave no rubs nor botches in the work,
    Fleance his son, that keeps him company,
    Whose absence is no less material to me
    Than is his father's, must embrace the fate   135
    Of that dark hour. Resolve yourselves apart;
    I'll come to you anon.

Both Murderers

                       We are resolv'd, my lord.

Macbeth

    I'll call upon you straight; abide within.

            [Exeunt MURDERERS.*]*

    It is concluded: Banquo, thy soul's flight
    If it find heaven must find it out to-night.   140

               [Exit.]

SCENE II

This scene shows a striking change in the relationship between Macbeth and his wife. They are both disillusioned about the power and position they have gained at so great a cost; they both say that it's better to be dead than suffer the misery they are going through now. However, this is about all they agree on. Lady Macbeth seems almost fatalistic ('what's done is done..') while Macbeth is desperately planning more crimes in order to protect his position and wipe out the possibility of Banquo's descendants inheriting the throne.

1. Lady Macbeth's first words suggest that she suspects her husband is plotting Banquo's death, but he has not told her about it.
3–4. *I would ... a few words* I should like to speak to him when he is free.

4–5. *Nought's had ... content* We have done our utmost and achieved nothing; we've got what we wanted, but it has given us no happiness.
6–7. She seems almost to envy the dead Duncan and she says that the murder has not brought her any steady contentment.
9. With your own miserable fantasies as your only form of company.

10–11. *those thoughts ... they think on* the fearful thoughts (of murder) should have stopped as soon as the murder was accomplished.

13. *scotch'd* slashed (i.e. cut without killing).
14. *close* join up again, healed itself.
14–15. *our poor malice ... former tooth*: our feeble ability to do harm
is vulnerable to its regained power.
16. *But let the frame ... suffer* 'But let the whole universe collapse, and heaven and earth be destroyed ...'

Scene II

Forres. The palace

[Enter LADY MACBETH and a SERVANT.]

Lady Macbeth
  Is Banquo gone from court?
Servant
  Ay, madam, but returns again to-night.
Lady Macbeth
  Say to the King I would attend his leisure
  For a few words.
Servant
                  Madam, I will.

                  [Exit.]

Lady Macbeth
                                   Nought's had, all's spent,
  Where our desire is got without content.   5
  'Tis safer to be that which we destroy,
  Than by destruction dwell in doubtful joy.

                  [Enter MACBETH.]

  How now, my lord! Why do you keep alone,
  Of sorriest fancies your companions making,
  Using those thoughts which should indeed have died   10
  With them they think on? Things without all remedy
  Should be without regard. What's done is done.
Macbeth
  We have scotch'd the snake, not kill'd it;
  She'll close, and be herself, whilst our poor malice
  Remains in danger of her former tooth.   15
  But let the frame of things disjoint, both the
      worlds suffer,
  Ere we will eat our meal in fear and sleep

19–22. *Better be ... restless ecstasy* Macbeth, without realizing it, repeats Lady Macbeth's thought in lines 6–7.

21. The image here is of a rack used to torture people.
22. *ecstasy* frenzy, a state of mental turmoil.

24–6. *nor steel ... touch him further* assassination attempts with weapon or poison, rebellion at home, attack from abroad – none of these now has the power to disturb Duncan.

27. *Gentle my lord* It was quite common in Shakespeare's time to put the adjective in this position. The modern order is, of course, 'My gentle lord'.
27. *sleek o'er your rugged looks* smooth away your worried looks.
30. Be particularly attentive to Banquo.
31. *Present him eminence* Honour him in your speech
32. *Unsafe the while ... what they are* We are so unsafe at the moment that we must preserve our honour by flattering others, and mask our true feelings.

35. *You must leave this* You must stop thinking like this.
38. Since Fleance is still very young, this certainly sounds like a hint to Macbeth that he can kill him (the 'copy' of his father?) and Banquo too. They are mortal (part of 'Nature'), and can die. Or perhaps she is probing to discover whether Macbeth is already committed to murdering them.
39. With her encouragement, Macbeth temporarily regains the feeling of partnership in hideous crime with his wife, and speaks of the planned murders in much the same way as he spoke of Duncan's as it approached – with disgust and yet with a kind of relish.
40. *jocund* joyful.
41. *cloister'd flight* because bats often live in church buildings and can be seen flying in the cloisters in the evening.
42. *shard–borne* the expression could mean either carried on wings like shards (pieces of pottery) or born in cow-dung. The second is the more likely meaning.
43. *night's yawning peal* the curfew-bell which announces the time for sleep.

In the affliction of these terrible dreams
That shake us nightly. Better be with the dead,
Whom we, to gain our peace, have sent to peace,   20
Than on the torture of the mind to lie
In restless ecstasy. Duncan is in his grave;
After life's fitful fever he sleeps well;
Treason has done his worst; nor steel, nor poison,
Malice domestic, foreign levy, nothing,   25
Can touch him further.

Lady Macbeth
                Come on.
Gentle my lord, sleek o'er your rugged looks;
Be bright and jovial among your guests to-night.

Macbeth
So shall I, love; and so, I pray, be you.
Let your remembrance apply to Banquo;   30
Present him eminence, both with eye and tongue –
Unsafe the while, that we
Must lave our honours in these flattering streams,
And make our faces vizards to our hearts,
Disguising what they are.

Lady Macbeth
                You must leave this.   35

Macbeth
O, full of scorpions is my mind, dear wife!
Thou know'st that Banquo, and his Fleance, lives.

Lady Macbeth
But in them nature's copy's not eterne.

Macbeth
There's comfort yet; they are assailable.
Then be thou jocund. Ere the bat hath flown   40
His cloister'd flight; ere to black Hecate's summons
The shard-borne beetle with his drowsy hums
Hath rung night's yawning peal, there shall be done
A deed of dreadful note.

Lady Macbeth
              What's to be done?

46–7. *Come ... day* Macbeth is appealing to the night to hide his fearful crime from the light as falconers used to stitch together *(seel)* the eyes of a hawk when training it.

49–50. *that great bond ... pale* what Shakespeare probably had in mind was the divine law against murder. Most moral laws seem to make Macbeth *pale* and fearful.

50. *thickens* grows dim.

50–1. *the crow ... rooky wood* the crow (or rook) flies to its wood, which is already black with many birds.

55. Macbeth seems to be getting his conscience under control, 'When one has done something evil to begin with, strength and security are gained by further evil'. The words seem to be said as some sort of reassurance: practice makes perfect, in evil as well as in good.

Macbeth

    Be innocent of the knowledge, dearest chuck,   45
    Till thou applaud the deed. Come, seeling night,
    Scarf up the tender eye of pitiful day,
    And with thy bloody and invisible hand
    Cancel and tear to pieces that great bond
    Which keeps me pale. Light thickens, and the crow   50
    Makes wing to th' rooky wood;
    Good things of day begin to droop and drowse,
    Whiles night's black agents to their preys do rouse.
    Thou marvell'st at my words; but hold thee still:
    Things bad begun make strong themselves by ill.   55
    So, prithee go with me.

            [Exeunt.]

SCENE III

The appearance of an unexpected Third Murderer perhaps gives us more insight into Macbeth's present state of mind. He is so full of suspicion that he sends another villain to check up on his hired thugs. Between them, the three are more than enough for Banquo, but Fleance manages to escape.

2–4. We need not be suspicious (of this newcomer) since he has just given us instructions which are exactly like those Macbeth gave us himself.

6. *lated traveller* one who is still journeying as night comes on.
7. *timely inn* the inn he reaches just in time (before night is fully come).
8. *The subject of our watch* Banquo.

10. *That ... expectation* That are expected (i.e. on the guest-list).

11. *go about* take a roundabout route.
12–14. The whole murder-plan depends on the fact that people who arrive at the castle usually leave their horses with grooms and walk the last few hundred yards.

Scene III

Forres. The approaches to the palace

[Enter three MURDERERS.]

First Murderer
  But who did bid thee join with us?
Third Murderer
                     Macbeth.
Second Murderer
  He needs not our mistrust, since he delivers
  Our offices, and what we have to do,
  To the direction just.
First Murderer
             Then stand with us.
  The west yet glimmers with some streaks of day;   5
  Now spurs the lated traveller apace
  To gain the timely inn, and near approaches
  The subject of our watch.
Third Murderer
                Hark! I hear horses.
Banquo
  [within] Give us a light there, ho!
Second Murderer
            Then 'tis he; the rest
  That are within the note of expectation   10
  Already are i' th' court.
First Murderer
           His horses go about.
Third Murderer
  Almost a mile; but he does usually,
  So all men do, from hence to th' palace gate
  Make it their walk.

    [Enter BANQUO, and FLEANCE with a torch.]

15. *Stand to't* Be at the ready to do the deed.

16. With black humour the First Murderer answers Banquo's comment on the weather with a remark that also refers to the rain of blows he and the others immediately deliver.

19. *Was't not the way*? Wasn't it the right thing to do?

20–1. Macbeth's emphasis on the need to kill Fleance as well as Banquo has clearly impressed itself on the murderers.

Second Murderer
  A light, a light!
Third Murderer
                  'Tis he.
First Murderer
  Stand to 't.   15
Banquo
  It will be rain to-night.
First Murderer
                  Let it come down.

                  [Stabs BANQUO.*]*
Banquo
  O, treachery! Fly, good Fleance, fly, fly, fly.
  Thou mayst revenge. O slave!

                  [Dies. FLEANCE *escapes.]*

Third Murderer
  Who did strike out the light?
First Murderer
                  Was't not the way?
Third Murderer
  There's but one down; the son is fled.
Second Murderer
                  We have lost   20
  Best half of our affair.
First Murderer
                  Well, let's away,
  And say how much is done.

                  [Exeunt.]

SCENE IV

Macbeth organised the second murder with far less anxiety than for the murder of Duncan but, during this scene, he once again loses control of himself and shows extreme fear. Are these the same sort of misgivings as he showed over Duncan? By the end of the scene how has he regained control? Has Lady Macbeth's help been vital, or does Macbeth finally control his feelings without her assistance?

The scene can be quite simply staged, with thrones for Macbeth and his wife and a large table for the state banquet. Banquo's ghost is sometimes presented with scientific ingenuity, using mirrors, but nothing of this kind was attempted in Shakespeare's theatre. What method would you choose if you were directing a modern production?

1. *degrees* respective rank, or seniority. This would determine where the guests sat at table.
2. From the beginning to the end of the banquet you are all heartily welcome.
4. *society* the assembled guests.
6. *keeps her state* stays seated on her throne. *in best time* at the right time.
7. *require her welcome* request her to welcome you.

11. There seem to be equal numbers on both sides of the table. Where is it that Macbeth decides to sit (*i'th'midst*)?
12. *large* generous (Macbeth encourages them to enjoy themselves freely, and to show it).
13. Macbeth sees one of the murderers at the door and moves over to speak to him.
15. 'I prefer the blood to be outside you, not inside him'; another example of Macbeth's peculiarly grim humour.

Scene IV

Forres. The palace

[Banquet prepared. Enter MACBETH, LADY MACBETH, ROSS, LENNOX, LORDS *and* ATTENDANTS.*]*

Macbeth
You know your own degrees, sit down.
At first and last the hearty welcome.
Lords
Thanks to your Majesty.
Macbeth
Our self will mingle with society
And play the humble host.   5
Our hostess keeps her state; but in best time
We will require her welcome.
Lady Macbeth
Pronounce it for me, sir, to all our friends;
For my heart speaks they are welcome.

[Enter FIRST MURDERER *to the door.]*
Macbeth
See, they encounter thee with their hearts' thanks.   10
Both sides are even; here I'll sit i' th' midst.
Be large in mirth; anon we'll drink a measure
The table round. *[Going to the door]*
There's blood upon thy face.
Murderer
                        'Tis Banquo's then.
Macbeth
'Tis better thee without than he within.   15
Is he despatch'd?
Murderer
                    My lord, his throat is cut;
That I did for him.
Macbeth
                    Thou art the best o' th' cut-throats;

19. *the nonpareil* the very best

21. *fit* spasm of fear.
21. *perfect* Macbeth seems to be continuing the health metaphor he used earlier (Act III, Scene i, lines 105–6).
22. *Whole* firm.
22. *founded* immovable.
23. As unlimited and free as the surrounding air.
24. *cabin'd, cribb'd, confin'd* all these words mean 'shut up in a small space'. The alliteration produces emphasis.
25. *saucy* impudent.
27. *trenched* deeply cut.
28. The least of the cuts enough to kill a man.

29. *worm* snake.
30. Will naturally, in time, develop the power to poison.
31–2. *to-morrow ... again* 'we'll meet and discuss the matter in detail'.

33. *give the cheer* 'give encouragement' (as a host should) or possibly 'propose a toast'.

37. *Sweet remembrancer!* Macbeth is thanking his wife for reminding him of his duties as host.

Yet he's good that did the like for Fleance.
If thou didst it, thou art the nonpareil.
Murderer
Most royal sir – Fleance is 'scap'd.   20
Macbeth
Then comes my fit again. I had else been perfect,
Whole as the marble, founded as the rock,
As broad and general as the casing air,
But now I am cabin'd, cribb'd, confin'd, bound in
To saucy doubts and fears. But Banquo's safe?   25
Murderer
Ay, my good lord. Safe in a ditch he bides,
With twenty trenched gashes on his head,
The least a death to nature.
Macbeth
                                    Thanks for that.
There the grown serpent lies; the worm that's fled
Hath nature that in time will venom breed,   30
No teeth for th' present. Get thee gone; to-morrow
We'll hear, ourselves, again.

                [Exit MURDERER.*]*

Lady Macbeth
                                    My royal lord,
You do not give the cheer; the feast is sold
That is not often vouch'd, while 'tis a-making,
'Tis given with welcome. To feed were best at home: 35
From thence the sauce to meat is ceremony;
Meeting were bare without it.

[Enter the GHOST OF BANQUO *and sits in* MACBETH'S *place.]*

Macbeth
                                    Sweet remembrancer!
Now good digestion wait on appetite,
And health on both!

40. *our country's honour* Macbeth's deliberately exaggerated way of referring to Banquo.

41. *grac'd* gracious.

42–3. Macbeth, with terrible insincerity, says that he hopes he can blame Banquo for bad manners, rather than feel anxious because ill fortune may have prevented him from attending.

43–4. *His absence ... promise* He shouldn't have said he was going to be present if he couldn't manage it.

46. Macbeth glances round the table and merely registers the fact that the seat he intended to sit in (the one *i'th' midst*) is now occupied. He doesn't at first see that Banquo's ghost is occupying it.

49. *Which of you have done this?* What does this mean? Is it possible that Macbeth really suspects that someone has tried to trick him by staging the appearance of Banquo's ghost? Or does he mean: *'Which of you killed Banquo?'*

50–1. Macbeth rejects the idea that he is responsible because he says he didn't actually do the killing himself.

52–5. Ross's remark about Macbeth's apparent illness gives Lady Macbeth an opportunity to make up a fairly convincing explanation on the spur of the moment.

55. *upon a thought* in a moment.

56–7. If you take a great deal of notice of him you will only annoy him and enrage him even more.

58. *Are you a man?* Lady Macbeth's main method to snap Macbeth out of his 'fit' is the 'Pull yourself together' one, shaming him with her contemptuous comments.

Lennox

May't please your Highness sit?

Macbeth

Here had we now our country's honour roof'd,   40
Were the grac'd person of our Banquo present;
Who may I rather challenge for unkindness
Thank pity for mischance.

Ross

His absence, sir,
Lays blame upon his promise. Please 't your Highness
To grace us with your royal company.   45

Macbeth

The table's full.

Lennox

Here is a place reserv'd, sir.

Macbeth

Where?

Lennox

Here, my good lord.
What is't that moves your Highness?

Macbeth

Which of you have done this?

Lords

What, my good lord?

Macbeth

Thou canst not say I did it; never shake   50
Thy gory locks at me.

Ross

Gentlemen, rise; his Highness is not well.

Lady Macbeth

Sit, worthy friends. My lord is often thus,
And hath been from his youth. Pray you, keep seat.
The fit is momentary; upon a thought   55
He will again be well. If much you note him,
You shall offend him and extend his passion.
Feed, and regard him not.—Are you a man?

60. *O proper stuff!* What you're saying is sheer rubbish!

61. *painting of your fear* an imaginary vision brought about by fear, not real at all.

62. *air-drawn* drawn in the air (and therefore unreal).

63. *flaws and starts* wild fits. *flaw* a sudden squall.

64. *Impostors to true fear* again, she means 'not the real thing' – his frightened behaviour isn't based on anything that would properly inspire fear.

65–6. *A woman's ... grandam* An old wives' tale passed down from a previous generation.

66. *Shame itself!* You are the personification of shame.

69. *how say you?* there, what do you say to that? It's making gestures now!

70. *nod* This often meant 'beckon' in Shakespeare's time. Perhaps Banquo's ghost is inviting Macbeth to join him in death.

71–3. *If charnel-houses ... kites* 'If men come back from the dead like this, the only way to dispose of a body completely will be to feed it to kites.' (Kites were common scavenger-birds in earlier times in England, as they still are in other parts of the world.)

71. *charnel-houses* stores of bones dug up by grave-diggers.

73. *maws* stomachs.

73. *unmanned* unmanly

74. *Fie* Shame!

76–80. *Ere humane statute ... an end* 'Murders were committed in previous ages, before civilized laws cleansed society and made it more gentle, and they have been committed in more recent times, too – murders too horrible to describe – but in the past the murdered men died when their brains were knocked out, and that was the end of them

81. *twenty mortal murders* see lines 27–8. *twenty trenched gashes ... The least a death to nature.*

81. *crowns* heads.

82. *strange* the word here, and in many other places in the play, means something like 'unnatural'.

Macbeth
> Ay, and a bold one that dare look on that
> Which might appal the devil.

Lady Macbeth
> O proper stuff!   60
> This is the very painting of your fear;
> This is the air-drawn dagger which you said
> Led you to Duncan. O, these flaws and starts –
> Impostors to true fear – would well become
> A woman's story at a winter's fire,   65
> Authoriz'd by her grandam. Shame itself!
> Why do you make such faces? When all's done,
> You look but on a stool.

Macbeth
> Prithee see there.
> Behold! look! lo! how say you?
> Why, what care I? If thou canst nod, speak, too.   70
> If charnel-houses and our graves must send
> Those that we bury back, our monuments
> Shall be the maws of kites. *[Exit GHOST]*

Lady Macbeth
> What, quite unmann'd in folly?

Macbeth
> If I stand here, I saw him.

Lady Macbeth
> Fie, for shame!

Macbeth
> Blood hath been shed ere now, i' th' olden time,   75
> Ere humane statute purg'd the gentle weal;
> Ay, and since too, murders have been perform'd
> Too terrible for the ear. The time has been
> That when the brains were out the man would die,
> And there an end; but now they rise again,   80
> With twenty mortal murders on their crowns,
> And push us from our stools. This is more strange
> Than such a murder is.

85. *muse at me* be astonished at me.

88. *Then I'll sit down* when the health has been drunk.

89–93. No-one but Macbeth sees the ghost. Do you think, then, that it is a fantasy present only in Macbeth's mind? Should it be visible to the audience?

91. *we thirst* we desire to drink.

92. *all to all* let us all drink to each other.

92. *Our duties, and the pledge* We offer our respects (to your Majesty) and drink the toast (you propose).

93. *Avaunt* go away. At this moment all the lords are on their feet, ready to drink the toast. When Macbeth's fit comes again, no doubt they remain standing, stunned. Then, perhaps, they mutter among themselves as he continues to rave.

93–4. *Let the earth ... cold* you're a corpse; you should be in a grave.

95. *speculation* light of intelligence.

97. *a thing of custom* a quite normal happening.

99. Macbeth continues to address the ghost, oblivious of Lady Macbeth's attempt to calm the horrified lords. Nevertheless he is partly answering her charge of not being a man.

100. If you came in the form of a shaggy Russian bear.

101. *arm'd* i.e. with a horn.

101. *Hyrcan tiger* a tiger from Hyrcania, a region near the Caspian Sea.

102. *but that* except the form of the dead Banquo.

104. Challenge me to fight with swords by ourselves in the desert.

105. *inhabit* stay at home. *protest* declare.

106. *The baby of a girl* a baby girl.

107. Lady Macbeth's insistence on the unreality of what he sees has had some effect on him. As soon as he asserts that the ghost is *Unreal,* it disappears.

Lady Macbeth
                    My worthy lord,
Your noble friends do lack you.
Macbeth
                         I do forget.
Do not muse at me, my most worthy friends;   85
I have a strange infirmity, which is nothing
To those that know me. Come, love and health to all;
Then I'll sit down. Give me some wine, fill full.

[Enter GHOST.*]*

I drink to the general Joy o' th' whole table,
And to our dear friend Banquo, whom we miss.   90
Would he were here! To all, and him, we thirst,
And all to all.
Lords
                    Our duties, and the pledge.
Macbeth
Avaunt, and quit my sight. Let the earth hide thee.
Thy bones are marrowless, thy blood is cold;
Thou hast no speculation in those eyes   95
Which thou dost glare with!
Lady Macbeth
                         Think of this, good peers,
But as a thing of custom. 'Tis no other;
Only it spoils the pleasure of the time.
Macbeth
What man dare, I dare.
Approach thou like the rugged Russian bear,   100
The arm'd rhinoceros, or th' Hyrcan tiger;
Take any shape but that, and my firm nerves
Shall never tremble. Or be alive again,
And dare me to the desert with thy sword;
If trembling I inhabit, then protest me   105
The baby of a girl. Hence, horrible shadow!
Unreal mock'ry, hence!

107. *being gone* now that it has gone.

109–10. You have destroyed the good humour and shattered a pleasant social occasion with mad behaviour that has astounded everyone.

111. *overcome* pass over.
112–13. *You make me strange ... owe* 'You (i.e. all those present) make me doubtful of my own nature.' (Because he is deeply frightened, while they seem undisturbed by what he saw.)
113. *I owe* that belongs to me.

116. *mine is blanch'd* my natural colour *(ruby)* has been replaced by paleness.

118–20. *Question enrages him ...* It is clear that Lady Macbeth is not going to allow her husband to incriminate himself any further. She makes sure that they all leave without delay.
118. *At once, good night* Let me say good-night to all of you together.
119. Don't bother about who is most senior as you leave.

121. As soon as she has ushered them all out she seems to be nervously exhausted. Her handling of this very difficult situation is in fact the last sign of her control of things.

122. *It* the murder of Banquo, or perhaps Banquo's ghost itself.

124–6. *Augurs ... man of blood* Drawing conclusions from omens.
125. *maggot-pies* magpies, *choughs* crows or jackdaws. The augurs, or Roman priests, often made predictions from what they observed of birds in flight.
126. *What is the night?* What time of night is it?

[Exit GHOST.*]*

                    Why, so; being gone,
I am a man again. Pray you, sit still.
Lady Macbeth
    You have displac'd the mirth, broke the good meeting,
    With most admir'd disorder.
Macbeth
                        Can such things be,   110
    And overcome us like a summer's cloud,
    Without our special wonder? You make me strange
    Even to the disposition that I owe,
    When now I think you can behold such sights
    And keep the natural ruby of your cheeks,   115
    When mine is blanch'd with fear.
Ross
                        What sights, my lord?

Lady Macbeth
    I pray you speak not; he grows worse and worse;
    Question enrages him. At once, good night.
    Stand not upon the order of your going,
    But go at once.
Lennox
                    Good night; and better health   120
    Attend his Majesty!
Lady Macbeth
                    A kind good night to all!

[Exeunt LORDS *and* ATTENDANTS.*]*
Macbeth
    It will have blood; they say blood will have blood.
    Stones have been known to move, and trees to speak;
    Augurs and understood relations have
    By maggot-pies and choughs and rooks brought
            forth   125
    The secret'st man of blood. What is the night?

127. *Almost at odds with morning* 'It's hard to say whether it's night or morning.' It has been pointed out that this is a symbolic moment, the centre point of the play, when the darkness represented by Macbeth is for the first time about to begin to fade as signs of opposition (representing a new dawn) are about to appear (notice Macduff's defiance, referred to in the next line).

131–2. Macbeth employs spies in the houses of all his thanes. The picture of a cruel dictatorship maintained by fear in an atmosphere of suspicion becomes more complete.

133. *betimes* early, very soon.

134. *bent* determined.

135–6. *For mine own good ... give way* Everything else must take second place to my welfare.

136–8. The image is, appropriately, of wading across a river of blood. He feels he is already wading so deeply that he may as well go on to the far side.

139–40. I have dark thoughts that will become deeds – the sort that have to be put into effect without being carefully considered first.

142–3. *My strange and self-abuse ... hard use* Those strange fantasies I thought I saw were merely the fears of a beginner lacking tough practice.

144. *We* the royal 'we' refers to Macbeth himself, as Lady Macbeth is now no longer part of his planning.

Lady Macbeth

Almost at odds with morning, which is which.

Macbeth

How say'st thou that Macduff denies his person
At our great bidding?

Lady Macbeth

Did you send to him, sir?

Macbeth

I hear it by the way; but I will send –   130
There's not a one of them but in his house
I keep a servant fee'd – I will to-morrow.
And betimes I will to the Weird Sisters:
More shall they speak; for now I am bent to know
By the worst means the worst. For mine own good   135
All causes shall give way. I am in blood
Stepp'd in so far that, should I wade no more,
Returning were as tedious as go o'er.
Strange things I have in head that will to hand,
Which must be acted ere they may be scann'd.   140

Lady Macbeth

You lack the season of all natures, sleep.

Macbeth

Come, well to sleep. My strange and self-abuse
Is the initiate fear that wants hard use.
We are yet but young in deed.

[Exeunt.]

SCENE V

It is unlikely that Shakespeare wrote this scene. The rhythm and style are quite different from those of the earlier scenes with the witches. Hecate's introduction into the play serves little purpose and the scene is usually cut in modern productions.

1. *Hecat* (or Hecate) a goddess of witchcraft in Greek mythology.
1. *angerly* angrily or, as we would say, 'angry'.
2. *beldams* hags, hideous old women.

6. *charms* magical powers.
7. Secret organiser of wickedness.

11. *wayward son* unreliable pupil.

15. *pit of Acheron* apparently the name of the witches' cave (*Acheron* was one of the rivers of Hell in classical legend).

20. *I am for th' air* 'I am going up into the air' (like the traditional witch on a broomstick).
21. *Unto a dismal ... end* On a disastrous and ominous purpose.
23–9. It was believed that the moon shed a kind of dew on certain plants, and this liquid was highly prized for its magic qualities.
24. *vap'rous drop profound* a drop of vapour with profound powers.

26. *sleights* arts.
27. *artificial sprites* spirits or apparitions conjured up by magic arts.

29. *confusion* ruin.

Scene V

A heath

[Thunder. Enter the three WITCHES, *meeting* HECATE.*]*

First Witch
  Why, how now, Hecat! You look angerly.
Hecate
  Have I not reason, beldams as you are,
  Saucy and overbold? How did you dare
  To trade and traffic with Macbeth
  In riddles and affairs of death;   5
  And I, the mistress of your charms,
  The close contriver of all harms,
  Was never call'd to bear my part,
  Or show the glory of our art?
  And, which is worse, all you have done   10
  Hath been but for a wayward son,
  Spiteful and wrathful; who, as others do,
  Loves for his own ends, not for you.
  But make amends now. Get you gone,
  And at the pit of Acheron   15
  Meet me i' the morning; thither he
  Will come to know his destiny.
  Your vessels and your spells provide,
  Your charms, and everything beside.
  I am for th' air; this night I'll spend   20
  Unto a dismal and a fatal end.
  Great business must be wrought ere noon.
  Upon the corner of the moon
  There hangs a vap'rous drop profound;
  I'll catch it ere it come to ground;   25
  And that, distill'd by magic sleights,
  Shall raise such artificial sprites
  As, by the strength of their illusion,
  Shall draw him on to his confusion.

30–1. *bear/His hopes … fear* he will become utterly careless of considerations such as commonsense. God's grace and natural fear, (swept away by the wild hopes the witches will give him.)
32. *security* over-confidence.

Stage Direction This song occurs in a play called *The Witch* by Middleton, a contemporary of Shakespeare.
34–5. *little spirit* Hecate's familiar.

He shall spurn fate, scorn death, and bear   30
His hopes 'bove wisdom, grace, and fear;
And you all know security
Is mortals' chiefest enemy.

[Music and a song within: 'Come away, come away, etc.']

Hark! I am call'd; my little spirit, see,
Sits in a foggy cloud, and stays for me.   35

[Exit.]

First Witch
Come, let's make haste; she'll soon be back again.

[Exeunt.]

SCENE VI

Since his last words in the Banquet Scene *(Good night; and better health Attend his Majesty!)* Lennox has obviously done some hard thinking. The deep irony of some of his remarks is very striking. Apart from the fact that some of the Scottish lords have now 'seen through' Macbeth, the scene provides the first real suggestion of better things to come.

1–3. *My former speeches ... borne* The remarks I have recently made have only put into words what you were thinking already. You can work out things in greater detail for yourself. All I say is that things have been carried on in a very odd way.

3–4. *The gracious Duncan ... Macbeth* The suggestion is that Macbeth could afford to pity Duncan when he was dead.

5–7. Macbeth had put the blame for Duncan's death on Malcolm and Donalbain, because they had fled to England. Lennox sarcastically suggests that it's just as reasonable to say that Fleance killed his father, as he has fled, too.

8–10. Who can help thinking how unnatural it was for Malcolm and Donalbain to kill their own father?

10. *fact* evil deed.

11. *straight* immediately.

12. *pious* loyal, patriotic.

12. *delinquents* those who have failed in their duty.

13. *thralls* can also mean slaves.

14–16. *Ay, and wisely ... men deny't* Without saying so, Lennox makes it clear that Macbeth was wise to kill the guards because they might have been able to convince people of their innocence.

17. *He has borne all things well* He has organized everything with remarkable skill.

18. *under his key* locked up.

19. *an't* if it.

20. Again very sarcastically, Lennox says that Macbeth would teach Malcolm, Donalbain and Fleance a lesson for killing their fathers (the 'lesson' being death!)

21. *broad* outspoken

23–4. *can you tell ... himself?* do you know where he's staying?

24–5. *The son of Duncan ... birth* Malcolm, from whom the dictator Macbeth withholds his rightful inheritance (the throne of Scotland).

Scene VI

Forres. The palace

[Enter LENNOX *and another* LORD.*]*

Lennox
My former speeches have but hit your thoughts,
Which can interpret farther. Only I say
Things have been strangely borne. The gracious Duncan
Was pitied of Macbeth. Marry, he was dead.
And the right-valiant Banquo walk'd too late;   5
Whom, you may say, ift please you, Fleance kill'd,
For Fleance fled. Men must not walk too late.
Who cannot want the thought how monstrous
It was for Malcolm and for Donalbain
To kill their gracious father? Damned fact!   10
How it did grieve Macbeth I Did he not straight,
In pious rage, the two delinquents tear,
That were the slaves of drink and thralls of sleep?
Was not that nobly done? Ay, and wisely too;
For 'twould have anger'd any heart alive   15
To hear the men deny't. So that, I say,
He has borne all things well; and I do think
That had he Duncan's sons under his key –
As, an't please heaven, he shall not – they should find
What 'twere to kill a father; so should Fleance.   20
But peace! For from broad words, and 'cause he fail'd
His presence at the tyrant's feast, I hear,
Macduff lives in disgrace. Sir, can you tell
Where he bestows himself?
Lord
                    The son of Duncan,
From whom this tyrant holds the due of birth,   25
Lives in the English court, and is receiv'd
Of the most pious Edward with such grace
That the malevolence of fortune nothing

28–9. *That the malevolence ... respect* the fact that he's had such ill fortune doesn't reduce in any way the honour he receives (in the English court).

30. *the holy King* Edward the Confessor, seen as holy and pious.

31. *wake* rouse. The Earl of Northumberland is later called 'Old Siward' and his *warlike* son 'Young Siward'.

32–3. *with Him above To ratify the work* with God to strengthen their activities.

34–6. Have good food on our tables again, sleep well at night, hold banquets without the fear of bloody murder, pay sincere respect to a rightful king and receive from him honours freely earned ...

38. *exasperate* exasperated, irritated.

40–3. Macbeth sent for Macduff, as he told Lady Macbeth he would (Act III, Scene iv, line 130), but Macduff flatly rejected the summons *(Sir, not I!)*; the surly *(cloudy)* messenger turned his back on Macduff and grunted, as if to say 'You'll live to regret burdening me with such an answer' (which suggests anyone who brought an unsatisfactory message to Macbeth was likely to suffer for it) .

43–5. *And that well might ... provide* That should be enough to warn Macduff to stay as far away as possible from Macbeth.

47. *His* Macduff's.

48–9. *our suffering country ... accursed!* our country, now suffering under a damned tyranny.

Takes from his high respect; thither Macduff
Is gone to pray the holy King upon his aid   30
To wake Northumberland and warlike Siward,
That by the help of these – with Him above
To ratify the work – we may again
Give to our tables meat, sleep to our nights,
Free from our feasts and banquets bloody knives,   35
Do faithful homage and receive free honours –
All which we pine for now. And this report
Hath so exasperate the King that he
Prepares for some attempt of war.

Lennox

                                    Sent he to Macduff?

Lord

He did; and with an absolute 'Sir, not I!'   40
The cloudy messenger turns me his back
And hums, as who should say 'You'll rue the time
That clogs me with this answer'.

Lennox

                                 And that well might

Advise him to a caution t' hold what distance
His wisdom can provide. Some holy angel   45
Fly to the court of England and unfold
His message ere he come, that a swift blessing
May soon return to this our suffering country
Under a hand accurs'd!
Lord I'll send my prayers with him.

[Exeunt.]

ACT IV SCENE I

The appearance of the witches in Act I, Scene iii, set in motion Macbeth's first steps in crime; now he seeks them out and they introduce his deeper and much more desperate involvement in evil.

1. *brinded* streaked. This cat (perhaps what we should call a tabby) is the First Witch's familiar, called Graymalkin, Act I, Scene i, line 9.
2. *hedge-pig* hedgehog.

3. *Harpier* the Third Witch's familiar. This is probably the mythical monster, a harpy, a creature with a woman's face and body and a bird's wings and claws. *Harpier* screams, and the Third Witch announces this as the signal to begin.

6–8. The toad has, while sleeping, sweated poison *(swelter'd venom sleeping got)* for 31 days and nights.

12. A slice of marsh-snake.

16. *fork* the forked tongue.
16. *blind-worm's sting* we know now that the blind-worm, or slow-worm, is not poisonous, but there was a firm belief in Shakespeare's time that it was.
17. *howlet's wing* owl's wing.
19. The witch commands the filthy mixture to seethe and gain evil power.

ACT FOUR
Scene I

A dark cave. In the middle, a cauldron boiling

[Thunder. Enter the three WITCHES.*]*

First Witch
    Thrice the brinded cat hath mew'd.
Second Witch
    Thrice and once the hedge-pig whin'd.
Third Witch
    Harpier cries; 'tis time, 'tis time.
First Witch
    Round about the cauldron go;
    In the poison'd entrails throw.   5
    Toad that under cold stone
    Days and nights has thirty-one
    Swelter'd venom sleeping got
    Boil thou first i th' charmed pot.
All
    Double, double toil and trouble;   10
    Fire burn, and cauldron bubble.
Second Witch
    Fillet of a fenny snake,
    In the cauldron boil and bake;
    Eye of newt, and toe of frog,
    Wool of bat, and tongue of dog,   15
    Adder's fork, and blind-worm's sting,
    Lizard's leg, and howlet's wing—
    For a charm of pow'rful trouble,
    Like a hell-broth boil and bubble.
All
    Double, double toil and trouble;   20
Third Witch
    Scale of dragon, tooth of wolf,

22. *Witch's mummy* dried flesh from a witch's body. (Dried human flesh was thought to have medicinal and magical powers.)

22. *maw and gulf* throat and stomach.

23. *ravin'd* stuffed with the flesh of its human victim.

24. The hemlock plant is in any case poisonous; digging it up at night was supposed to increase its powers.

25–30. The Jew, the Turk, the Tartar and the baby strangled at birth would all be seen in Shakespeare's time as anti-Christian or non-Christian, and certainly un-christened.

26. *slips of yew* cuttings from a yew-tree, which is associated with churchyards and is also poisonous (cattle sometimes become ill through eating yew-leaves).

27. Cut off during an eclipse of the moon (considered a time of misfortune to the superstitious).

30. Born to a prostitute, in a ditch.

31. *gruel;* a soupy mixture.

31. *slab* slimy and sticky.

32. *tiger's chaudron* a tiger's guts.

33. *ingredience* we would write 'ingredients'.

38–42. It is unlikely that these lines and stage directions are by Shakespeare.

43. There is an old superstition that sudden unexpected pains are omens of coming events.

Witch's mummy, maw and gulf
Of the ravin'd salt-sea shark,
Root of hemlock digged i' th' dark,
Liver of blaspheming Jew,   25
Gall of goat, and slips of yew
Sliver'd in the moon's eclipse,
Nose of Turk, and Tartar's lips,
Finger of birth-strangled babe
Ditch-deliver'd by a drab –   30
Make the gruel thick and slab;
Add thereto a tiger's chaudron,
For th' ingredience of our cauldron.

All
Double, double toil and trouble;
Fire burn, and cauldron bubble.   35

Second Witch
Cool it with a baboon's blood,
Then the charm is firm and good.

[Enter HECATE.*]*

Hecate
O well done! I commend your pains;
And every one shall share i' th' gains.
And now about the cauldron sing,   40
Like elves and fairies in a ring,
Enchanting all that you put in.

[Music and a song: 'Black Spirits, etc.' Exit HECATE*]*

Second Witch
By the pricking of my thumbs,
Something wicked this way comes. *[Knocking]*
Open, locks, whoever knocks.   45

[Enter MACBETH.*]*

Macbeth
How now, you secret, black, and midnight hags!

47. *A deed ... name* It's too horrible to be described.

48. I call upon you in the name of your devilish art

50–1. *let them fight ... churches* again, the anti-Christian nature of witchcraft is emphasized.
51. *yesty* frothing, like fermenting yeast.
52. *swallow navigation up* wreck ships.
53. *Though bladed corn be lodg'd* though the corn is blown flat even before the ears are formed.
54. *their warders' heads* the heads of those who guard them.
55–6. *Slope ... foundations* bend down to their bases, i.e. are blown flat.
56–7. *Though ... together* Macbeth's obsessive interest in his own position has now gone to extremes. He has reached the desperate state of a crazy dictator who doesn't mind if the universe is destroyed as long as he gets his own way.
57. *nature's germens* the very seeds of life.
58. *till destruction sicken* destruction is personified as a violent man who finally becomes disgusted by his own deeds, like one who eats so much that he makes himself sick.

61. *our masters* the devils whom the witches serve.

63. *farrow* piglets (the number 9 – 3 times 3 – was particularly potent in magic).
63. *sweaten* sweated, oozed out.
64. *gibbet* gallows.
66. Show yourself, and at the same time go through your performance efficiently.

Macbeth

What is't you do?

All

A deed without a name.

Macbeth

I conjure you by that which you profess –
Howe'er you come to know it – answer me.
Though you untie the winds and let them fight   50
Against the churches; though the yesty waves
Confound and swallow navigation up;
Though bladed corn be lodg'd and trees blown down;
Though castles topple on their warders' heads;
Though palaces and pyramids do slope   55
Their heads to their foundations; though the treasure
Of nature's germens tumble all together,
Even till destruction sicken – answer me
To what I ask you.

First Witch

Speak.

Second Witch

Demand.

Third Witch

We'll answer.

First Witch

Say, if thou'dst rather hear it from our mouths,   60
Or from our masters?

Macbeth

Call 'em; let me see 'em.

First Witch

Pour in sow's blood that hath eaten
Her nine farrow; grease that's sweaten
From the murderer's gibbet throw
Into the flame.

All

Come, high or low;   65
Thyself and office deftly show.

Stage Direction The ***Armed Head*** might well be the helmeted head of Macbeth as it is when Macduff cuts it off later. However, for the moment it has no special meaning for Macbeth (***thou unknown power***, line 67).

72. *harp'd* guessed.

Stage Direction The ***Bloody Child*** is Macduff as a baby from his mother's womb ***untimely ripp'd*** (Act V, Scene viii, lines 15–16).

76. *Had I three ears ...* Macbeth's grim humour suggests that he retains some of his old confidence; later he falls into a state of hopelessness

82. *take a bond of fate* hold Fate itself to its word, by killing Macduff.
83. So that I can prove that my weak fears are unjustified.
84. He hears the thunder of the Stage Direction as he speaks. Thunder was often regarded as the voice of an angry god.

Stage Direction The ***Child Crowned*** is probably Malcolm, who later orders his troops to use branches from Birnam Wood as camouflage.

85. *issue* child.

[Thunder. FIRST APPARITION, *an Armed Head.]*
Macbeth
    Tell me, thou unknown power –
First Witch
                        He knows thy thought.
    Hear his speech, but say thou nought.
Apparition
    Macbeth! Macbeth! Macbeth! Beware Macduff;
    Beware the Thane of Fife. Dismiss me. Enough.   70

              [He descends.]
Macbeth
    Whate'er thou art, for thy good caution, thanks;
    Thou hast harp'd my fear aright. But one word more –
First Witch
    He will not be commanded. Here's another,
    More potent than the first.

    [Thunder. SECOND APPARITION, *a Bloody Child.]*

Apparition
    Macbeth! Macbeth! Macbeth! Macbeth   75
    Had I three ears, I'd hear thee.
Apparition
    Be bloody, bold, and resolute; laugh to scorn
    The pow'r of man, for none of woman born
    Shall harm Macbeth. *[Descends]*
Macbeth
    Then live, Macduff; what need I fear of thee?   80
    But yet I'll make assurance double sure
    And take a bond of fate. Thou shalt not live;
    That I may tell pale-hearted fear it lies,
    And sleep in spite of thunder.

[Thunder. THIRD APPARITION, *a Child Crowned, with a tree*
in his hand.]

                  What is this
    That rises like the issue of a king,   85

86–7. *round And top* a very Shakespearian phrase, full of meaning. A crown is literally round and is worn on top of the head, but also (especially in Macbeth's eyes) it is metaphorically the 'rounding-off' and summit of all ambition.

89. *Who chafes, who frets* who rages and storms.

91. Birnam and Dunsinane are about twelve miles apart. You may think that Shakespeare gives the impression that they are much closer than this in Act V.

92. *That will never be* Macbeth takes the apparitions' words very literally and unquestioningly. Perhaps he simply dares not take them otherwise?

93. *impress* conscript, i.e. make the trees march.

94. *bodements* prophecies.

95. *Rebellion's head* the forces which may rise to remove Macbeth from the throne.

97. *Shall live the lease of nature* a complete human lifetime

97–8. *pay his breath … custom* stop breathing in the course of time, i.e. die a natural death.

100–1. After a show of returning confidence Macbeth cannot resist asking the question regarding Fleance's escape which has grown in his mind; 'Have I committed these crimes merely for another man's sons to inherit the throne?'

Stage Direction *Hautboys* the hautboy was a high-pitched wooden instrument, as the name suggests. The modern form of the word is 'oboe'.

104. *noise* music.

And wears upon his baby brow the round
And top of sovereignty?
All

Listen, but speak not to't.
Apparition
Be lion-mettled, proud, and take no care
Who chafes, who frets, or where conspirers are:
Macbeth shall never vanquish'd be until   90
Great Birnam wood to high Dunsinane Hill
Shall come against him. *[Descends]*
Macbeth

That will never be.
Who can impress the forest, bid the tree
Unfix his earth-bound root? Sweet bodements, good!
Rebellion's head rise never till the wood   95
Of Birnam rise, and our high-plac'd Macbeth
Shall live the lease of nature, pay his breath
To time and mortal custom. Yet my heart
Throbs to know one thing; tell me, if your art
Can tell so much – shall Banquo's issue ever   100
Reign in this kingdom?
All

Seek to know no more.
Macbeth
I will be satisfied. Deny me this,
And an eternal curse fall on you! Let me know.
Why sinks that cauldron? And what noise is this?

[Hautboys.]
First Witch
Show!   105
Second Witch
Show!
Third Witch
Show!
All
Show his eyes, and grieve his heart;

Stage Direction *A Show of eight Kings* a dumb–show, or mime, was a regular feature in plays of Shakespeare's time. In this one Banquo mocks Macbeth by introducing him to a line of eight Stuart kings who are all descendants of his. This seems to be roughly historically accurate, except that there is no mention of Mary, Queen of Scots. During the show Macbeth goes through a variety of strong emotions, horror, rage, despair and finally blank depression.

111. *thy hair* This probably means 'your general appearance or character'.

114. *Start, eyes* Macbeth would rather that his eyes should pop from his head than that he should see any more.

115. *th' crack of doom* Doomsday, the moment when the world will come to an end.

117–19. The mirror carried by the eighth shows Macbeth many Banquo-like figures, including some who carry *two-fold balls* (double orbs representing the union of England and Scotland) and *treble sceptres* (signifying rule over England, Scotland and Ireland). Such a description applied to James I, who was descended from Banquo, and who probably saw the play at some time.

121. *blood-bolter'd* with hair plastered in blood

128. *antic round* grotesque dance.

129–30. It is possible that these words were really addressed to James I seated in the audience or perhaps they are an ironic comment on Macbeth.

131–2. Macbeth is getting into the habit of uttering hideous but empty curses.

133. It is interesting to note that Lennox still serves Macbeth, in spite of the doubts he expressed about him in Act III, Scene vi.

Come like shadows, so depart!

[A Show of eight Kings, and BANQUO *last; the last king
with a glass in his hand.]*

Macbeth
> Thou art too like the spirit of Banquo; down!　　110
> Thy crown does sear mine eye-balls. And thy hair,
> Thou other gold-bound brow, is like the first.
> A third is like the former. Filthy hags!
> Why do you show me this? A fourth? Start, eyes.
> What, will the line stretch out to th' crack of doom?　115
> Another yet? A seventh? I'll see no more.
> And yet the eighth appears, who bears a glass
> Which shows me many more; and some I see
> That two-fold balls and treble sceptres carry.
> Horrible sight! Now I see 'tis true;　　120
> For the blood-bolter'd Banquo smiles upon me,
> And points at them for his. *[The show vanishes]*
> 　　What! is this so?

First Witch
> Ay, sir, all this is so. But why
> Stands Macbeth thus amazedly?
> Come, sisters, cheer we up his sprites,　　125
> And show the best of our delights;
> I'll charm the air to give a sound,
> While you perform your antic round;
> That this great king may kindly say,
> Our duties did his welcome pay.　　130

[Music. The WITCHES *dance, and vanish.]*

Macbeth
> Where are they? Gone? Let this pernicious hour
> Stand aye accursed in the calendar.
> Come in, without there.

[Enter LENNOX.*]*

Lennox
> 　　　　What's your Grace's will?

136–7. More curses!

139–40. Macbeth is shocked that the prophecies seem already to be making sense.

142. Time is holding him back – he was planning to kill Macduff, but he has escaped to England.
143–4. 'The only way of making sure that an intention becomes reality is to act as soon as you think of it'. In the next sentence Macbeth resolves to go one better; to act on emotion *(firstlings of my heart)* without thinking purposefully at all.

148. *surprise* take by surprise.

151. *trace* follow.

Macbeth
　Saw you the Weird Sisters?
Lennox
　　　　　　　No, my lord.

Macbeth
　Came they not by you?
Lennox
　　　　　　　No, indeed, my lord.　　　　　135

Macbeth
　Infected be the air whereon they ride;
　And damn'd all those that trust them! I did hear
　The galloping of horse. Who was't came by?
Lennox
　'Tis two or three, my lord, that bring you word
　Macduff is fled to England.
Macbeth
　　　　　　　Fled to England!　　　　　140
Lennox
　Ay, my good lord.
Macbeth
　[aside] Time, thou anticipat'st my dread exploits.
　The flighty purpose never is o'ertook
　Unless the deed go with it. From this moment
　The very firstlings of my heart shall be　　　　145
　The firstlings of my hand. And even now,
　To crown my thoughts with acts, be it thought
　　　　and done
　The castle of Macduff I will surprise,
　Seize upon Fife, give to the edge o' th' sword
　His wife, his babes, and all unfortunate souls　　150
　That trace him in his line. No boasting like a fool:
　This deed I'll do before this purpose cool.
　But no more sights! – Where are these gentlemen?
　Come, bring me where they are.　　　　155

　　　　　[Exeunt.]

SCENE II

Macduff has fled to England, without telling his wife. She is naturally bitter about this, and seems to think he is a coward. It is often suggested that he went secretly so that Macbeth would have no excuse for harming his wife and children. Examine the evidence as it comes out and try to decide whether Macduff's action is justifiable. And how are we to view Ross and the Messenger, here? Yes, they seem to warn Lady Macduff, but could they have done more? Or are they just ordinary decent men bewildered by an evil political regime.

3–4. When our actions … traitors Lady Macduff thinks that her husband has not actually plotted against Macbeth, but that he has fled through fear and as a result laid himself open to the charge of treachery.

7. titles his estates and possessions.
9. He wants the natural touch a terrible accusation from a wife, equivalent to saying 'he hasn't any normal feelings of love and protectiveness'. Does she really mean this?
10. most diminutive tiniest.
12–14. 'His fear for his own skin has driven out all love for his family. What's more, the same fear has driven out all sense, too; what reason is there for such a flight ?' This gives Ross his cue to suggest that Macduff may have very good reasons for fleeing.
14. coz an affectionate term, applied in a variety of relationships.
15. school control.
15. for as for, concerning.
17. The fits o' th' season the violent disturbances of the time.
18–19. when we are traitors … ourselves when we're regarded as traitors without knowing it.
19–20. when we hold rumour … fear when we believe the stories we hear, because we're afraid, without knowing what there is to be afraid of.
22. Each way and none the general idea seems to be that frightened people are tossed backwards and forwards on the sea of fear without getting anywhere.

Scene II

Fife. Macduff's castle

[Enter LADY MACDUFF, *her* SON, *and* ROSS.*]*

Lady Macduff
  What had he done to make him fly the land?
Ross
  You must have patience, madam.
Lady Macduff
                     He had none;
  His flight was madness. When our actions do not,
  Our fears do make us traitors.
Ross
                 You know not
  Whether it was his wisdom or his fear.   5
Lady Macduff
  Wisdom! To leave his wife, to leave his babes,
  His mansion, and his titles, in a place
  From whence himself does fly? He loves us not;
  He wants the natural touch; for the poor wren,
  The most diminutive of birds, will fight,   10
  Her young ones in her nest, against the owl.
  All is the fear, and nothing is the love;
  As little is the wisdom, where the flight
  So runs against all reason,
Ross
              My dearest coz,
  I pray you, school yourself. But, for your husband, 15
  He is noble, wise, judicious, and best knows
  The fits o' th' season. I dare not speak much further;
  But cruel are the times, when we are traitors
  And do not know ourselves; when we hold rumour
  From what we fear, yet know not what we fear, 20
  But float upon a wild and violent sea
  Each way and none. I take my leave of you;

24–5. Ross's wise remark suggests to the audience that some change in fortune may be about to occur.

28–9. Ross means that he feels like crying and would embarrass Lady Macduff by doing so if he stayed any longer.

30–63. Macduff's small son, with his precocious questions and answers, provides an interval of partly comic Shakespearian 'back-chat' which brings out the horror of the end of the scene.
30. *Sirrah* a term used by parents to children (and also by masters to servants).
30. *dead* as good as dead. She doesn't expect to see him again.

34. *lime* bird-lime, a sticky substance spread to catch birds.
35. *The pitfall … the gin* two other methods of catching birds – a disguised hole in the ground (presumably for flightless birds) and a snare.
36. *Poor birds … for* the boy is saying, shrewdly, 'If I'm a poor bird, as you say, I'm in no danger; no-one's silly enough to set traps for *poor* birds!'

41. *Then you'll buy …* If they're as easy to get as all that, they won't be worth keeping.

Shall not be long but I'll be here again.
Things at the worst will cease, or else climb upward
To what they were before. – My pretty cousin,   25
Blessing upon you!

Lady Macduff
Father'd he is, and yet he's fatherless.

Ross
I am so much a fool, should I stay longer,
It would be my disgrace and your discomfort.
I take my leave at once.

[Exit.]

Lady Macduff
                              Sirrah, your father's dead;   30
And what will you do now? How will you live?

Son
As birds do, mother.

Lady Macduff
                    What, with worms and flies?

Son
With what I get, I mean; and so do they.

Lady Macduff
Poor bird! thou'dst never fear the net nor lime,
The pitfall nor the gin.   35

Son
Why should I, mother? Poor birds they are not set for.
My father is not dead, for all your saying.

Lady Macduff
Yes, he is dead. How wilt thou do for a father?

Son
Nay, how will you do for a husband?

Lady Macduff
Why, I can buy me twenty at any market.   40

Son
Then you'll buy 'em to sell again.

42–3. *Thou speak'st ... thee* You're not talking very sensibly – but perhaps sensibly enough, considering how young you are.

45. She is probably referring to her husband's running away and leaving her, which she sees as treachery. In line 47 she suggests that he has broken his marriage-vow by leaving her.

55. *enow* enough.

57. *poor monkey!* an affectionate phrase, showing her amusement at her son's clever chatter. But immediately after it she becomes sad and serious again.

Lady Macduff

Thou speak'st with all thy wit; and yet, i' faith,
With wit enough for thee.

Son

Was my father a traitor, mother?

Lady Macduff

Ay, that he was.   45

Son

What is a traitor?

Lady Macduff

Why, one that swears and lies.

Son

And be all traitors that do so?

Lady Macduff

Every one that does so is a traitor, and must be
            hang'd.

Son

And must they all be hang'd that swear and lie?   50

Lady Macduff

Every one.

Son

Who must hang them?

Lady Macduff

Why, the honest men.

Son

Then the liars and swearers are fools; for there are
liars and swearers enow to beat the honest men and   55
hang up them.

Lady Macduff

Now, God help thee, poor monkey! But how wilt
thou do for a father?

Son

If he were dead, you'd weep for him; if you would not,
it were a good sign that I should quickly have a new   60
father.

Lady Macduff

Poor prattler, how thou talk'st!

63. Ross's warnings were vague, but this Messenger's are much more urgent. The pace of the scene changes abruptly.

64. *Though in your state ... perfect* Although I know your honourable status very well.

65. *I doubt* I am afraid.

66. *homely* humble.

70–71. 'It is cruel of me to frighten you in this way; to do worse to you would be monstrous'. He makes it plain in the next line that someone is likely to *do worse* to her soon.

73–5. *where to do harm ... folly* 'where doing harm often receives praise, and doing good is regarded as dangerous and stupid'. The complete reversal of values under Macbeth's tyranny is made clear.

81. *shag-ear'd* if this is the word Shakespeare actually wrote (which is doubtful) it probably means 'with hair sprouting from the ears' – the kind of thing a child might well notice.

81–2. *egg* and *fry* These are contemptuous terms applied to Lady Macduff's son because of his youthfulness and small stature.

[Enter a MESSENGER.*]*

Messenger
    Bless you, fair dame! I am not to you known,
    Though in your state of honour I am perfect.
    I doubt some danger does approach you nearly.   65
    If you will take a homely man's advice,
    Be not found here; hence, with your little ones.
    To fright you thus, methinks, I am too savage;
    To do worse to you were fell cruelty,
    Which is too nigh your person. Heaven preserve you   70
    I dare abide no longer.

[Exit.]

Lady Macduff
                Whither should I fly?
    I have done no harm. But I remember now
    I am in this earthly world, where to do harm
    Is often laudable, to do good sometime
    Accounted dangerous folly. Why then, alas,   75
    Do I put up that unmanly defence
    To say I have done no harm?

[Enter MURDERERS.*]*

                What are these faces?

First Murderer
    Where is your husband?

Lady Macduff
    I hope, in no place so unsanctified
    Where such as thou mayst find him.

First Murderer
                He's a traitor.   80

Son
    Thou liest, thou shag-ear' d villain.

First Murderer
                What, you egg?

82. *fry* baby fish.

[stabbing him]
Young fry of treachery!

Son

He has kill'd me, mother.
Run away, I pray you.

[Dies. Exit LADY MACDUFF, *crying 'Murder!'.]*

SCENE III

Macbeth, the tyrant, now has a firm hold on Scotland. Malcolm, in the safety of the English court, naturally suspects anyone who comes from Scotland to persuade him to go back there, and he therefore tests Macduff's honesty.

1–2. Malcolm puts on a show of indicating that he has no hope and can only accept the situation passively. Macduff, on the other hand, urges active opposition to Macbeth.

3. *the mortal sword* the sword that kills.

4. *Bestride ... birthdom* defend our native country in its misfortune

5–8. *new sorrows ... dolour* woeful cries at fresh miseries are a blow (a 'slap in the face') to the forces of goodness. Heaven echoes with similar *(Like)* wails, in sympathy with Scotland.

8–17. Malcolm replies cautiously, almost as though he is saying; 'I regret any unhappiness that can be proved to have occurred, and I'll put right anything I can, if a suitable time *(time to friend)* comes.' Then he quite openly expresses his doubts about Macduff (lines 12–13); 'People once believed what Macbeth said—and you have shown respect and loyalty to him in the past. What's more, it's suspicious that he hasn't harmed you. I may seem gullible, but I can see that you might win favour with Macbeth by harming me. It might be in your interest to sacrifice a helpless creature (like me) to placate him.'

19–20. *A good ... charge* even a good man may falter and step back (into evil ways) when a king gives the orders.

21. *transpose* change. Malcolm means 'You are what you are; my suspicions of you won't make you vicious'.

22. *the brightest* Lucifer, who turned against God and was cast out.

Scene III

England. Before King Edward's palace

[*Enter* MALCOLM *and* MACDUFF.]

Malcolm
Let us seek out some desolate shade, and there
Weep our sad bosoms empty.
Macduff
                               Let us rather
Hold fast the mortal sword, and like good men
Bestride our down-fall'n birthdom. Each new morn
New widows howl, new orphans cry; new sorrows   5
Strike heaven on the face, that it resounds
As if it felt with Scotland and yell'd out
Like syllable of dolour.
Malcolm
                               What I believe, I'll wail;
What know, believe: and what I can redress,
As I shall find the time to friend, I will.   10
What you have spoke, it may be so perchance.
This tyrant, whose sole name blisters our tongues,
Was once thought honest; you have lov'd him well;
He hath not touch'd you yet. I am young; but
    something
You may deserve of him through'me; and wisdom   15
To offer up a weak, poor, innocent lamb
T' appease an angry god.
Macduff
I am not treacherous.
Malcolm
                               But Macbeth is.
A good and virtuous nature may recoil
In an imperial charge. But I shall crave your pardon;   20
That which you are, my thoughts cannot transpose;
Angels are bright still, though the brightest fell.

25. The thought in Malcolm's mind seems to be that perhaps Macbeth promised Macduff that his family would be left unharmed if he betrayed Malcolm.

26. *rawness* unprotected state.

29–31. 'Don't let my suspicions alone dishonour you. I'm simply protecting myself by voicing them'. He ends, apologetically, by saying that Macduff may very well be an honest man, in spite of *these* suspicions.

33. *For goodness ... thee* Macduff bitterly accuses Malcolm of being too feeble to oppose Macbeth.

33–4. *Wear thou ... affeer'd* (the 'thou' here is Macbeth) go on enjoying the fruits of your crimes; you're undisputed master now.

34. *affeer'd* a legal term meaning 'confirmed'.

34. Macduff gives up the attempt and turns to go. But Malcolm has by no means completed his testing yet.

37. The Elizabethans thought of the East as the main source of gold and precious stones.

37. *to boot* as well.

39. *sinks beneath the yoke* The country is like an ill-treated animal pulling a heavy load.

41. *withal* moreover.

42. That people would support my cause.

43. *gracious England* King Edward the Confessor, who has God's grace.

44. From this point onwards Malcolm deliberately paints a frightful portrait of himself. He wants to see if Macduff would accept him as king, however evil he is; if so, then his suspicions will be proved to be correct – Macduff has come to trap him.

44. *for all this* in spite of all this.

Though all things foul would wear the brows of grace,
Yet grace must still look so.

Macduff
                              I have lost my hopes.

Malcolm
Perchance even there where I did find my doubts.   25
Why in that rawness left you wife and child,
Those precious motives, those strong knots of love,
Without leave-taking? I pray you,
Let not my jealousies be your dishonours,
But mine own safeties. You may be rightly just,   30
Whatever I shall think.

Macduff
                         Bleed, bleed, poor country.
Great tyranny, lay thou thy basis sure,
For goodness dare not check thee. Wear thou thy
                    wrongs,
The title is affeer'd. Fare thee well, lord.
I would not be the villain that thou think'st   35
For the whole space that's in the tyrant's grasp
And the rich East to boot.

Malcolm
                       Be not offended.
I speak not as in absolute fear of you.
I think our country sinks beneath the yoke;
It weeps, it bleeds; and each new day a gash   40
Is added to her wounds. I think withal
There would be hands uplifted in my right;
And here, from gracious England, have I offer
Of goodly thousands. But, for all this,
When I shall tread upon the tyrant's head,   45
Or wear it on my sword, yet my poor country
Shall have more vices than it had before;
More suffer, and more sundry ways than ever,
By him that shall succeed.

Macduff
                     What should he be?

51. *particulars* detailed varieties.
51. *grafted* included, attached

54–5. *Esteem him ... harms* Think of Macbeth as being as innocent as a lamb, in contrast with my unlimited *(confineless)* vices.

58. *Luxurious* lustful.
58. *avaricious* miserly.
There is no evidence that Macbeth has either of these faults, but Malcolm is now presenting a kind of 'fantasy Macbeth', the sum of all evils, in order to declare himself even worse!
59. *Sudden* violent.
59. *smacking* tasting.
60–1. *but ... voluptuousness* my lustfulness has no limit.
63–5. *my desire ... my will* my lust would overcome all attempts to limit it.
66. We may imagine Macduff being silent for a few moments, not knowing what to say to such an astonishing piece of self-criticism. Then he admits that lustfulness has been the downfall of many rulers; nevertheless, even this may not rule Malcolm out as an improvement upon Macbeth as King of Scotland!
70–2. You may satisfy all your sexual desires lavishly in secret, preserving a reputation for self-control, by deceiving everyone.

73–6. That greedy creature, your lust, can't possibly take as many women as are willing to offer themselves to a king ...

76–84. Malcolm now moves on to the second major vice he accuses himself of – greed for possessions *(avarice)*.
77. *ill–compos'd affection* unbalanced character

Malcolm
It is myself I mean; in whom I know 50
All the particulars of vice so grafted
That, when they shall be open'd, black Macbeth
Will seem as pure as snow; and the poor state
Esteem him as a lamb, being compar'd
With my confineless harms.
Macduff
Not in the legions 55
Of horrid hell can come a devil more damn'd
In evils to top Macbeth.
Malcolm
I grant him bloody,
Luxurious, avaricious, false, deceitful,
Sudden, malicious, smacking of every sin
That has a name; but there's no bottom, none, 60
In my voluptuousness. Your wives, your daughters,
Your matrons, and your maids, could not fill up
The cistern of my lust; and my desire
All continent impediments would o'erbear
That did oppose my will. Better Macbeth 65
Than such an one to reign.
Macduff
Boundless intemperance
In nature is a tyranny; it hath been
Th' untimely emptying of the happy throne
And fall of many kings. But fear not yet
To take upon you what is yours. You may 70
Convey your pleasures in a spacious plenty,
And yet seem cold, the tune you may so hoodwink.
We have willing dames enough; there cannot be
That vulture in you to devour so many
As will to greatness dedicate themselves, 75
Finding it so inclin'd.
Malcolm
With this there grows
In my most ill-compos'd affection such

78. *stanchless* uncontrollable.
79. *cut off* kill.
80. *his* one nobleman's.

82–3. *that I should ... unjust* make up false complaints (as excuses for robbing them).

86–9. *summer-seeming* Macduff's point is that lust isn't likely to last throughout a man's life (it will pass, like summer), but avarice is different, and worse. Even so, Scotland can probably cope with this, too.
88. *foisons* plentiful resources.
89. *Of your mere own* out of what really belongs to you (as king).
89. *portable* bearable.
92. *verity*: truthfulness.
93. *Bounty* generosity.

95. *I have no relish of them* I haven't a scrap of any of these in me.
96. In variations of every possible sin.

97–100. This is just the kind of conclusive, all-embracingly destructive threat that Macbeth makes at his most desperate moments (see Act IV, Scene i, lines 57–60). Malcolm still seems to be using the tyrant as his model of wickedness.
98. *concord* harmony.
99. *Uproar* throw into chaos.

102. Macduff has now had enough, and gives up his attempt to persuade Malcolm.
104. *untitled* not entitled to the throne.

A stanchless avarice that, were I King,
I should cut off the nobles for their lands,
Desire his jewels, and this other's house;   80
And my more-having would be as a sauce
To make me hunger more, that I should forge
Quarrels unjust against the good and loyal,
Destroying them for wealth.

Macduff
                  This avarice
Sticks deeper, grows with more pernicious root   85
Than summer-seeming lust; and it hath been
The sword of our slain kings. Yet do not fear;
Scotland hath foisons to fill up your will
Of your mere own. All these are portable,
With other graces weigh'd.   90

Malcolm
But I have none. The king-becoming graces,
As justice, verity, temp'rance, stableness,
Bounty, perseverance, mercy, lowliness,
Devotion, patience, courage, fortitude,
I have no relish of them; but abound   95
In the division of each several crime,
Acting it many ways. Nay, had I pow'r, I should
Pour the sweet milk of concord into hell,
Uproar the universal peace, confound
All unity on earth.

Macduff
             O Scotland, Scotland!   100

Malcolm
If such a one be fit to govern, speak.
I am as I have spoken.

Macduff
             Fit to govern!
No, not to live! O nation miserable,
With an untitled tyrant bloody-scept'red,
When shalt thou see thy wholesome days again,   105
Since that the truest issue of thy throne

107. *interdiction* condemnation.
108. *blaspheme his breed* disgrace his family.

111. *Died every day she liv'd* she was so devout that she lived every day as if it were her last.
112–13. *These evils ... Hath* we now regard *Hath* as a singular verb, but it was often used with a plural subject in Shakespeare's time.
113. *breast* heart (thought to be the source of feelings).

115. *Child of integrity* i.e. 'which was inspired by your honest nature'. Malcolm is now satisfied that Macduff is not acting a sinister part.
116. *black scruples* dark suspicions.
118. *trains* tricks, schemes.
119–20. *and modest wisdom ... haste* commonsense has prevented me from believing things too easily.
120–1. Malcolm's appeal to God's grace, putting fears and doubts away in the process, sets the tone for the remainder of the play, as the forces of good seek to overthrow the forces of evil represented by Macbeth.
123. *Unspeak mine own detraction* take back the things I accused myself of.
123. *abjure* deny.
125. *For strangers ... nature* as qualities quite foreign to me.
126. *Unknown to woman* virginal.
126. *never was forsworn* never dishonoured by being false.
127. Far from wanting things, Malcolm declares he doesn't particularly value his own possessions, let alone those of others.

135. *at a point* fully prepared for action.
136–7. *the chance of goodness ... quarrel!* may our chances of success be as great as the justice of our cause'

138–9. It is not hard to sympathize with Macduff's bewilderment. But could Malcolm have tested him in any more effective way?

By his own interdiction stands accurs'd
And does blaspheme his breed? Thy royal father
Was a most sainted king; the queen that bore thee,
Oft'ner upon her knees than on her feet,　　　　　110
Died every day she liv'd. Fare thee well!
These evils thou repeat'st upon thyself
Hath banish'd me from Scotland. O my breast,
Thy hope ends here!

Malcolm

　　　　　　　　　Macduff, this noble passion,
Child of integrity, hath from my soul　　　　　115
Wip'd the black scruples, reconcil'd my thoughts
To thy good truth and honour. Devilish Macbeth
By many of these trains hath sought to win me
Into his power; and modest wisdom plucks me
From over-credulous haste. But God above　　　120
Deal between thee and me; for even now
I put myself to thy direction, and
Unspeak mine own detraction, here abjure
The taints and blames I laid upon myself
For strangers to my nature. I am yet　　　　　125
Unknown to woman, never was forsworn,
Scarcely have coveted what was mine own,
At no time broke my faith, would not betray
The devil to his fellow, and delight
No less in truth than life. My first false speaking　130
Was this upon myself. What I am truly
Is thine and my poor country's to command:
Whither indeed, before thy here-approach,
Old Siward with ten thousand warlike men
Already at a point was setting forth.　　　　　135
Now we'll together; and the chance of goodness
Be like our warranted quarrel! Why are you silent?

Macduff

Such welcome and unwelcome things at once
'Tis hard to reconcile.

140–59. In this passage Edward the Confessor (the King of England) is presented as a source of healing. Not only can he heal the glandular disease, scrofula (the tradition that English sovereigns possessed this power continued until at least Queen Anne's time), but it is also implied that he can heal political and social evils, like Macbeth's regime. It is the support of Edward's soldiers that make it possible for Malcolm to return powerfully to Scotland.

142. *stay his cure* wait for him to cure them.

142–3. *Convinces … art* defeats all the skill of trained doctors.

145. *presently amend* immediately get better.

146. Scrofula is often called 'the King's Evil'.

149. *solicits heaven* secures help from God.

150. *strangely-visited* horribly afflicted.

152. *mere* sheer.

153. *stamp* coin.

155–6. His successors on the throne will inherit his blessed healing power.

160. Apparently Malcolm sees that Ross is wearing Scottish clothes, but does not at first recognize him, although we know they have met before (see Act I, Scene vi). Perhaps he is again suspicious of a visitor from Scotland, until Macduff greets him warmly.

[Enter a DOCTOR.]

Malcolm
Well; more anon. Comes the King forth, I pray you?   140

Doctor
Ay, sir. There are a crew of wretched souls
That stay his cure. Their malady convinces
The great assay of art; but at his touch,
Such sanctity hath heaven given his hand,
They presently amend.

Malcolm
                              I thank you, doctor.   145

[Exit DOCTOR.]

Macduff
What's the disease he means?

Malcolm
                              'Tis called the evil:
A most miraculous work in this good king,
Which often since my hero-remain in England
I have seen him do. How he solicits heaven,
Himself best knows; but strangely-visited people,   150
All swoln and ulcerous, pitiful to the eye,
The mere despair of surgery, he cures,
Hanging a golden stamp about their necks,
Put on with holy prayers; and 'tis spoken,
To the succeeding royalty he leaves   155
The healing benediction. With this strange virtue,
He hath a heavenly gift of prophecy;
And sundry blessings hang about his throne
That speak him full of grace.

[Enter ROSS.]

Macduff
                              See, who comes here?

Malcolm
My countryman; but yet I know him not.   160

162. *betimes* quickly.
163. The things (such as a foul dictatorship) which make men suspicious of each other.

166–7. *nothing ... knows nothing* no-one except the *most* ignorant person (e.g. an imbecile).
168. *rent* rend.
169. *Are made, not mark'd* uttered, but not noticed (because agonized cries are so common).
170. *A modem ecstasy* a familiar emotion, something like 'a fashionable disease'.
170–1. *the dead man's knell ... for who* people hardly bother to ask who's dead when they hear the bell tolling.
173. 'Dying before they fall ill' – probably because so many are being 'liquidated' by Macbeth's agents.
173–4. *O, relation ... true!* Your account is too full of horrid detail, but undeniably true.

175. Any news an hour old earns the teller hisses (because it's stale. Evil things are happening all the time).
176. *teems* gives birth to.
176–240. In the rest of the scene Ross finds it difficult to break the news of the slaughter of Macduff's family, and when he does so Macduff is at first almost struck dumb with horror. Only when he expresses his feelings of sorrow and anger can he cope with the dreadful event. Then he is ready to seek a righteous revenge.

Macduff
My ever gentle cousin, welcome hither.
Malcolm
I know him now. Good God betimes remove
The means that makes us strangers!
Ross
                              Sir, amen.
Macduff
Stands Scotland where it did?
Ross
                    Alas, poor country,
Almost afraid to know itself! It cannot   165
Be call'd our mother, but our grave; where nothing,
But who knows nothing, is once seen to smile;
Where sighs, and groans, and shrieks, that rent the air,
Are made, not mark'd; where violent sorrow seems
A modern ecstasy; the dead man's knell   170
Is there scarce ask'd for who; and good men's lives
Expire before the flowers in their caps,
Dying or ere they sicken.
Macduff
                    O, relation
Too nice, and yet too true!
Malcolm
                    What's the newest grief?
Ross
That of an hour's age doth hiss the speaker: 175
Each minute teems a new one.
Macduff
                    How does my wife?
Ross
Why, well.
Macduff
          And all my children?
Ross
                         Well too.

179. *well at peace* It seems cruel to use a pun at such a time; but it does convey Ross's uneasiness and unwillingness to lie or reveal the dreadful news.

180. *a niggard of your speech* so reluctant to speak.

181–3. *the tidings* probably the news of the death of Lady Macduff and her children which he is yet to reveal.

183. *were out* had left their homes to oppose Macbeth.

185. *the tyrant's power afoot* Macbeth's army mobilized.

186. *your eye ...* Ross has turned from Macduff, only too glad to avoid conversation with him, and is addressing Malcolm.

188. *To doff ... distresses* To get rid of their troubles, as though throwing off clothes.

189. Exactly the same phrase was used of King Edward in line 43.

191. *older* more experienced.

192. *gives out* proclaims.

195. *Where hearing ... them* Where they wouldn't be heard by anyone.

195. *latch* catch.

196–7. *a fee-grief ... breast?* a sorrow belonging to one particular person.

197–8. *No mind ... some woe* All decent people feel sympathy for those who suffer, and thus suffer themselves.

199. *pertains* relates

Macduff
    The tyrant has not batter'd at their peace?
Ross
    No; they were well at peace when I did leave 'em.
Macduff
    Be not a niggard of your speech. How goes't?   180
Ross
    When I came hither to transport the tidings,
    Which I have heavily borne, there ran a rumour
    Of many worthy fellows that were out;
    Which was to my belief witnessed the rather
    For that I saw the tyrant's power afoot.   185
    Now is the time of help; your eye in Scotland
    Would create soldiers, make our women fight,
    To doff their dire distresses.
Malcolm
                        Be't their comfort
    We are coming thither. Gracious England hath
    Lent us good Siward and ten thousand men –   190
    An older and a better soldier none
    That Christendom gives out.
Ross
                        Would I could answer
    This comfort with the like! But I have words
    That would be howl'd out in the desert air,
    Where hearing should not latch them.
Macduff
                        What concern they?   195
    The general cause, or is it a fee-grief
    Due to some single breast?
Ross
                        No mind that's honest
    But in it shares some woe, though the main part
    Pertains to you alone.
Macduff
                    If it be mine.
    Keep it not from me; quickly let me have it.   200

202. *possess them* inform them.

205–7. *To relate ... death of you* To tell you in detail how it happened would add your death to the deaths of those you loved.
206. *quarry* means a heap of animals killed in hunting, and *deer* is a deeply sympathetic pun on 'dear'.

208–9. Macduff has tried not to show his feelings to the others, by hiding his face. Malcolm knows that he must express what he feels *(Give sorrow words...)*.
210. *o'erfraught* overburdened.

212. *And I must ... thence!* And I had to be absent at the time!

216. *He has no children* There are several possible explanations of this remark, the most likely being that it is addressed to Macbeth and means that Macduff cannot take an appropriate revenge ('tit for tat'). It might, alternatively, be addressed to Ross or himself and refer to Malcolm who doesn't yet know what it is to have a father's feelings.
217. *hell–kite* a devilish bird of prey, raiding a chicken-run and killing all the birds.
218. *dam* mother.

Ross
Let not your ears despise my tongue for ever,
Which shall possess them with the heaviest sound
That ever yet they heard.
Macduff
                              Humph guess at it.
Ross
Your castle is surpris'd; your wife and babes
Savagely slaughter'd. To relate the manner,   205
Were, on the quarry of these murder'd deer,
To add the death of you.
Malcolm
                              Merciful heaven!
What, man! Ne'er pull your hat upon your brows;
Give sorrow words. The grief that does not speak
Whispers the o'erfraught heart and bids it break.   210
Macduff
My children too?
Ross
                    Wife, children, servants, all
That could be found.
Macduff
                         And I must be from thence!
My wife kill'd too?
Ross
                   I have said.
Malcolm
                                Be comforted.
Let's make us med'cines of our great revenge
To cure this deadly grief.   215
Macduff
He has no children. All my pretty ones?
Did you say all? O hell-kite! All?
What, all my pretty chickens and their dam
At one fell swoop?
Malcolm
Dispute it like a man.

222. *things* beings (i.e. Lady Macduff and the children).

225. *nought* evil.

226–7. *Not for their own ... souls* 'They died because of my sinfulness, not their own'. Macduff sees their deaths as the consequence of his own sins, but he is probably not blaming himself for having left his family in Scotland – that was an unfortunate necessity.

228. *whetstone* a piece of stone on which knives (and swords) are sharpened.

229. *blunt not ... it* don't tone down your feelings; express them in full force.

230–1. Macduff declares that he could easily act like a woman (by weeping) or like a boaster (by merely saying what he will do); instead, he intends to return to Scotland and get his revenge.

232. *Cut short all intermission* cut out all delay.

232. *front to front* face to face.

235. *Heaven forgive him too!* He means that if Macbeth escapes with his life it will mean that he, Macduff, has first forgiven him.

235. *This tune goes manly* This is a proper, manly way of speaking.

237. *Our lack ... leave* The only thing left to do is to say our farewells.

237–9. *Macbeth ... their instruments* Macbeth is compared to a ripe fruit which is ready to fall.

238–9. *the pow'rs above ... instruments* he means that God has selected them as the agents of divine vengeance.

240. He implies that dawn (which will bring light and therefore hope) will soon break and that the fortunes of all good, true people in Scottish society are about to change.

Macduff

                    I shall do so;   220
But I must also feel it as a man.
I cannot but remember such things were
That were most precious to me. Did heaven look on,
And would not take their part? Sinful Macduff,
They were all struck for thee – nought that I am;   225
Not for their own demerits, but for mine,
Fell slaughter on their souls. Heaven rest them now!

Malcolm

Be this the whetstone of your sword. Let grief
Convert to anger; blunt not the heart, enrage it.

Macduff

O, I could play the woman with mine eyes   230
And braggart with my tongue! But, gentle heavens,
Cut short all intermission; front to front
Bring thou this fiend of Scotland and myself;
Within my sword's length set him; if he scape,
Heaven forgive him too!

Malcolm

               This tune goes manly.   235
Come, go we to the King. Our power is ready;
Our lack is nothing but our leave. Macbeth
Is ripe for shaking, and the pow'rs above
Put on their instruments. Receive what cheer you may;
The night is long that never finds the day.   240

[Exeunt.]

ACT V SCENE I

We have not seen Lady Macbeth since the middle of Act III. At that point (Scene iv) she was still trying to comfort and strengthen her husband (*You lack the season of all natures, sleep* were her last words then), but he was beginning to act alone, without communication with her. Now it is she who cannot sleep and who lives in a dreadful world of guilty visions. The scene is introduced almost like a documentary by the Doctor and the Gentlewoman, preparing the way for Lady Macbeth's wild but significant remarks.

1. *watch'd* stayed up at night to watch.

3. *went into the field* led his army against the rebels.

5. *closet* a writing-cabinet. What do you imagine Lady Macbeth wrote?

8–9. *A great perturbation ... watching!* A terrible disorder, to be asleep yet at the same time to act as though awake!
11. *actual performances* actions.

14. *meet* correct, fitting.
15–16. The Gentlewoman has more sense, in Macbeth's Scotland, with secret agents everywhere, than to say anything which can't be conclusively proved.

17. *This is her very guise* This is exactly as she looked before.
18. *stand close* stay hidden.

ACT FIVE
Scene I

Dunsinane. Macbeth's castle

[Enter a DOCTOR OF PHYSIC *and a* WAITING-GENTLEWOMAN.*]*

Doctor

I have two nights watch'd with you, but can perceive
no truth in your report. When was it she last walk'd?

Gentle-woman

Since his Majesty went into the field, I have seen her
rise from her bed, throw her nightgown upon her,
unlock her closet, take forth paper, fold it, write   5
upon't, read it, afterwards seal it, and again return to
bed; yet all this while in a most fast sleep.

Doctor

A great perturbation in nature, to receive at once the
benefit of sleep and do the effects of watching! In this
slumb'ry agitation, besides her walking and other   10
actual performances, what, at any time, have you
heard her say?

Gentlewoman

That, sir, which I will not report after her.

Doctor

You may to me; and 'tis most meet you should.

Gentlewoman

Neither to you nor any one, having no witness to   15
confirm my speech.

[Enter LADY MACBETH, *with a taper.]*

Lo you, here she comes! This is her very guise; and,
upon my life, fast asleep. Observe her; stand close.

Doctor

How came she by that nght?

20–1. There is a horrible irony in the fact that the woman who said *Come, thick night. And pall thee in the dunnest smoke of hell* (Act I, Scene v, lines 50–1) should now be, like a nervous child, afraid of the dark. On the other hand it might be said that she herself is now *in the dunnest smoke of hell.*

24–8. She stops at this point, puts down the candle, and stands desperately going through the motions of washing—an *accustomed action* since her 'nervous breakdown'.

29. *Yet* still, even now.

29. *a spot of* blood (though she had told her husband *A little water clears us of this deed.* Act II, Scene ii, line 67).

31. *satisfy my remembrance* back up and confirm what I remember later.

32. *One, two* either the bell she struck as a signal for Macbeth (Act II, Scene i, lines 31–2) or, more likely, the clock striking in the night when Duncan was murdered.

33. *Hell is murky* i.e. the hell she is now in. Her broken speeches are a mix of her past, cold comments when she encouraged Macbeth to act, and horrified remarks which show the more sensitive womanly nature she deliberately repressed. Do you think we are getting a more accurate picture of her as a person now than when we watched her behaving like a monster before?

39. *The Thane of Fife* … now? What effect does the 'nursery rhyme' have?

41–2. *you mar all with this starting* She recalls her anger and dismay when Macbeth broke down at the banquet, and said he saw Banquo's ghost.

43. *Go to, go to* The Doctor can't resist expressing his deep concern about the deeds her words hint at.

Gentlewoman

    Why, it stood by her. She has light by her continually;   20
'tis her command.

Doctor

    You see her eyes are open.

Gentlewoman

    Ay, but their sense is shut.

Doctor

    What is it she does now? Look how she rubs her
hands.   25

Gentlewoman

    It is an accustomed action with her, to seem thus
washing her hands; I have known her continue in
this a quarter of an hour.

Lady Macbeth

    Yet here's a spot.

Doctor

    Hark, she speaks. I will set down what comes from   30
her, to satisfy my remembrance the more strongly.

Lady Macbeth

    Out, damned spot! Out, I say! One, two; why then
'tis time to do't. Hell is murky. Fie, my lord, fie! a
soldier, and afeard? What need we fear who knows
it, when none can call our pow'r to account? Yet who   35
would have thought the old man to have had so
much blood in him?

Doctor

    Do you mark that?

Lady Macbeth

    The Thane of Fife had a wife; where is she now?
What, will these hands ne'er be clean? No more o'   40
that, my lord, no more o' that; you mar all with this
starting.

Doctor

    Go to, go to; you have known what you should not.

Gentlewoman

    She has spoke what she should not, I am sure of that.

46–7. *All the perfumes ... hand* a close parallel with the similar hopelessness of Macbeth's *Will all great Neptune's ocean wash this blood Clean from my hand?* (Act II, Scene ii, lines 60–1.)

50. *dignity* value, rank or position.
51–2. Even in such a small part as the Gentlewoman's, we notice she has a talent for shrewd and sharp comment.

53. *my practice* my medical expertise.

58. *out on's grave* out of his grave.

61–2. *What's done cannot be undone* There is, again, deep irony in such shoulder-shrugging words coming from a woman broken by the deeds she dismisses.

65. *Foul whisperings are abroad* evil rumours are going around.
65–6. *Unnatural deeds ... troubles* the unnatural deeds of leaders like Macbeth lead to unnatural events like rebellion (anything which breaks public order being, in a sense, unnatural).

Heaven knows what she has known.   45
Lady Macbeth
Here's the smell of the blood still. All the perfumes
of Arabia will not sweeten this little hand. Oh, oh,
oh!
Doctor
What a sigh is there! The heart is sorely charg'd.
Gentlewoman
I would not have such a heart in my bosom for the
dignity of the whole body.   50
Doctor
Well, well, well.
Gentlewoman
Pray God it be, sir.
Doctor
This disease is beyond my practice. Yet I have known
those which have walk'd in their sleep who have
died holily in their beds.   55
Lady Macbeth
Wash your hands, put on your nightgown, look not
so pale. I tell you yet again, Banquo's buried; he can-
not come out on's grave.
Doctor
Even so?
Lady Macbeth
To bed, to bed; there's knocking at the gate. Come,   60
come, come, come, give me your hand. What's done
cannot be undone. To bed, to bed, to bed.

[Exit.]

Doctor
Will she go now to bed?
Gentlewoman
Directly.
Doctor
Foul whisp'rings are abroad. Unnatural deeds   65

66. *infected minds* diseased or corrupted minds, like Lady Macbeth's.

68. She needs a priest to save her soul, rather than a doctor to heal her body.

70. *means of all annoyance* all means of injuring herself (in particular, of committing suicide).

71. *still* always, constantly.

72. *mated* bewildered.

Do breed unnatural troubles; infected minds
To their deaf pillows will discharge their secrets.
More needs she the divine than the physician.
God, God forgive us all. Look after her;
Remove from her the means of all annoyance,   70
And still keep eyes upon her. So, good night.
My mind she has mated, and amaz'd my sight.
I think, but dare not speak. Gentlewoman
Good night, good doctor.

                    [Exeunt.]

SCENE II

The purpose of this short scene is to show that there are other Scotsmen who are prepared to work tirelessly to rid their country of tyranny. Malcolm and Macduff can expect considerable assistance from inside their own country, as well as from outside.

3–5. *for their dear causes ... man* for their heartfelt causes would bring to life even a dead man to fight the bloody battle.
6. *Shall we well meet them* we are likely to meet them.

8. *file* list.
10. *unrough* smooth-cheeked (too young to shave yet).

11. *Protest ... manhood* insist on showing (by fighting) that they are now men.

15–16. *He cannot buckle ... rule* 'He can no longer impose his will on a failing situation' (the image is of a plump man – perhaps swollen with dropsy – trying to control his waistline.)
17. *sticking on his hands* i.e. the blood shed in the murders.
18–20. *Now minutely ... love* Minute by minute men desert him, reflecting and condemning his own treachery (when he betrayed his king). Those who remain faithful on the surface obey him only because they are under orders, not because they love him.
20–2. *Now does ... thief.* He has put on royal robes, but he lacks the royal nature to fill them.

Scene II

The country near Dunsinane

[Drum and colours. Enter MENTEITH, CAITHNESS, ANGUS, LENNOX *and* SOLDIERS.*]*

Menteith
    The English pow'r is near, led on by Malcolm,
    His uncle Siward, and the good Macduff.
    Revenges burn in them; for their dear causes
    Would to the bleeding and the grim alarm
    Excite the mortified man.

Angus
                     Near Birnam wood   5
    Shall we well meet them; that way are they coming.

Caithness
    Who knows if Donalbain be with his brother?

Lennox
    For certain, sir, he is not; I have a file
    Of all the gentry. There is Siward's son,
    And many unrough youths that even now   10
    Protest their first of manhood.

Menteith
                   What does the tyrant?

Caithness
    Great Dunsinane he strongly fortifies.
    Some say he's mad; others, that lesser hate him,
    Do call it valiant fury; but for certain
    He cannot buckle his distempered cause   15
    Within the bete of rule.

Angus
                  Now does he feel
    His secret murders sticking on his hands;
    Now minutely revolts upbraid his faith-breach;
    Those he commands move only in command,
    Nothing in love. Now does he feel his title   20

22–5. *Who then ... being there?* Who could blame Macbeth's own troubled senses for reacting violently when they condemn themselves for belonging to him..

27. *med'cine* probably, as in French, 'doctor'– referring to Malcolm, who has come to heal the state *(sickly weal)*.

28–9. They will shed their blood, which is Scottish, in order to cure Scotland of its disease. (Bleeding was an important form of treatment for many illnesses.)

30. To make Malcolm's cause flourish and to destroy Macbeth and those who support him.

Hang loose about him, like a giant's robe
Upon a dwarfish thief.
Menteith
                          Who then shall blame
His pester'd senses to recoil and start,
When all that is within him does condemn
Itself for being there?
Caithness
                          Well, march we on   25
To give obedience where 'tis truly ow'd.
Meet we the med'cine of the sickly weal;
And with him pour we in our country's purge
Each drop of us.
Lennox
                  Or so much as it needs
To dew the sovereign flower and drown the weeds.   30
Make we our march towards Birnam.

        [Exeunt, marching.]

SCENE III

Macbeth drives himself on by referring to the witches' most recent prophecies, but he is increasingly desperate and has little else to encourage him: his wife is mentally unstable, he has no real friends, and his castle is being hemmed in by the English forces under Malcolm, Siward and Macduff, and by those Scots who have already rebelled.

1. *let them fly all* (I don't care) if all my thanes leave me.
3. *taint with fear* be weakened by the disease of fear.

4–5. *The spirits ... consequences* The witches who know everything that is going to happen to human beings.

8. *epicures* luxury-loving people: the tough Scots perhaps tended to look on the English as pampered Southerners.
9. *sway by* rule myself with.

11–19. The number of times Macbcth refers to the messenger's (not surprising) paleness is quite astonishing, *cream-fac'd, goose look, prick thy face, and over-red thy fear, lily-liver'd,* possibly *patch* (which can mean 'plaster' as well as 'fool' or 'clown'), *linen cheeks,* and *whey-face.* Such crazy repetition may suggest Macbeth's obsessive nature.
11. *loon* rogue.

17. *Are counsellors to fear* make other people afraid.
17. *whey-face* a fellow with a face the colour of skimmed milk.

Scene III

Dunsinane. Macbeth's castle

[Enter MACBETH, DOCTOR *and* ATTENDANTS.*]*

Macbeth
Bring me no more reports; let them fly all.
Till Birnam wood remove to Dunsinane
I cannot taint with fear. What's the boy Malcolm?
Was he not born of woman? The spirits that know
All mortal consequences have pronounc'd me thus: 5
'Fear not, Macbeth; no man that's born of woman
Shall e'er have power upon thee'. Then fly, false thane
And mingle with the English epicures.
The mind I sway by and the heart I bear
Shall never sag with doubt nor shake with fear.   10

[Enter SERVANT.*]*

The devil damn thee black, thou cream-fac'd loon!
Where got'st thou that goose look?

Servant
There is ten thousand –
Macbeth
                    Geese, villain?
Servant
                                Soldiers, sir.
Macbeth
Go, prick thy face, and over-red thy fear,
Thou lily-liver'd boy. What soldiers, patch?   15
Death of thy soul! Those linen cheeks of thine
Are counsellors to fear. What soldiers, whey-face?
Servant
The English force, so please you.
Macbeth
Take thy face hence.

20. *push* attack.

21. *disseat* remove from the throne.

22–8. It is some time since we have felt sympathy for Macbeth, but we might admire here his remarkable clear-sightedness when analysing himself and his life.

23. *Is fall'n ... leaf* Has come to autumn, the time of withered, yellow leaves.

23–6. Macbeth cannot hope to have any of the compensations of old age enjoyed by most reasonably happy men.

27. *mouth-honour* i.e. respectful words spoken but not meant.
breath This conveys the same idea.

28. *Which the poor ... dare not* Which the faint-hearted speaker would like to hold back.

31. Presumably the arrival of the English army, and its size.

35. *moe* more.

35. *skirr* scour.

37. There is no real need for the doctor to come on until now, and in some productions this is how it is arranged.

[Exit SERVANT.]

Seyton! – I am sick at heart,

When I behold – Seyton, I say! – This push   20
Will cheer me ever, or disseat me now.
I have liv'd long enough. My way of life
Is fall'n into the sear, the yellow leaf;
And that which should accompany old age,
As honour, love, obedience, troops of friends,   25
I must not look to have; but, in their stead,
Curses not loud but deep, mouth-honour, breath,
Which the poor heart would fain deny, and dare not.
Seyton!

[Enter SEYTON.]

Seyton
What's your gracious pleasure?
Macbeth

What news more?   30

Seyton
All is confirm'd, my lord, which was reported.
Macbeth
I'll fight till from my bones my flesh be hack'd.
Give me my armour.
Seyton

'Tis not needed yet.

Macbeth
I'd put it on.
Send out moe horses, skirr the country round;   35
Hang those that talk of fear. Give me mine armour.
How does your patient, doctor
Doctor

Not so sick, my lord,

As she is troubled with thick-coming fancies
That keep her from her rest.
Macbeth

Cure her of that.

40–5. What Macbeth suggests that his wife needs is the skill of a modern psychiatrist, but certainly not of a medieval doctor.

42. *Raze out* erase.

43. *oblivious antidote* a medicine that will make the patient forget.

44. *stuff'd* overloaded.

47. *physic* the art of the doctor.

48. *staff* the symbol of his rank as commander-in-chief (the equivalent of a modern Field-Marshal's baton).

49. *Doctor ... from me* What has this to do with the doctor?

50. *Come, sir, dispatch* 'Hurry up and get on with it' (addressed to Seyton).

50–1. *Cast ... disease* diagnose the disease by examining the patient's urine. But the patient now is Scotland; Lady Macbeth has passed from his mind.

52. *pristine health* the health the country once enjoyed. *pristine* former.

53–4. *I would applaud ... again* I would applaud you so enthusiastically that the echoes would then applaud you too.

54. *Pull't off, I say* Macbeth seems to have changed his mind, and now tells Seyton to take his armour off again.

55. *rhubarb, senna, purgative drugs* ... These are all laxatives. Macbeth wants something to purge the body of Scotland of the English intruders

58. *it* his armour, or a piece of it.

59. *bane* destruction.

61. Probably both 'safe' ('in the clear') and 'unstained by evil'.

Canst thou not minister to a mind diseas'd,   40
Pluck from the memory a rooted sorrow,
Raze out the written troubles of the brain,
And with some sweet oblivious antidote
Cleanse the stuff'd bosom of that perilous stuff
Which weighs upon the heart?
Doctor

                    Therein the patient   45
Must minister to himself.
Macbeth

Throw physic to the dogs – I'll none of it.
Come, put mine armour on; give me my staff.
Seyton, send out. Doctor, the thanes fly from me.
Come, sir, dispatch. If thou couldst, doctor, cast   50
The water of my land, find her disease,
And purge it to a sound and pristine health,
I would applaud thee to the very echo,
That should applaud again.—Pull't off, I say. –
What rhubarb, senna, or what purgative drug,   55
Would scour these English hence? Hear'st thou of
    them?
Doctor

Ay, my good lord. Your royal preparation
Makes us hear something.
Macbeth

                Bring it after me.
I will not be afraid of death and bane
Till Birnam Forest come to Dunsinane.   60

[Exeunt all but the DOCTOR.]

Doctor

Were I from Dunsinane away and clear,
Profit again should hardly draw me here.

[Exit.]

SCENE IV

The combined Scottish and English forces are now marching towards Dunsinane and are near Birnam Wood.

Stage Direction *colours* flags.

2. *That chambers will be safe* i.e. when people can sleep safely in their bedrooms again (unlike Duncan).
doubt it nothing have no doubt that it will be so.

5. *shadow* hide
6. *host* army.
6–7. *make discovery ... of us* cause the enemy's scouts to make false reports about us.

8–10. *We learn. ... before't* All reports agree that the confident Macbeth stays all the time in the castle of Dunsinane and will allow us to besiege it (without leaving the castle to oppose us).

10. *'Tis his main hope* i.e. to 'sit tight', defending his castle.
11–12. For whenever any opportunity has presented itself, both high and low-ranking soldiers have deserted him . ..
13. *constrained things* wretched creatures forced to obey him.
14–16. *Let our just censures ... soldiership* Let us delay giving our opinions until we see how things turn out. In the meantime let's do our jobs as efficient soldiers.

Scene IV

Before Birnam Wood

[Drum and colours. Enter MALCOLM, SIWARD, MACDUFF, SIWARD'S SON, MENTEITH, CAITHNESS, ANGUS, LENNOX, ROSS *and* SOLDIERS, *marching.]*

Malcolm
    Cousins, I hope the days are near at hand
    That chambers will be safe.
Menteith
                    We doubt it nothing.
Siward
    What wood is this before us?
Menteith
                    The wood of Birnam.
Malcolm
    Let every soldier hew him down a bough
    And bear't before him; thereby shall we shadow   5
    The numbers of our host, and make discovery
    Err in report of us.
Soldiers
               It shall be done.
Siward
    We learn no other but the confident tyrant
    Keeps still in Dunsinane, and will endure
    Our setting down before't.
Malcolm
                'Tis his main hope;   10
    For where there is advantage to be given,
    Both more and less have given him the revolt;
    And none serve with him but constrained things
    Whose hearts are absent too.
Macduff
               Let our just censures
    Attend the true event, and put we on   15

16–18. ***The time approaches ... we owe*** Soon, when fate has decided the event, we shall be able to separate our hopes (***What we shall say we have***) and our actual achievements *(what we owe)*.

19–20. Talking can only raise fragile hopes. Fighting *(strokes)* is the way to decide the issue beyond doubt.

Industrious soldiership.
Siward.

                    The time approaches
That will with due decision make us know
What we shall say we have, and what we owe.
Thoughts speculative their unsure hopes relate,
But certain issue strokes must arbitrate; 20
Towards which advance the war.

       [Exeunt, marching.]

SCENE V

Macbeth does at first seem the *confident tyrant* that Siward called him. It appears that he has overcome his old concerns and is now tough and indifferent to what happens to him. Is this impression confirmed as the scene goes on, or are there deeper, different emotions we begin to see?

3. *let them lie* let the besieging forces stay.
4. *ague* fever (infectious fevers of several kinds were very common in armies in those days).
5. *forc'd* reinforced.
5. *those that should be ours* Macbeth's way of referring to the *more and less who have given him the revolt.*
6. *dareful* defiantly.
6. *beard to beard* face to face.

10–13. *The time has been ... were in't* 'Formerly I would have shivered with fear at a cry in the night, and the hair would have stood up on my scalp as though it had a life of its own, when I heard a horrifying story.'
11. *fell* any skin with fur or hair on it.
14–15. *Direness ... start me* Horror, which has become a common part of my murderous thoughts, has no power now to startle me.

Scene V

Dunsinane. Macbeth's castle

[Enter MACBETH, SEYTON and SOLDIERS, with drum and colours.]

Macbeth
Hang out our banners on the outward walls;
The cry is still 'They come'. Our castle's strength
Will laugh a siege to scorn. Here let them lie
Till famine and the ague eat them up.
Were they not forc'd with those that should be ours,   5
We might have met them dareful, beard to beard,
And beat them backward home.

[A cry within of women.]

What is that noise?
Seyton
It is the cry of women, my good lord.

[Exit]

Macbeth
I have almost forgot the taste of fears.
The time has been my senses would have cool'd   10
To hear a night-shriek, and my fell of hair
Would at a dismal treatise rouse and stir
As life were in't. I have supp'd full with horrors;
Direness, familiar to my slaughterous thoughts,
Cannot once start me.

[Re-enter SEYTON.]

Wherefore was that cry?   15
Seyton
The Queen, my lord, is dead.

17–28. Although he seemed concerned about his wife's health in Scene iii, his reaction to her death is strangely emotionless, yet it leads to a beautifully simple speech about the futility of life.

17–18. It would have been better if she had died later on, at a more convenient time for such news.

19. Notice how well this line puts across the plodding monotony of dreary days succeeding each other in a meaningless life.

21. *To the last syllable ... time* i.e. until the very last word of human history is written.

22–3. *And all ... death* And every day in the past stupid human beings have been able to see just well enough to move to their deaths and crumble to dust in their graves.

23. *Out, out, brief candle!* Macbeth's farewell to his wife.

24–6. *walking shadow* and *poor player* both are ways of referring to an actor. Shakespeare often refers to acting in a way which stresses its unreality and how it is impossible to present life meaningfully on the stage

25. *struts and frets* the activity is hectic, but in no way significant.

26–8. *it is a tale ... nothing* a statement of extreme despair.

29. Do you think there should be a long pause after Macbeth's last words?

30. *Gracious my lord* 'My gracious lord.' Although there is no sign of grace in Macbeth now he is still the king and must be addressed in an appropriate manner.

39. *next* nearest.

40. *Till famine cling thee* Until starvation shrivels you up.

40. *If thy speech be sooth* If what you say is true.

Macbeth
> She should have died hereafter;
> There would have been a time for such a word.
> To-morrow, and to-morrow, and to-morrow,
> Creeps in this petty pace from day to day   20
> To the last syllable of recorded time,
> And all our yesterdays have lighted fools
> The way to dusty death. Out, out, brief candle!
> Life's but a walking shadow, a poor player,
> That struts and frets his hour upon the stage,   25
> And then is heard no more; it is a tale
> Told by an idiot, full of sound and fury,
> Signifying nothing.

[Enter a MESSENGER.*]*

> Thou com'st to use thy tongue; thy story quickly.
Messenger
> Gracious my lord,   30
> I should report that which I say I saw,
> But know not how to do't.
Macbeth
>   Well, say, sir.
Messenger
> As I did stand my watch upon the hill,
> I look'd toward Birnam, and anon methought
> The wood began to move.
Macbeth
>   Liar and slave!   35
Messenger
> Let me endure your wrath, if't be not so.
> Within this three mile may you see it coming;
> I say, a moving grove.
Macbeth
>   If thou speak'st false,
> Upon the next tree shalt thou hang alive,
> Till famine cling thee. If thy speech be sooth,   40

41. I don't care if you do the same to me (i.e. bind me alive to a tree).

42–4. *I pull in … like truth* I find I doubt my own certainty and begin to wonder whether the Devil (speaking in the form of the Third Apparition, the Child Crowned) mislead me by lying, even though seeming to tell the truth.

46. *Arm, arm, and out* He shouts orders to make an attack on the besieging army.

47–8. *If this … tarry here* i.e. If what this messenger says is true. It won't make any difference whether we try to escape or stay here in the castle.

49. *gin* begin.

50. *th'estate o' th' world* the ordered universe.

51. *the alarum bell* the bell warning the men in the castle that an attack is coming.

51. *wrack* destruction.

52. *harness* armour. Macbeth regains a touch of his old courage and zest for battle.

I care not if thou dost for me as much.
I pull in resolution, and begin
To doubt th' equivocation of the fiend
That lies like truth. 'Fear not, till Birnam wood
Do come to Dunsinane.' And now a wood   45
Comes toward Dunsinane. Arm, arm, and out.
If this which he avouches does appear,
There is nor flying hence nor tarrying here.
I gin to be aweary of the sun,
And wish th' estate o' th' world were now undone.   50
Ring the alarum bell. Blow wind, come wrack;
At least we'll die with harness on our back.

[Exeunt.]

SCENE VI

Malcolm is already showing the calmness and confidence of genuine authority.

1. *leavy* leafy.
2. *show like those you are* i.e. the soldiers are to reveal themselves; the camouflage has served its purpose.

4. *battle* section of the army. Notice that Malcolm now uses the royal *we*. He is growing into his rightful role.

6. *our order* our plan of battle.
7–8. If we can only bring the tyrant's army to battle tonight we will accept defeat if we cannot fight worthily.

10. *clamorous harbingers* noisy heralds, or forerunners.

Scene VI

Dunsinane. Before the castle

[Drum and colours. Enter MALCOLM, SIWARD, MACDUFF *and their* ARMY *with boughs.]*

Malcolm
Now near enough; your leavy screens throw down,
And show like those you are. You, worthy uncle,
Shall with my cousin, your right noble son,
Lead our first battle; worthy Macduff and we
Shall take upon's what else remains to do,   5
According to our order.
Siward
                                    Fare you well.
Do we but find the tyrant's power to-night,
Let us be beaten, if we cannot fight.
Macduff
Make all our trumpets speak; give them all breath,
Those clamorous harbingers of blood and death.

                         [Exeunt.]

SCENE VII

Battle is about to begin. Macbeth is still depending on the only saying of the witches that has not yet been proved false *(none of woman born Shall harm Macbeth,* Act IV, Scene i, lines 79–80).

The battle is presented in the usual manner of the Elizabethan and Jacobean stage. Brief incidents, involving very small numbers of combatants, rapidly follow one after to the other, to produce a sense of excitement and expectation in the audience.

1–2. The image is from a favourite Elizabethan sport, bear-baiting, in which a bear was tied to a stake while dogs attacked it.
2. *course* a round or bout.

6–7. It sounds as though Young Siward already suspects that he is facing Macbeth.

10. *abhorred* hated, loathed.
10–11. *with my sword ... thou speak'st* I'll show you by the way I fight that you lie in suggesting I'm afraid of your name.

12–13. Macbeth still seems invincible. At least he has once more convinced himself that he is.

Scene VII

Another part of the field

[Enter MACBETH.]

Macbeth
They have tied me to a stake; I cannot fly,
But bear-like I must fight the course. What's he
That was not born of woman? Such a one
Am I to fear, or none.

[Enter YOUNG SIWARD.]

Young Siward
What is thy name?
Macbeth
                    Thou'lt be afraid to hear it.   5
Young Siward
No; though thou call'st thyself a hotter name
Than any is in hell.
Macbeth
                  My name's Macbeth.
Young Siward
The devil himself could not pronounce a title
More hateful to mine ear.
Macbeth
                    No, nor more fearful.
Young Siward
Thou liest, abhorred tyrant; with my sword   10
I'll prove the lie thou speak'st.

[Fight, and YOUNG SIWARD slain.]

Macbeth
                Thou wast born of woman.
But swords I smile at, weapons laugh to scorn,
Brandish'd by man that's of a woman born.

16. *still* for ever.

17. *kerns* Irish foot-soldiers, paid to fight, as Macduff says.

18. *staves* shafts of spears

18–20. *either thou, Macbeth ... undeeded* Macduff now will not fight anyone but Macbeth. His overwhelming desire is to take revenge for the fate of his family.

20. *undeeded* without having done any deeds in battle.

20. *There thou shouldst be* That's where you're likely to be.

22. *bruited* announced by noise.

Stage Direction *Exit* Macduff goes off, seeking Macbeth, and the audience is left in suspense.

24. *The castle's gently render'd* 'The castle has been surrendered with remarkably little resistance'.

25. We have already heard, from Macbeth himself, that many of his men have gone over to the other side (Act V, Scene iii, lines 7–8). The process must have sped up by now.

27. *The day ... yours* i.e. Your victory is now almost won.

28–9. *foes That strike beside us* enemy soldiers who deliberately miss with their sword thrusts.

[Exit. Alarums. Enter MACDUFF.*]*

Macduff
    That way the noise is. Tyrant, show thy face.
    If thou beest slain and with no stroke of mine,   15
    My wife and children's ghosts will haunt me still.
    I cannot strike at wretched kerns whose arms
    Are hir'd to bear their staves; either thou, Macbeth,
    Or else my sword with an unbattered edge
    I sheathe again undeeded. There thou shouldst be;   20
    By this great clatter, one of greatest note
    Seems bruited. Let me find him. Fortune,
    And more I beg not.

    [Exit. Alarums. Enter MALCOLM *and old* SIWARD.*]*

Siward
    This way, my lord. The castle's gently rend'red;
    The tyrant's people on both sides do fight;   25
    The noble thanes do bravely in the war;
    The day almost itself professes yours,
    And little is to do.
Malcolm
                We have met with foes
    That strike beside us.
Siward
                Enter, sir, the castle.

    [Exeunt, Alarum.]

SCENE VIII

Macbeth's death leaves mixed feelings in most people's minds. You will find this discussed in the Summing-up.

1. *play the Roman fool* When an honourable Roman faced defeat he usually thought it his duty to commit suicide (see Shakespeare's *Julius Caesar*).

2–3. *Whiles I see lives ... upon them* As long as I see enemies who are still alive, mortal wounds are better on their bodies than on mine.

4. *Of all men else* More than any other man.

5–6. *my soul ... already* Are we to take this as a sign of lingering human feelings (remorse, for example) in Macbeth? Does the comment change your attitude to him at this point?

8. *terms* words. *Thou losest labour* You're wasting your efforts.

9–10. You can just as easily make a mark with your sharp sword on the uncuttable air as make me bleed.

11. *vulnerable crests* the helmets of men who can be wounded.

12. *a charmed life* a life protected by a magic spell.

12. *must not* cannot.

13. *Despair thy charm* Give up any faith you might have had in your magical protection.

14. *angel* evil spirit. (Angels could be good or bad.)

14. *still* always.

16. *Untimely* prematurely (i.e. before he was ready to be born naturally).

Scene VIII

Another part of the field

[Enter MACBETH.*]*

Macbeth
    Why should I play the Roman fool, and die
    On mine own sword? Whiles I see lives, the gashes
    Do better upon them.

[Enter MACDUFF.*]*

Macduff
                  Turn, hell-hound, turn.

Macbeth
    Of all men else I have avoided thee.
    But get thee back; my soul is too much charg'd   5
    With blood of thine already.

Macduff
                I have no words –
    My voice is in my sword: thou bloodier villain
    Than terms can give thee out.

[Fight. Alarum.]

Macbeth
              Thou losest labour.
    As easy mayst thou the intrenchant air
    With thy keen sword impress as make me bleed.   10
    Let fall thy blade on vulnerable crests;
    I bear a charmed life, which must not yield
    To one of woman born.

Macduff
            Despair thy charm;
    And let the angel whom thou still hast serv'd
    Tell thee Macduff was from his mother's womb   15
    Untimely ripp'd.

18. *cow'd my better part of man* crushed my spirit.

19. *juggling* cheating.

20. 'That trick us by saying things that have two meanings'. This is the point at which Macbeth finally gives up reliance on the witches.

21–2. *That keep the word ... our hope!* i.e. their words turn out to be literally true, but the other possible meaning, which inspired hope, proves false.

24. *the show and gaze o' th' time* a popular public spectacle (as at a fair).

25. *rarer monsters* 'strangest freaks'. Monsters, in this sense, such as calves with two heads, were frequently shown at fairs.

26. Sideshows were advertised by paintings on cloth hung from poles. Macduff goes on to describe the caption written under the picture.

27. *Here* in the tent where the freak is exhibited.

29. *baited with the rabble's curse* irritated by the crowd's curses (Macbeth is again comparing himself with a bear; see Scene vii, lines 1–2).

31. *And thou opposed* And though you are here opposed to me.

32. *Yet I will try the last* I will nevertheless go to the very limit (that is, fight to the death).

32–3. *Before my body ... shield* i.e. I hold my shield in front of my body.

33. *Lay on* fight.

35. Malcolm is referring to men who have not reported from the battle – that is, those who may have been killed or wounded.

36. *go off* be killed.

36. *by these I see* judging by the (number of) men I see around here ...

38. *your noble son* Young Siward.

39. *paid a soldier's debt* 'given his life'.

40. he had only just become an adult.

Macbeth

Accursed be that tongue that tells me so,
For it hath cow'd my better part of man;
And be these juggling fiends no more believ'd
That palter with us in a double sense,   20
That keep the word of promise to our ear,
And break it to our hope! I'll not fight with thee.

Macduff

Then yield thee, coward,
And live to be the show and gaze o' th' time.
We'll have thee, as our rarer monsters are,   25
Painted upon a pole, and underwrit
'Here may you see the tyrant'.

Macbeth

                  I will not yield,
To kiss the ground before young Malcolm's feet
And to be baited with the rabble's curse.
Though Birnam wood be come to Dunsinane,   30
And thou oppos'd, being of no woman born,
Yet I will try the last. Before my body
I throw my warlike shield. Lay on, Macduff;
And damn'd be him that first cries 'Hold, enough!'

[Exeunt, fighting. Alarums]

[Retreat and flourish. Enter, with drum and colours,
MALCOLM, SIWARD, ROSS, LENNOX, ANGUS, CAITHNESS,
MENTEITH *and* SOLDIERS.*]*

Malcolm

I would the friends we miss were safe arriv'd.   35

Siward

Some must go off; and yet, by these I see,
So great a day as this is cheaply bought.

Malcolm

Macduff is missing, and your noble son.

Ross

Your son, my lord, has paid a soldier's debt:

41–3. *The which no sooner ... died* Immediately he had proved his manhood by his fighting quality in carrying out his duty without shrinking, there and then he died like a man.

46–50. Siward's reaction to his son's death is a tough soldier's attitude, but undoubtedly sincere. It is typical of men dedicated to service and is not unlike Macbeth's own view of the soldier's profession when he was honoured and praised at the beginning of the play.

48. *hairs* a pun on 'heirs' – another example of a serious pun.

50. *his knell is knoll'd* his death-bell has been tolled (that is, all necessary formalities have been carried out).

52. *parted* departed.

52. *paid his score* settled all his debts (by doing his duty as a soldier).

55. *The time* The world in our time.

56. *compass'd with thy kingdom's pearl* surrounded by the jewels of your kingdom (the faithful thanes standing around).

57. i.e. they are all thinking what Macduff is putting into words.

He only liv'd but till he was a man;   40
The which no sooner had his prowess confirm'd
In the unshrinking station where he fought,
But like a man he died.

Siward
                 Then he is dead?

Ross
Ay, and brought off the field. Your cause of sorrow
Must not be measur'd by his worth, for then   45
It hath no end.

Siward
             Had he his hurts before?

Ross
Ay, on the front.

Siward
                Why, then. God's soldier be he!
Had I as many sons as I have hairs,
I would not wish them to a fairer death.
And so his knell is knoll'd.

Malcolm
                  He's worth more sorrow,   50
And that I'll spend for him.

Siward
                 He's worth no more.
They say he parted well and paid his score;
And so. God be with him! Here comes newer comfort

[Re-enter MACDUFF, with MACBETH's head.]

Macduff
Hail, King! for so thou art. Behold where stands
Th' usurper's cursed head. The time is free.   55
I see thee compass'd with thy kingdom's pearl
That speak my salutation in their minds;
Whose voices I desire aloud with mine –
Hail, King of Scotland!

All
              Hail, King of Scotland! *[Flourish]*

61. 'Before I, the king, settle the debt I owe you, by rewarding you for your services'. The short time he mentions is in fact only a few seconds. He rewards them by making them earls. This action also symbolizes his gratitude to King Edward of England, because the rank of earl was an English one.

64–5. *What's more ... time* Whatever else I have to do, which ought to be begun appropriately in a new regime ...

68. *Producing forth* Finding and arresting.

69. Is Malcolm's summing-up of Macbeth and his wife an accurate description of them?

70–1. *by self ... her life* committed suicide.

72. *by the grace of Grace* The personification of grace is God himself.

73. *in measure, time and place* 'in the right proportion, at the right time, in the right place'. Malcolm will be the restorer of order in Scottish society.

Malcolm
> We shall not spend a large expense of time   60
> Before we reckon with your several loves,
> And make us even with you. My Thanes and kinsmen
> Henceforth be Earls, the first that ever Scotland
> In such an honour nam'd. What's more to do,
> Which would be planted newly with the time –   65
> As calling home our exil'd friends abroad
> That fled the snares of watchful tyranny;
> Producing forth the cruel ministers
> Of this dead butcher, and his fiend-like queen,
> Who, as 'tis thought, by self and violent hands   70
> Took off her life – this, and what needful else
> That calls upon us, by the grace of Grace,
> We will perform in measure, time, and place.
> So thanks to all at once and to each one,
> Whom we invite to see us crown'd at Scone.   75

[Flourish. Exeunt.]

SUMMING UP

The man Macbeth He is the first person named in the play, and with his wife, the last to be referred to: *this dead butcher, and his fiend-like queen.* The play is, in a very real sense, about a man named Macbeth. Lady Macbeth is interesting and influential, but Macbeth is the centre of attention throughout. If your final judgment of him is similar to Malcolm's *this dead butcher*, you will probably have found the play both fascinating and horrifying. But it is likely that you will have seen more in him than that – perhaps felt the tragedy of the decline and ruin of a brave, talented, even affectionate man, and understood something of the mystery of good and evil mingled in human experience.

It is the witches who mention him first, and that within ten lines of the beginning. After associating themselves with disturbance in the elements (*In thunder, lightning, or in rain?*) and with human confusion (*When the battle's lost and won*), they significantly state their intention to *meet with Macbeth.* So, from the start, there is a question mark against the man: what can such evil creatures want with a Scottish hero fresh from his greatest triumph ? They speak almost as though they have an appointment with him, or he with them. In contrast, in the second scene, Macbeth receives glowing commendation from the Sergeant, from King Duncan and from Ross, but it is noticeable that the sole basis of the recommendation is his tremendous fighting spirit, amounting to unique ferocity. The Sergeant becomes incoherent in his efforts to describe the behaviour of Macbeth and Banquo on the battlefield. He is forced into comparisons which certainly make a doubtful impression on modern readers:

> *Except they meant to bathe in reeking wounds,*
> *Or memorize another Golgotha,*
> *I cannot tell –*

> (Act I, Scene ii, lines 39–41)

Even in an age when military prowess was more whole-heartedly admired than in our own, surely a conflict so bloody as to recall the Crucifixion, with all that has meant to Christians throughout the centuries, must raise questions about the motives of those involved?

There is the same suggestion of abnormally violent courage in Ross's address to Macbeth when he brings the news that the king has made him Thane of Cawdor:

> *Nothing afeard of what thyself didst make,*
> *Strange images of death.*
>
> (Act I Scene iii, lines 96–7)

Banquo is soon cleared of any suspicion by his loyalty to the good Duncan and by his self-identification with the divine:

> *In the great hand of God I stand, and thence*
> *Against the undivulg'd pretence I fight*
> *Of treasonous malice*
>
> (Act II, Scene iii, lines 130–2)

His partner, however, from the time of the first encounter with the witches (that is, on the very first occasion when we see him) responds to tests and temptations very differently. Banquo unhesitatingly associates the witches with the devil:

> *What can the devil speak true?*
>
> (Act I, Scene iii, line 107)

Macbeth, however, on hearing the first prophecies, seems afraid and, when the first one comes true so quickly and unexpectedly, sinks into a troubled reverie full of nightmarish visions (Act I, Scene iii, lines 131–43). The two men, heroes of the war, are already differentiated, their paths already diverging.

Macbeth and destiny One other aspect of the early impression made by Macbeth must be mentioned. The Sergeant commented (Act I, Scene ii, lines 14–24) that Macbeth disdained Fortune when he pursued and killed the traitor Macdonwald in the battle. There is a significant distinction to be made here: to defy Fortune in such a cause is widely and perhaps rightly admired. But there is a state of mind in which a man may stubbornly refuse to accept anything which destiny seems to hold out to him. In this state of mind a man may strike out wildly in every direction and on every occasion, until he is finally overwhelmed by disillusion and despair. This is Macbeth's mentality, as opposed to Banquo's, and it is well illustrated when the first prophecy of the witches comes true. Banquo talks about trust:

> That, trusted home,
> Might yet enkindle you unto the crown ...
>
> (Act I, Scene iii, lines 120–1)

while Macbeth immediately considers assisting Fortune by committing murder:

> My thought, whose murder yet is but fantastical,
> Shakes so my single state of man
> That function is smother'd in surmise,
> And nothing is but what is not.
>
> (Act I, Scene iii, lines 139–42)

He brushes aside the 'accepting' thought that his destiny may in any case be a great one:

> If chance will have me King, why, chance may crown me,
> Without my stir.
>
> (Act I, Scene iii, lines 144–5)

and takes things into his own hands.

Macbeth's view of right and wrong. If Macbeth is presented, from the very beginning of the story, as vulnerable to evil promptings from without and from within, it is also clear that he knows right from wrong. Even if the balance of his mind is at times disturbed, he is not the sort of criminal who could or would plead that he didn't know what he was doing. In the soliloquy *If it were done when 'tis done ...* (Act I, Scene vii, lines 1–28) he takes it for granted that a king should be able to trust one of his subjects, and particularly a man who is also his relative and his host, to protect and cherish him – certainly not to murder him in his sleep. Further, Macbeth has a positive appreciation of Duncan's human qualities:

> *this Duncan*
> *Hath borne his faculties so meek, hath been*
> *So clear in his great office*
>
> (Act I, Scene vii, lines 16–18)

and, at the end of his terrible career, his underlying sense of what is true and fitting reasserts itself when he speaks sadly and movingly of the fulfilments of the good life that he has cast away:

> *... that which should accompany old age,*
> *As honour, love, obedience, troops of friends,*
> *I must not look to have ...*
>
> (Act V, Scene iii, lines 24–6)

The meaning of manliness Another important question for us, as observers of the play, is this: how can a man who knows the meaning of love, honour and virtue, who admires his truly admirable king and fights bravely for him, destroy that same king in a most treacherous way? How can he then go on to destroy his best friend, and many others, including women and children? The answer seems to lie in deep confusion about what being a man means. This, of course, links up directly with the image of the ferocious soldier in the first few scenes, which we examined in the first section of this summing-up. There have been men in our own century who were honoured and praised for violent deeds in war, but who failed to adjust to peacetime, having acquired a taste for violence, and became deadly criminals. Macbeth seems to be in this category. Some might want to delve a little deeper into the character of such a man and say that he was one who had to prove something to himself. In this connection it is interesting to see that, just after he has uttered the true and heartfelt words:

> *I dare do all that may become a man;*

> *Who dares do more is none.*
> (Act I, Scene vii, lines 46–7)

in reply to Lady Macbeth's fierce taunting, he is almost immediately converted to committing the murder by her twisted definition of manliness (in the course of which she horribly denies her own essential womanliness):

> *When you durst do it, then you were a man;*
> *And to be more than what you were, you would*
> *Be so much more the man ...*
>   *I have given suck, and know*
> *How tender 'tis to love the babe that milks me –*
> *I would, while it was smiling in my face,*
> *Have pluck'd my nipple from his boneless gums,*
> *And dash'd the brains out, had I so sworn*
> *As you have done to this.*
> (Act I, Scene vii, lines 49–59)

The same warped reasoning is used when Macbeth bullies the murderers into killing Banquo. His strange speech about the various kinds of dogs, lifted from its context, might be thought to be an exhortation by an honourable man to other potentially honourable men:

> *... If you have a station in the file,*
> *Not i' th' worst rank of manhood, say't;*
> (Act III, Scene i, lines 100–1)

and again:

> *Your spirits shine through you.*
> (Act III, Scene i, line 126)

The whole elaborate image presents a world in which *bounteous nature* has arranged an appropriate function for every creature, and in which leaders can respect and love their subjects, grappling them *to the heart and love of us*, as Macbeth himself puts it. But the man who speaks is a foul tyrant and he is speaking to hired thugs. The speaker's main argument is that any man who allows himself to be ruled by patience when he is – supposedly – being ill-treated by another, can't call himself a man at all. It is exactly the same argument that was so effective when used on Macbeth by his wife.

Macbeth's increasing self-centredness During the course of the play Macbeth moves from preoccupation with himself and his situation to total self-obsession. At no point does he seem to be a man who relates easily to others. Banquo, his fellow-soldier, who has shared the kind of experiences that bind men together, calls him *Worthy Macbeth* and *My noble partner*, but they do not seem to be close friends. The only person to whom Macbeth talks freely – at first – is his wife, though the way they speak to each other is curious. Nearly all Lady Macbeth's forms of address to her husband refer to his rank or title: *Great Glamis, worthy Cawdor, worthy Thane, my royal Lord*; only once does she call him husband. He, on the other hand, is usually much more affectionate; *my dearest partner, my dearest love, dear wife, dearest chuck*. The contrast suggests that Lady Macbeth's feeling for her husband has come to be expressed overwhelmingly in terms of attention to his 'getting on in the world' (like a modern wife who – with 'ulterior motives' – invites her husband's boss to dinner), a concentration which leads her to a deliberate appeal to evil spirits to *unsex* her, and symbolically to pervert her own maternal instincts:

> … *Come to my woman's breasts,*
> *And take my milk for gall, you murd'ring ministers …*
> (Act I, Scene v, lines 47–8)

Macbeth, however, seems to look upon his marriage-partner primarily as a wife and the potential mother of his children:

> *Bring forth men-children only …*
> (Act I, Scene vii, line, 73)

A well-known critic, L. C. Knights, once made fun of other critics of a pedantic kind by pointing out how futile it is to wonder how many children Lady Macbeth had had (since she said she had *given suck*). All that really matters is that there is no sign of a young Macbeth to inherit the throne of Scotland;

that Macbeth is very much concerned that the prophecy about Banquo's children should not come true, and that he no doubt hopes for an heir (to fight as he does, Macbeth must be a young man: modern stage make-up often obscures this truth). This makes Lady Macbeth's denial or distortion of her sexuality particularly unfortunate for him. They begin to drift apart before the death of Banquo (see Act III, Scene ii). The partnership in greatness they had both looked forward to comes to nothing. The deed divides them, and Macbeth is left to brood darkly on further crimes, an even more lonely man than before. His wife asks:

> *Why do you keep alone,*
> *Of sorriest fancies your companions making?*
>
> (Act III, Scene ii, lines 8–9)

At this mid-point in the play, then, with Banquo's death already planned, three of Macbeth's most significant characteristics, all related to each other, have become accentuated. He is more withdrawn and out of touch with his fellow human beings; he relies less and less on Fortune or destiny to direct the course of his life, and yet, as a paradoxical consequence, has less and less control over it; and he puts even more trust than before in violence as the only solution. In other words, he is becoming perceptibly less human. All this is well illustrated in the banquet scene (Act III, Scene iv); throughout he is trying desperately to act a part – the part of Duncan, the king he has killed and replaced – and failing. Macbeth's words and actions arc designed to convey the benevolence of a confident ruler of a society in which the subjects know their own degrees and serve in mutual respect and love. But first he has to excuse himself to hear what the murderers have to say about the fate of Banquo and Fleance; then Banquo's ghost comes to haunt him at the moment when Macbeth is trying hardest to seem hospitable and natural:

> *Here had we now our country's honour roof'd,*
> *Were the graced person of our Banquo present;*
>
> (Act III, Scene iv, lines 40–1)

> *I drink to the general joy o' th' whole table,*
> *And to our dear friend Banquo ...*
>
> (Act III, Scene iv, lines 89–90)

Instead of presiding over an occasion to mark a happy state of order in the kingdom, Macbeth has:

> *broke the good meeting,*
> *With most admir'd disorder.*
>
> (Act III, Scene iv, lines 109–10)

and from this time onward reduces the entire country to the same sort of chaos, and worse. Indeed, his self-centredness becomes so intense that his words at the end of the banquet scene:

> *For mine own good*
> *All causes shall give way ...*
>
> (Act III, Scene iv, lines 135–6)

become a motto for the rest of his life, amplified in Act IV, Scene i, when he sees the witches again, in a speech of pure megalomania:

> *Though you untie the winds and let them fight*
> *Against the churches; though the yesty waves*
> *Confound and swallow navigation up;*
> *Though bladed corn be lodg'd and trees blown down;*
> *Though castles topple on their warders' heads;*
> *Though palaces and pyramids do slope*
> *Their heads to their foundations; though the treasure*
> *Of nature's germens tumble all together,*
> *Even till destruction sicken – answer me*
> *To what I ask you.*
>
> (Act IV, Scene i, lines 51–60)

Through Shakespeare's skill with words we here see into the soul of all power-crazy men through the ages, from the wilder Roman Emperors to Hitler and Stalin. For although this summing-up began with the statement that the play is 'about a man named Macbeth', it clearly has a wider significance. In

Macbeth and his wife are embodied tendencies that are either familiar to us, or accessible to our imaginations. Malcolm's final judgment on the Macbeths as a *dead butcher* and *his fiend-like queen* is perfectly understandable from his point of view, but those who see and read the play are unlikely to dismiss them so sweepingly. Shakespeare's creatures have enabled us to see more deeply into some of the mysteries and contradictions of life.

The side of goodness Long before the end of the play the human tendencies embodied in Macbeth and his wife have been reduced to almost exclusively evil ones. The characters who represent goodness are not nearly so fully individualized. The best two are a king (Duncan) who appears in only three scenes and is dead by the middle of the Second Act, and another king (Edward the Confessor) who never makes an appearance. The two main instruments of Macbeth's downfall, Malcolm and Macduff, are both firmly on the side of goodness by the end, but earlier on they are involved in the confusion of values by their escapes from Scotland, actions which are justified by events but which appear dubious at the time. Banquo, as has already been suggested, seems reluctant to involve himself in action against Macbeth, in spite of his highmindedness. The powers of goodness are conveyed more by symbols and by imagery than by the deeds of individuals comparable in importance to the Macbeths. Nature often illustrates the human and supernatural war that is being waged throughout the play: a study of the varied uses of the word 'nature' can be very illuminating, and some suggestions for such studies are provided in the Theme Index.

The wider context In spite of the gloom and doubt that pervades most of the scenes, and in spite of the depths of human depravity that are explored, *Macbeth* is a play of hope and faith. There is a fine irony about the ending. The theme of 'appearance and reality', which runs through the story, is almost always used as an instrument of disillusionment. The reality is usually worse than the appearance (Duncan is actually dead, not asleep; Macbeth looks like a real king but isn't) yet the overall impression, that evil has the most powerful weapons and protagonists, proves to be untrue. At the close, Macduff addressing Malcolm, says:

> The time is free.
> I see thee compassed with thy kingdom's pearl
> > (Act V, Scene viii, lines 55–6)

and Malcolm himself promises:

> ... what needful else
> That calls upon us, by the grace of Grace,
> We will perform in measure, time, and place.
> > (Act V, Scene viii, lines 71–3)

There is very much more that could be said about the play; whole books are frequently written on it. The purpose of this summing-up is simply to suggest some of the aspects which are likely to arouse the interest of any thoughtful person. The remaining sections and the Theme Index hint at ways of widening and deepening the reader's approach.

THEME INDEX

Certain themes or recurrent ideas are very noticeable in *Macbeth*, and awareness of them can deepen a reader's understanding of the play. The fundamental notion seems to be the contrast between good and evil, but closely bound up with this is the fact that one can be confused with the other. In other words 'good' and 'evil' sometimes seem ambiguous terms, and this ambiguity may even extend throughout a human being's experience of life. Similarly, there are times when the meanings of words like 'nature' and 'honour' may become blurred, and what one man thinks of as 'order' can be labelled 'repression' by another. During the course of this play such ideas are constantly being presented and represented until, at the end, a glimpse is given of a new and happy 'order' under a trustworthy new king: man's true nature is affirmed, the two meanings of honour come together, and goodness has defeated evil.

The following list of references gives a few examples of the complex way in which Shakespeare presents the contrast and the ambiguity. Some of these examples are overt, that is, they are demonstrated openly or stated directly; others are embedded in the language of the play in the form of images and suggestions. The main division between 'contrast' and 'ambiguity' is only made for convenience; the two ideas frequently overlap.

Contrast

Grace and sin I vi 30; II ii 24–33; II iii 130–2; II iv 40–1; III i 65–8; III i 86–9; III iv 41 & 45; III vi 26–9; IV i 45; IV i 104; IV i 132–3 & 137–8; IV ii 80–1; IV iii 23–4; IV iii 43; IV iii 91–5; IV iii 108–11; IV iii 144–5 & 155–9; IV iii 189–92; V iii 26–7; Vviii 71–3.

Hell and heaven I vii 7; II i 63–4; II hi 1–20; III i 139–40; IIIvi 19; IV iii 223–7 ;Vi 33.

Angels and devils II iii 4 & 7; III iv 59; III vi 45–9; IV iii 22; IV iii 117; V vii 8; Vviii 3.

Life and death II ii 6–8; II iii 67–8 & 75–6; II iii 92–7; III ii 19–26; III v 4–5; IV iii 165–6 & 171–3; V viii 39–50.

Health and disease I iii 23–4; II ii 45–6; II iii 48; III i 105–6; III iv 53–6 & 86–7; IV iii 141–59; IV iii 214–5; V i 53 & 68; V ii 27–30; V iii 39–47 & 50–6.

Fair weather and foul I iii 12–30; I iii 39; II iii 53–4; IV i 51–7; IV ii 20–2.

Light and darkness; day and night I iv 50–1; I v 50–4; I v 59–61; II i 1–5; II i 49–56; II iii 54–62; II iv 1–9; III i 26–7; III i 129 & 136; III ii 40–56; III iii 9 & 14; III iv 126–7; IV i 25 & 28; IV i 47; IV iii 240. Order and disorder I iv 24–7; III i 91–101; III ii 16–19; III ii 24–6; III iv 1; III iv 76; III iv 109–10; III iv 119–20; III vi 33–7; IV i 51–9; IV ii 55–7; IV iii 4–8; IV iii 66–9 & 78–84; IV iii 97–100; V v 50.

Desire and performance; intention and action I vii 39–41; II iii 26–8; III ii 4–5; IV i 144–53.

Appearance and reality I iii 42–3 & 46–7; I iii 82–3; I iv 11 –12; I v 65–6; I vii 83; II ii 12–13; II ii 53–5; II ii 70–1; II iii 75–6; II iii 101; II iii 136–7; II iv 6–10; III i 74–7; III i 120–1; III ii 27–8 & 32–5; III iv 61 & 68; III iv 107; V iii 26–8; V iv 4–7;Vvii–2.

Clothes and the man wearing them I iii 9–10; I iii 147–8; II iv 37–8; Vii 20–2.

Ambiguity

Equivocation I iii 123–7; II iii 8–11 & 28–34; IV i 79–80 & 91–3; Vv 42–6; Vviii 12–22.

Punning and word–play I v 17–25; I vii 1–7; II ii 55–7; III iv 15; Vviii 48.

Dramatic irony I vi 20–4; II iii 42–3; II iii 83–6; III i 126; III iv 90–1.

Nature I iii 138; I iv 28–9 & 32–3; I v 15–17; I v 40–50; I vi 1–10; I vii 13–20; I vii 46–7; I vii 54–9; II i 7–9; II ii 14–16; II ii 39–40;

II iii 57–60; II iv 10–20; II iv 27–9; III i 29–32; III i 47–9; III i 95–7; III iv 28 & 30; III iv 78–83; III iv 115; III iv 141; III vi 8–10; IV i 97–9; IV ii 8–11; V i 65–7. Honour I ii 44; I iii 105–8; I iii 146; I iv 39–42; I vi 10; I vi 17–18; I vii 32–5; II i 25–9; III ii 33; III iv 40; III vi 36; IV ii 65; IV iii 117; V iii 25; V viii 63–4.

Shakespeare: Words and Phrases

adapted from the Collins English Dictionary

abate 1 VERB to abate here means to lessen or diminish ❑ *There lives within the very flame of love/A kind of wick or snuff that will abate it* (*Hamlet 4.7*) 2 VERB to abate here means to shorten ❑ *Abate thy hours* (*A Midsummer Night's Dream 3.2*) 3 VERB to abate here means to deprive ❑ *She hath abated me of half my train* (*King Lear 2.4*)

abjure VERB to abjure means to renounce or give up ❑ *this rough magic I here abjure* (*Tempest 5.1*)

abroad ADV abroad means elsewhere or everywhere ❑ *You have heard of the news abroad* (*King Lear 2.1*)

abrogate VERB to abrogate means to put an end to ❑ *so it shall praise you to abrogate scurrility* (*Love's Labours Lost 4.2*)

abuse 1 NOUN abuse in this context means deception or fraud ❑ *What should this mean? Are all the rest come back?/Or is it some abuse, and no such thing?* (*Hamlet 4.7*) 2 NOUN an abuse in this context means insult or offence ❑ *I will be deaf to pleading and excuses/Nor tears nor prayers shall purchase our abuses* (*Romeo and Juliet 3.1*) 3 NOUN an abuse in this context means using something improperly ❑ *we'll digest/Th'abuse*

of distance (*Henry II Chorus*) 4 NOUN an abuse in this context means doing something which is corrupt or dishonest ❑ *Come, bring them away: if these be good people in a commonweal that do nothing but their abuses in common houses, I know no law: bring them away.* (*Measure for Measure 2.1*)

abuser NOUN the abuser here is someone who betrays, a betrayer ❑ *I ... do attach thee/For an abuser of the world* (*Othello 1.2*)

accent NOUN accent here means language ❑ *In states unborn, and accents yet unknown* (*Julius Caesar 3.1*)

accident NOUN an accident in this context is an event or something that happened ❑ *think no more of this night's accidents* (*A Midsummer Night's Dream 4.1*)

accommodate VERB to accommodate in this context means to equip or to give someone the equipment to do something ❑ *The safer sense will ne'er accommodate/His master thus.* (*King Lear 4.6*)

according ADJ according means sympathetic or ready to agree ❑ *within the scope of choice/Lies* *my consent and fair according voice* (*Romeo and Juliet 1.2*)

account NOUN account often means judgement (by God) or reckoning ❑ *No reckoning made, but sent to my account/ With all my imperfections on my head* (*Hamlet 1.5*)

accountant ADJ accountant here means answerable or accountable ❑ *his offence is… /Accountant to the law* (*Measure for Measure 2.4*)

ace NOUN ace here means one or first referring to the lowest score on a dice ❑ *No die, but an ace, for him; for he is but one./ Less than an ace, man; for he is dead; he is nothing.* (*A Midsummer Night's Dream 5.1*)

acquit VERB here acquit means to be rid of or free of. It is related to the verb quit ❑ *I am glad I am so acquit of this tinderbox* (*The Merry Wives of Windsor 1.3*)

afeard ADJ afeard means afraid or frightened ❑ *Nothing afeard of what thyself didst make* (*Macbeth 1.3*)

affiance NOUN affiance means confidence or trust ❑ *O how hast thou with jealousy infected/ The sweetness of affiance* (*Henry V 2.2*)

affinity NOUN in this context, affinity means important connections, or relationships with important people ❑ *The Moor replies/ That he you hurt is of great fame in Cyprus,/ And great affinity* (*Othello 3.1*)

agnize VERB to agnize is an old word that means that you recognize or acknowledge something ❑ *I do agnize/ A natural and prompt alacrity I find in hardness* (*Othello 1.3*)

ague NOUN an ague is a fever in which the patient has hot and cold

shivers one after the other ❑ *This is some monster of the isle with four legs, who hath got … an ague* (*The Tempest 2.2*)

alarm, alarum NOUN an alarm or alarum is a call to arms or a signal for soldiers to prepare to fight ❑ *Whence cometh this alarum and the noise?* (*Henry VI part I 1.4*)

Albion NOUN Albion is another word for England ❑ *but I will sell my dukedom,/ To buy a slobbery and a dirty farm In that nook-shotten isle of Albion* (*Henry V 3.5*)

all of all PHRASE all of all means everything, or the sum of all things ❑ *The very all of all* (*Love's Labours Lost 5.1*)

amend VERB amend in this context means to get better or to heal ❑ *at his touch… They presently amend* (*Macbeth 4.3*)

anchor VERB if you anchor on something you concentrate on it or fix on it ❑ *My invention … Anchors on Isabel* (*Measure for Measure 2.4*)

anon ADV anon was a common word for soon ❑ *You shall see anon how the murderer gets the love of Gonzago's wife* (*Hamlet 3.2*)

antic 1 ADJ antic here means weird or strange ❑ *I'll charm the air to give a sound/ While you perform your antic round* (*Macbeth 4.1*) 2 NOUN in this context antic means a clown or a strange, unattractive creature ❑ *If black, why nature, drawing an antic,/ Made a foul blot* (*Much Ado About Nothing 3.1*)

apace ADV apace was a common word for quickly ❑ *Come apace* (*As You Like It 3.3*)

apparel NOUN apparel means clothes or clothing ❑ *one suit of apparel* (*Hamlet 3.2*)

appliance NOUN appliance here means cure ❑ *Diseases desperate grown/ By desperate appliance are relieved* (*Hamlet 4.3*)

argument NOUN argument here means a topic of conversation or the subject ❑ *Why 'tis the rarest argument of wonder that hath shot out in our latter times* (*All's Well That Ends Well 2.3*)

arrant ADJ arrant means absolute, complete. It strengthens the meaning of a noun ❑ *Fortune, that arrant whore* (*King Lear 2.4*)

arras NOUN an arras is a tapestry, a large cloth with a picture sewn on it using coloured thread ❑ *Behind the arras I'll convey myself/ To hear the process* (*Hamlet 3.3*)

art 1 NOUN art in this context means knowledge ❑ *Their malady convinces/ The great essay of art* (*Macbeth 4.3*) 2 NOUN art can also mean skill as it does here ❑ *He ... gave you such a masterly report/ For art and exercise in your defence* (*Hamlet 4.7*) 3 NOUN art here means magic ❑ *Now I want/ Spirits to enforce, art to enchant* (*The Tempest 5 Epilogue*)

assay 1 NOUN an assay was an attempt, a try ❑ *Make assay./ Bow, stubborn knees* (*Hamlet 3.3*) 2 NOUN assay can also mean a test or a trial ❑ *he hath made assay of her virtue* (*Measure for Measure 3.1*)

attend (on/upon) VERB attend on means to wait for or to expect ❑ *Tarry I here, I but attend on death* (*Two Gentlemen of Verona 3.1*)

auditor NOUN an auditor was a member of an audience or someone who listens ❑ *I'll be an auditor* (*A Midsummer Night's Dream 3.1*)

aught NOUN aught was a common word which meant anything ❑ *if my love thou holdest at aught* (*Hamlet 4.3*)

aunt 1 NOUN an aunt was another word for an old woman and also means someone who talks a lot or a gossip ❑ *The wisest aunt telling the saddest tale* (*A Midsummer Night's Dream 2.1*) 2 NOUN aunt could also mean a mistress or a prostitute ❑ *the thrush and the jay/ Are summer songs for me and my aunts/ While we lie tumbling in the hay* (*The Winter's Tale 4.3*)

avaunt EXCLAM avaunt was a common word which meant go away ❑ *Avaunt, you curs!* (*King Lear 3.6*)

aye ADV here aye means always or ever ❑ *Whose state and honour I for aye allow* (*Richard II 5.2*)

baffle VERB baffle meant to be disgraced in public or humiliated ❑ *I am disgraced, impeached, and baffled here* (*Richard II 1.1*)

bald ADJ bald means trivial or silly ❑ *I knew 'twould be a bald conclusion* (*The Comedy of Errors 2.2*)

ban NOUN a ban was a curse or an evil spell ❑ *Sometimes with lunatic bans... Enforce their charity* (*King Lear 2.3*)

barren ADJ barren meant empty or hollow ❑ *now I let go your hand, I am barren.* (*Twelfth Night 1.3*)

base ADJ base is an adjective that means unworthy or dishonourable ❑ *civet is of a baser birth than tar* (*As You Like It 3.2*)

base 1 ADJ base can also mean of low social standing or someone who was not part of the ruling class ❑ *Why brand they us with 'base'?* (*King Lear 1.2*) 2 ADJ here base means poor quality ❑ *Base cousin,/ Darest thou break first?* (*Two Noble Kinsmen 3.3*)

bawdy NOUN bawdy means obscene or rude ❑ *Bloody, bawdy villain!* (*Hamlet 2.2*)

bear in hand PHRASE bear in hand means taken advantage of or fooled ❑ *This I made good to you In our last conference, passed in probation with you/How you were borne in hand* (*Macbeth 3.1*)

beard VERB to beard someone was to oppose or confront them ❑ *Com'st thou to beard me in Denmark?* (*Hamlet 2.2*)

beard, in one's PHRASE if you say something in someone's beard you say it to their face ❑ *I will verify as much in his beard* (*Henry V 3.2*)

beaver NOUN a beaver was a visor on a battle helmet ❑ *O yes, my lord, he wore his beaver up* (*Hamlet 1.2*)

become VERB if something becomes you it suits you or is appropriate to you ❑ *Nothing in his life became him like the leaving it* (*Macbeth 1.4*)

bed, brought to PHRASE to be brought to bed means to give birth ❑ *His wife but yesternight was brought to bed* (*Titus Andronicus 4.2*)

bedabbled ADJ if something is bedabbled it is sprinkled ❑ *Bedabbled with the dew, and torn with briers* (*A Midsummer Night's Dream 3.2*)

Bedlam NOUN Bedlam was a word used for Bethlehem Hospital which was a place the insane were sent to ❑ *The country give me proof and precedent/Of Bedlam beggars* (*King Lear 2.3*)

bed-swerver N a bed-swerver was someone who was unfaithful in marriage, an adulterer ❑ *she's/A bed-swerver* (*Winter's Tale 2.1*)

befall 1 VERB to befall is to happen, occur or take place ❑ *In this same interlude it doth befall/That I present a wall* (*A Midsummer Night's Dream 5.1*) 2 VERB to befall can also mean to happen to someone or something ❑ *fair befall thee and thy noble house* (*Richard III 1.3*)

behoof NOUN behoof was an advantage or benefit ❑ *All our surgeons/Convent in their behoof* (*Two Noble Kinsmen 1.4*)

beldam NOUN a beldam was a witch or old woman ❑ *Have I not reason, beldams as you are?* (*Macbeth 3.5*)

belike ADV belike meant probably, perhaps or presumably ❑ *belike he likes it not* (*Hamlet 3.2*)

bent 1 NOUN bent means a preference or a direction ❑ *Let me work,/For I can give his humour true bent,/And I will bring him to the Capitol* (*Julius Caesar 2.1*) 2 ADJ if you are bent on something you are determined to do it ❑ *for now I am bent to know/By the worst means the worst.* (*Macbeth 3.4*)

beshrew VERB beshrew meant to curse or wish evil on someone ❑ *much beshrew my manners and my pride/If Hermia meant to say Lysander lied* (*A Midsummer Night's Dream 2.2*)

betime (s) ADV betime means early ❑ *To business that we love we rise betime* (*Antony and Cleopatra 4.4*)

bevy NOUN bevy meant type or sort, it was also used to mean company ❑ *many more of the same bevy* (*Hamlet 5.2*)

blazon VERB to blazon something meant to display or show it ❑ *that thy skill be more to blazon it* (*Romeo and Juliet 2.6*)

blind ADJ if you are blind when you do something you are reckless or do not care about the consequences ❑ *are you yet to your own souls so blind/That two you will war with God by murdering me* (*Richard III 1.4*)

bombast NOUN bombast was wool stuffing (used in a cushion for example) and so it came to mean padded out or long-winded. Here it means someone who talks a lot about nothing in particular ❑ *How now my sweet creature of bombast* (*Henry IV part I 2.4*)

bond 1 NOUN a bond is a contract or legal deed ❑ *Well, then, your bond, and let me see* (*Merchant of Venice 1.3*) 2 NOUN bond could also mean duty or commitment ❑ *I love your majesty/According to my bond* (*King Lear 1.1*)

bottom NOUN here bottom means essence, main point or intent ❑ *Now I see/The bottom of your purpose* (*All's Well That Ends Well 3.7*)

bounteously ADV bounteously means plentifully, abundantly ❑ *I prithee, and I'll pay thee bounteously* (*Twelfth Night 1.2*)

brace 1 NOUN a brace is a couple or two ❑ *Have lost a brace of kinsmen* (*Romeo and Juliet 5.3*) 2 NOUN if you are in a brace position it means you are ready ❑ *For that it stands not in such warlike brace* (*Othello 1.3*)

brand VERB to mark permanently like the markings on cattle ❑ *the wheeled seat/Of fortunate Caesar ... branded his baseness that ensued* (*Anthony and Cleopatra 4.14*)

brave ADJ brave meant fine, excellent or splendid ❑ *O brave new world/That has such people in't* (*The Tempest 5.1*)

brine NOUN brine is sea-water ❑ *He shall drink nought brine, for I'll not show him/Where the quick freshes are* (*The Tempest 3.2*)

brow NOUN brow in this context means appearance ❑ *doth hourly grow/Out of his brows* (*Hamlet 3.3*)

burden 1 NOUN the burden here is a chorus ❑ *I would sing my song without a burden* (*As You Like It 3.2*) 2 NOUN burden means load or weight (this is the current meaning) ❑ *the scarfs and the bannerets about thee did manifoldly dissuade me from believing thee a vessel of too great a burden* (*All's Well that Ends Well 2.3*)

buttons, in one's PHRASE this is a phrase that means clear, easy to see ❑ *Tis in his buttons he will carry't* (*The Merry Wives of Windsor 3.2*)

cable NOUN cable here means scope or reach ❑ *The law ... Will give her cable* (*Othello 1.2*)

cadent ADJ if something is cadent it is falling or dropping ❑ *With cadent tears fret channels in her cheeks* (*King Lear 1.4*)

canker VERB to canker is to decay, become corrupt ❑ *And, as with age his body uglier grows,/ So his mind cankers* (*The Tempest* 4.1)

canon, from the PHRASE from the canon is an expression meaning out of order, improper ❑ *Twas from the canon* (*Coriolanus* 3.1)

cap-a-pie ADV cap-a-pie means from head to foot, completely ❑ *I am courtier cap-a-pie* (*The Winter's Tale* 4.4)

carbonadoed ADJ if something is carbonadoed it is cut or scored (scratched) with a knife ❑ *it is your carbonadoed* (*All's Well That Ends Well* 4.5)

carouse VERB to carouse is to drink at length, party ❑ *They cast their caps up and carouse together* (*Anthony and Cleopatra* 4.12)

carrack NOUN a carrack was a large old ship, a galleon ❑ *Faith, he tonight hath boarded a land-carrack* (*Othello* 1.2)

cassock NOUN a cassock here means a military cloak, long coat ❑ *half of the which dare not shake the snow from off their cassocks lest they shake themselves to pieces* (*All's Well That Ends Well* 4.3)

catastrophe NOUN catastrophe here means conclusion or end ❑ *pat he comes, like the catastrophe of the old comedy* (*King Lear* 1.2)

cautel NOUN a cautel was a trick or a deceptive act ❑ *Perhaps he loves you now/ And now no soil not cautel doth besmirch* (*Hamlet* 1.2)

celerity NOUN celerity was a common word for speed, swiftness ❑ *Hence hath offence his quick celerity/ When it is borne in high authority* (*Measure for Measure* 4.2)

chafe NOUN chafe meant anger or temper ❑ *this Herculean Roman does become/ The carriage of his chafe* (*Anthony and Cleopatra* 1.3)

chanson NOUN chanson was an old word for a song ❑ *The first row of the pious chanson will show you more* (*Hamlet* 2.2)

chapman NOUN a chapman was a trader or merchant ❑ *Not uttered by base sale of chapman's tongues* (*Love's Labours Lost* 2.1)

chaps, chops NOUN chaps (and chops) was a word for jaws ❑ *Which ne'er shook hands nor bade farewell to him/ Till he unseamed him from the nave to th' chops* (*Macbeth* 1.2)

chattels NOUN chattels were your moveable possessions. The word is used in the traditional marriage ceremony ❑ *She is my goods, my chattels* (*The Taming of the Shrew* 3.3)

chide VERB if you are chided by someone you are told off or reprimanded ❑ *Now I but chide, but I should use thee worse* (*A Midsummer Night's Dream* 3.2)

chinks NOUN chinks was a word for cash or money ❑ *he that can lay hold of her/ Shall have the chinks* (*Romeo and Juliet* 1.5)

choleric ADJ if something was called choleric it meant that they were quick to get angry ❑ *therewithal unruly waywardness that infirm and choleric years bring with them* (*King Lear* 1.1)

chuff NOUN a chuff was a miser,

someone who clings to his or her money ❑ *ye fat chuffs* (*Henry IV part I 2.2*)

cipher NOUN cipher here means nothing ❑ *Mine were the very cipher of a function* (*Measure for Measure 2.2*)

circummured ADJ circummured means that something is surrounded with a wall ❑ *He hath a garden circummured with brick* (*Measure for Measure 4.1*)

civet NOUN a civet is a type of scent or perfume ❑ *Give me an ounce of civet* (*King Lear 4.6*)

clamorous ADJ clamorous means noisy or boisterous ❑ *Be clamorous and leap all civil bounds* (*Twelfth Night 1.4*)

clangour, clangor NOUN clangour is a word that means ringing (the sound that bells make) ❑ *Like to a dismal clangour heard from far* (*Henry VI part III 2.3*)

cleave VERB if you cleave to something you stick to it or are faithful to it ❑ *Thy thoughts I cleave to* (*The Tempest 4.1*)

clock and clock, 'twixt PHRASE from hour to hour, without stopping or continuously ❑ *To weep 'twixt clock and clock* (*Cymbeline 3.4*)

close ADJ here close means hidden ❑ *Stand close; this is the same Athenian* (*A Midsummer Night's Dream 3.2*)

cloud NOUN a cloud on your face means that you have a troubled, unhappy expression ❑ *He has cloud in's face* (*Anthony and Cleopatra 3.2*)

cloy VERB if you cloy an appetite you satisfy it ❑ *Other women cloy/ The*

appetites they feed (*Anthony and Cleopatra 2.2*)

cock-a-hoop, set PHRASE if you set cock-a-hoop you become free of everything ❑ *You will set cock-a-hoop* (*Romeo and Juliet 1.5*)

colours NOUN colours is a word used to describe battle-flags or banners. Sometimes we still say that we nail our colours to the mast if we are stating which team or side of an argument we support ❑ *the approbation of those that weep this lamentable divorce under her colours* (*Cymbeline 1.5*)

combustion NOUN combustion was a word meaning disorder or chaos ❑ *prophesying ... Of dire combustion and confused events* (*Macbeth 2.3*)

comely ADJ if you are or something is comely you or it is lovely, beautiful, graceful ❑ *O, what a world is this, when what is comely/ Envenoms him that bears it!* (*As You Like It 2.3*)

commend VERB if you commend yourself to someone you send greetings to them ❑ *Commend me to my brother* (*Measure for Measure 1.4*)

compact NOUN a compact is an agreement or a contract ❑ *what compact mean you to have with us?* (*Julius Caesar 3.1*)

compass 1 NOUN here compass means range or scope ❑ *you would sound me from my lowest note to the top of my compass* (*Hamlet 3.2*) 2 VERB to compass here means to achieve, bring about or make happen ❑ *How now shall this be compassed?/ Canst thou bring me to the party?* (*Tempest 3.2*)

comptible ADJ comptible is an old word meaning sensitive ❑ *I am very comptible, even to the least sinister usage.* (*Twelfth Night 1.5*)

confederacy NOUN a confederacy is a group of people usually joined together to commit a crime. It is another word for a conspiracy ❑ *Lo, she is one of this confederacy!* (*A Midsummer Night's Dream 3.2*)

confound VERB if you confound something you confuse it or mix it up; it also means to stop or prevent ❑ *A million fail, confounding oath on oath.* (*A Midsummer Night's Dream 3.2*)

contagion N contagion is an old word for disease or poison ❑ *hell itself breathes out/ Contagion to this world* (*Hamlet 3.2*)

contumely NOUN contumely is an old word for an insult ❑ *the proud man's contumely* (*Hamlet 3.1*)

counterfeit 1 VERB if you counterfeit something you copy or imitate it ❑ *Meantime your cheeks do counterfeit our roses* (*Henry VI part I 2.4*) 2 VERB in this context counterfeit means to pretend or make believe ❑ *I will counterfeit the bewitchment of some popular man* (*Coriolanus*)

coz NOUN coz was a shortened form of the word cousin ❑ *sweet my coz, be merry* (*As You Like It 1.2*)

cozenage NOUN cozenage is an old word meaning cheating or a deception ❑ *Thrown out his angle for my proper life,/ And with such coz'nage* (*Hamlet 5.2*)

crave VERB crave used to mean to beg or request ❑ *I crave your pardon* (*The Comedy of Errors 1.2*)

crotchet NOUN crotchets are strange ideas or whims ❑ *thou hast some strange crotchets in thy head now* (*The Merry Wives of Windsor 2.1*)

cuckold NOUN a cuckold is a man whose wife has been unfaithful to him ❑ *As there is no true cuckold but calamity* (*Twelfth Night 1.5*)

cuffs, go to PHRASE this phrase meant to fight ❑ *the player went to cuffs in the question* (*Hamlet 2.2*)

cup VERB in this context cup is a verb which means to pour drink or fill glasses with alcohol ❑ *cup us til the world go round* (*Anthony and Cleopatra 2.7*)

cur NOUN cur is an insult meaning dog and is also used to mean coward ❑ *Out, dog! out, cur! Thou drivest me past the bounds/ Of maiden's patience* (*A Midsummer Night's Dream 3.2*)

curiously ADV in this context curiously means carefully or skilfully ❑ *The sleeves curiously cut* (*The Taming of the Shrew 4.3*)

curry VERB curry means to flatter or to praise someone more than they are worth ❑ *I would curry with Master Shallow that no man could better command his servants* (*Henry IV part II 5.1*)

custom NOUN custom is a habit or a usual practice ❑ *Hath not old custom made this life more sweet/ Than that of painted pomp?* (*As You Like It 2.1*)

cutpurse NOUN a cutpurse is an old word for a thief. Men used to carry their money in small bags (purse) that hung from their belts; thieves would cut the purse from the belt and steal their money ❑ *A cutpurse of the empire and the rule* (*Hamlet 3.4*)

dainty ADJ dainty used to mean splendid, fine ❑ *Why, that's my dainty Ariel!* (*Tempest* 5.1)

dally VERB if you dally with something you play with it or tease it ❑ *They that dally nicely with words may quickly make them wanton* (*Twelfth Night* 3.1)

damask COLOUR damask is a light-red or pink colour ❑ *Twas just the difference/Betwixt the constant red and mingled damask* (*As You Like It* 3.5)

dare 1 VERB dare means to challeng or, confront ❑ *He goes before me, and still dares me on* (*A Midsummer Night's Dream* 3.3) 2 VERB dare in this context means to present, deliver or inflict ❑ *all that fortune, death, and danger dare* (*Hamlet* 4.4)

darkly ADV darkly was used in this context to mean secretly or cunningly ❑ *I will go darkly to work with her* (*Measure for Measure* 5.1)

daw NOUN a daw was a slang term for idiot or fool (after the bird jackdaw which was famous for its stupidity) ❑ *Yea, just so much as you may take upon a knife's point and choke a daw withal* (*Much Ado About Nothing* 3.1)

debile ADJ debile meant weak or feeble ❑ *And debile minister great power* (*All's Well That Ends Well* 2.3)

deboshed ADJ deboshed was another way of saying corrupted or debauched ❑ *Men so disordered, deboshed and bold* (*King Lear* 1.4)

decoct VERB to decoct was to heat up, warm something ❑ *Can sodden water,/A drench for sur-reained jades ... Decoct their cold blood to such valiant heat?* (*Henry V* 3.5)

deep-revolving ADJ deep-revolving here uses the idea that you turn something over in your mind when you are thinking hard about it and so means deep-thinking, meditating ❑ *The deep-revolving Buckingham/No more shall be the neighbour to my counsels* (*Richard III* 4.2)

defect NOUN defect here means shortcoming or something that is not right ❑ *Being unprepared/Our will became the servant to defect* (*Macbeth* 2.1)

degree 1 NOUN degree here means rank, standing or station ❑ *Should a like language use to all degrees,/ And mannerly distinguishment leave out/Betwixt the prince and beggar* (*The Winter's Tale* 2.1) 2 NOUN in this context, degree means extent or measure ❑ *her offence/Must be of such unnatural degree* (*King Lear* 1.1)

deify VERB if you deify something or someone you worship it or them as a God ❑ *all.. deifying the name of Rosalind* (*As You Like It* 3.2)

delated ADJ delated here means detailed ❑ *the scope/Of these delated articles* (*Hamlet* 1.2)

delicate ADJ if something was described as delicate it meant it was of fine quality or valuable ❑ *thou wast a spirit too delicate* (*The Tempest* 1.2)

demise VERB in this context demise means to transmit, give or convey ❑ *what state ... Canst thou demise to any child of mine?* (*Richard III* 4.4)

deplore VERB to deplore means to express with grief or sorrow ❏ *Never more/ Will I my master's tears to you deplore* (*Twelfth Night 3.1*)

depose VERB if you depose someone you make them take an oath, or swear something to be true ❏ *Depose him in the justice of his cause* (*Richard II 1.3*)

depositary NOUN a depositary is a trustee ❏ *Made you ... my depositary* (*King Lear 2.4*)

derive 1 VERB to derive means to comes from or to descend (it usually applies to people) ❏ *No part of it is mine,/ This shame derives itself from unknown loins.* (*Much Ado About Nothing 4.1*) 2 VERB if you derive something from someone you inherit it ❏ *Treason is not inherited ...Or, if we derive it from our friends/ What's that to me?* (*As You Like It 1.3*)

descry VERB to see or catch sight of ❏ *The news is true, my lord. He is descried* (*Anthony and Cleopatra 3.7*)

desert 1 NOUN desert means worth or merit ❏ *That dost in vile misproson shackle up/ My love and her desert* (*All's Well That Ends Well 2.3*) 2 ADJ desert is used here to mean lonely or isolated ❏ *if that love or gold/ Can in this desert place buy entertainment* (*As You LIke It 2.4*)

design 1 VERB to design means to indicate or point out ❏ *we shall see/ Justice design the victor's chivalry* (*Richard II 1.1*) 2 NOUN a design is a plan, an intention or an undertaking ❏ *hinder not the honour of his design* (*All's Well That Ends Well 3.6*)

designment NOUN a designment was a plan or undertaking ❏ *The desperate tempest hath so bang'd the Turks,/ That their designment halts* (*Othello 2.1*)

despite VERB despite here means to spite or attempt to thwart a plan ❏ *Only to despite them I will endeavour anything* (*Much Ado About Nothing 2.2*)

device NOUN a device is a plan, plot or trick ❏ *Excellent, I smell a device* (*Twelfth Night 2.3*)

disable VERB to disable here means to devalue or make little of ❏ *he disabled my judgement* (*As You Like It 5.4*)

discandy VERB here discandy means to melt away or dissolve ❏ *The hearts ... do discandy , melt their sweets* (*Anthony and Cleopatra 4.12*)

disciple VERB to disciple is to teach or train ❏ *He ...was/ Discipled of the bravest* (*All's Well That Ends Well 1.2*)

discommend VERB if you discommend something you criticize it ❏ *my dialect which you discommend so much* (*King Lear 2.2*)

discourse NOUN discourse means conversation, talk or chat ❏ *which part of it I'll waste/ With such discourse as I not doubt shall make it/ Go quick away* (*The Tempest 5.1*)

discover VERB discover used to mean to reveal or show ❏ *the Prince discovered to Claudio that he loved my niece* (*Much Ado About Nothing 1.2*)

disliken VERB disguise, make unlike ❏ *disliken/ The truth of your own seeming* (*The Winter's Tale 4.4*)

dismantle VERB to dismantle is to remove or take away ❏ *Commit a thing so monstrous to dismantle/*

So many folds of favour (*King Lear* 1.1)

disponge VERB disponge means to pour out or rain down ❑ *The poisonous damp of night disponge upon me* (*Anthony and Cleopatra* 4.9)

distrain VERB to distrain something is to confiscate it ❑ *My father's goods are all distrained and sold* (*Richard II* 2.3)

divers ADJ divers is an old word for various ❑ *I will give out divers schedules of my beauty* (*Twelfth Night* 1.5)

doff VERB to doff is to get rid of or dispose ❑ *make our women fight/ To doff their dire distresses* (*Macbeth* 4.3)

dog VERB if you dog someone or something you follow them or it closely ❑ *I will rather leave to see Hector than not to dog him* (*Troilus and Cressida* 5.1)

dotage NOUN dotage here means infatuation ❑ *Her dotage now I do begin to pity* (*A Midsummer Night's Dream* 4.1)

dotard NOUN a dotard was an old fool ❑ *I speak not like a dotard nor a fool* (*Much Ado About Nothing* 5.1)

dote VERB to dote is to love, cherish, care without seeing any fault ❑ *And won her soul; and she, sweet lady, dotes,/ Devoutly dotes, dotes in idolatry* (*A Midsummer Night's Dream* 1.1)

doublet NOUN a doublet was a man's close-fitting jacket with short skirt ❑ *Lord Hamlet, with his doublet all unbraced* (*Hamlet* 2.1)

dowager NOUN a dowager is a widow ❑ *Like to a step-dame or a dowage* (*A Midsummer Night's Dream* 1.1)

dowdy NOUN a dowdy was an ugly woman ❑ *Dido was a dowdy* (*Romeo and Juliet* 2.4)

dower NOUN a dower (or dowery) is the riches or property given by the father of a bride to her husband-to-be ❑ *Thy truth then by they dower* (*King Lear* 1.1)

dram NOUN a dram is a tiny amount ❑ *Why, everything adheres together that no dram of a scruple* (*Twelfth Night* 3.4)

drift NOUN drift is a plan, scheme or intention ❑ *Shall Romeo by my letters know our drift* (*Romeo and Juliet* 4.1)

dropsied ADJ dropsied means pretentious ❑ *Where great additions swell's and virtues none/ It is a dropsied honour* (*All's Well That Ends Well* 2.3)

drudge NOUN a drudge was a slave, servant ❑ *If I be his cuckold, he's my drudge* (*All's Well That Ends Well* 1.3)

dwell VERB to dwell sometimes meant to exist, to be ❑ *I'd rather dwell in my necessity* (*Merchant of Venice* 1.3)

earnest ADJ an earnest was a pledge to pay or a payment in advance ❑ *for an earnest of a greater honour/ He bade me from him call thee Thane of Cawdor* (*Macbeth* 1.3)

ecstasy NOUN madness ❑ *This is the very ecstasy of love* (*Hamlet* 2.1)

edict NOUN law or declaration ❑ *It stands as an edict in destiny.* (*A Midsummer Night's Dream* 1.1)

egall ADJ egall is an old word meaning equal ❑ *companions/Whose souls do bear an egall yoke of love* (Merchant of Venice 2.4)

eisel NOUN eisel meant vinegar ❑ *Woo't drink up eisel?* (Hamlet 5.1)

eke, eke out VERB eke meant to add to, to increase. Eke out nowadays means to make something last as long as possible – particularly in the sense of making money last a long time ❑ *Still be kind/And eke out our performance with your mind* (Henry V Chorus)

elbow, out at PHRASE out at elbow is an old phrase meaning in poor condition – as when your jacket sleeves are worn at the elbow which shows that it is an old jacket ❑ *He cannot, sir. He's out at elbow* (Measure for Measure 2.1)

element NOUN elements were thought to be the things from which all things were made. They were: air, earth, water and fire ❑ *Does not our lives consist of the four elements?* (Twelfth Night 2.3)

elf VERB to elf was to tangle ❑ *I'll ... elf all my hairs in knots* (King Lear 2.3)

embassy NOUN an embassy was a message ❑ *We'll once more hear Orsino's embassy.* (Twelfth Night 1.5)

emphasis NOUN emphasis here means a forceful expression or strong statement ❑ *What is he whose grief/Bears such an emphasis* (Hamlet 5.1)

empiric NOUN an empiric was an untrained doctor sometimes called a quack ❑ *we must not ... prostitute our past-cure malady/To empirics* (All's Well That Ends Well 2.1)

emulate ADJ emulate here means envious ❑ *pricked on by a most emulate pride* (Hamlet 1.1)

enchant VERB to enchant meant to put a magic spell on ❑ *Damn'd as thou art, thou hast enchanted her,/For I'll refer me to all things of sense* (Othello 1.2)

enclog VERB to enclog was to hinder something or to provide an obstacle to it ❑ *Traitors enscarped to enclog the guitless keel* (Othello 1.2)

endure VERB to endure was to allow or to permit ❑ *and will endure/Our setting down before't.* (Macbeth 5.4)

enfranchise VERB if you enfranchised something you set it free ❑ *Do this or this;/Take in that kingdom and enfranchise that;/Perform't, or else we damn thee.'* (Anthony and Cleopatra 1.1)

engage VERB to engage here means to pledge or to promise ❑ *This to be true I do engage my life* (As You Like It 5.4)

engaol VERB to lock up or put in prison ❑ *Within my mouth you have engaoled my tongue* (Richard II 1.3)

engine NOUN an engine was a plot, device or a machine ❑ *their promises, enticements, oaths, tokens, and all these engines, of lust, are not the things they go under* (All's Well That Ends Well 3.5)

englut VERB if you were engulfed you were swallowed up or eaten whole ❑ *For certainly thou art so near the gulf,/Thou needs must be englutted.* (Henry V 4.3)

enjoined ADJ enjoined describes people joined together for the same reason ❑ *Of enjoined penitents/*

There's four or five (*All's Well That Ends Well* 3.5)

entertain 1 VERB to entertain here means to welcome or receive ❏ *Approach, rich Ceres, her to entertain.* (*The Tempest* 4.1) 2 VERB to entertain in this context means to cherish, hold in high regard or to respect ❏ *and I quake,/ Lest thou a feverous life shouldst entertain/ And six or seven winters more respect/ Than a perpetual honour.* (*Measure for Measure* 3.1) 3 VERB to entertain means here to give something consideration ❏ *But entertain it,/ And though you think me poor, I am the man/ Will give thee all the world.* (*Anthony and Cleopatra* 2.7) 4 VERB to entertain here means to treat or handle ❏ *your highness is not entertained with that ceremonious affection as you were wont* (*King Lear* 1.4)

envious ADJ envious meant spiteful or vindictive ❏ *he shall appear to the envious a scholar* (*Measure for Measure* 3.2)

ere PREP ere was a common word for before ❏ *ere this I should ha' fatted all the region kites* (*Hamlet* 2.2)

err VERB to err means to go astray, to make a mistake ❏ *And as he errs, doting on Hermia's eyes* (*A Midsummer Night's Dream* 1.1)

erst ADV erst was a common word for once or before ❏ *that erst brought sweetly forth/ The freckled cowslip* (*Henry V* 5.2)

eschew VERB if you eschew something you deliberately avoid doing it ❏ *What cannot be eschewed must be embraced* (*The Merry Wives of Windsor* 5.5)

escote VERB to escote meant to pay for, support ❏ *How are they escoted?* (*Hamlet* 2.2)

estimable ADJ estimable meant appreciative ❏ *I could not with such estimable wonder over-far believe that* (*Twelfth Night* 2.1)

extenuate VERB extenuate means to lessen ❏ *Which by no means we may extenuate* (*A Midsummer Night's Dream* 1.1)

fain ADV fain was a common word meaning gladly or willingly ❏ *I would fain prove so* (*Hamlet* 2.2)

fall NOUN in a voice or music fall meant going higher and lower ❏ *and so die/ That strain again! it had a dying fall* (*Twelfth Night* 1.1)

false ADJ false was a common word for treacherous ❏ *this is counter, you false Danish dogs!* (*Hamlet* 4.5)

fare VERB fare means to get on or manage ❏ *I fare well* (*The Taming of the Shrew Introduction* 2)

feign VERB to feign was to make up, pretend or fake ❏ *It is the more like to be feigned* (*Twelfth Night* 1.5)

fie EXCLAM fie was an exclamation of disgust ❏ *Fie, that you'll say so!* (*Twelfth Night* 1.3)

figure VERB to figure was to symbolize or look like ❏ *Wings and no eyes, figure unheedy haste* (*A Midsummer Night's Dream* 1.1)

filch VERB if you filch something you steal it ❏ *With cunning hast thou filch'd my daughter's heart* (*A Midsummer Night's Dream* 1.1)

flout VERB to flout something meant to scorn it ❏ *Why will you suffer her to flout me thus?* (*A Midsummer Night's Dream* 3.2)

fond ADJ fond was a common word meaning foolish ❏ *Shall we their fond pageant see?* (*A Midsummer Night's Dream 3.2*)

footing 1 NOUN footing meant landing on shore, arrival, disembarkation ❏ *Whose footing here anticipates our thoughts/A se'nnight's speed.* (*Othello 2.1*) 2 NOUN footing also means support ❏ *there your charity would have lacked footing* (*Winter's Tale 3.3*)

forsooth ADV in truth, certainly, truly
❏ *I had rather, forsooth, go before you like a man* (*The Merry Wives of Windsor 3.2*)

forswear VERB if you forswear you lie, swear falsely or break your word ❏ *he swore a thing to me on Monday night, which he forswore on Tuesday morning* (*Much Ado About Nothing 5.1*)

freshes NOUN a fresh is a fresh water stream ❏ *He shall drink nought brine, for I'll not show him/Where the quick freshes are.* (*Tempest 3.2*)

furlong NOUN a furlong is a measure of distance. It is the equivalent on one eight of a mile ❏ *Now would I give a thousand furlongs of sea for an acre of barren ground* (*Tempest 1.1*)

gaberdine NOUN a gaberdine is a cloak ❏ *My best way is to creep under his gaberdine* (*Tempest 2.2*)

gage NOUN a gage was a challenge to duel or fight ❏ *There is my gage, Aumerle, in gage to thine* (*Richard II 4.1*)

gait NOUN your gait is your way of walking or step ❏ *I know her by her gait* (*Tempest 4.1*)

gall VERB to gall is to annoy or irritate ❏ *Let it not gall your patience, good Iago,/ That I extend my manners* (*Othello 2.1*)

gambol NOUN frolic or play ❏ *Hop in his walks, and gambol in his eyes* (*A Midsummer Night's Dream 3.1*)

gaskins NOUN gaskins is an old word for trousers ❏ *or, if both break, your gaskins fall.* (*Twelfth Night 1.5*)

gentle ADJ gentle means noble or well-born ❏ *thrice-gentle Cassio!* (*Othello 3.4*)

glass NOUN a glass was another word for a mirror ❏ *no woman's face remember/Save from my glass, mine own* (*Tempest 3.1*)

gleek VERB to gleek means to make a joke or jibe ❏ *Nay, I can gleek upon occasion* (*A Midsummer Night's Dream 3.1*)

gust NOUN gust meant taste, desire or enjoyment. We still say that if you do something with gusto you do it with enjoyment or enthusiasm ❏ *the gust he hath in quarrelling* (*Twelfth Night 1.3*)

habit NOUN habit means clothes ❏ *You know me by my habit* (*Henry V 3.6*)

heaviness NOUN heaviness means sadness or grief ❏ *So sorrow's heaviness doth heavier grow/For debt that bankrupt sleep doth sorrow owe* (*A Midsummer Night's Dream 3.2*)

heavy ADJ if you are heavy you are said to be sad or sorrowful ❏ *Away from light steals home my heavy son* (*Romeo and Juliet 1.1*)

hie VERB to hie meant to hurry ❏ *My husband hies him home* (*All Well That Ends Well 4.4*)

hollowly ADV if you did something hollowly you did it insincerely ❑ *If hollowly invert/What best is boded me to mischief!* (Tempest 3.1)

holy-water, court PHRASE if you court holy water you make empty promises, or make statements which sound good but have no real meaning ❑ *court holy-water in a dry house is better than this rain-water out o'door* (King Lear 3.2)

howsoever ADV howsoever was often used instead of however ❑ *But howsoever strange and admirable* (A Midsummer Night's Dream 5.1)

humour NOUN your humour was your mood, frame of mind or temperament ❑ *it fits my humour well* (As You Like It 3.2)

ill ADJ ill means bad ❑ *I must thank him only,/Let my remembrance suffer ill report* (Antony and Cleopatra 2.2)

indistinct ADJ inseparable or unable to see a difference ❑ *Even till we make the main and the aerial blue/An indistinct regard.* (Othello 2.1)

indulgence NOUN indulgence meant approval ❑ *As you from crimes would pardoned be,/Let your indulgence set me free* (The Tempest Epilogue)

infirmity NOUN infirmity was weakness or fraility ❑ *Be not disturbed with my infirmity* (The Tempest 4.1)

intelligence NOUN here intelligence means information ❑ *Pursue her; and for this intelligence/If I have thanks* (A Midsummer Night's Dream 1.1)

inwards NOUN inwards meant someone's internal organs ❑ *the thought whereof/Doth like a poisonous mineral gnaw my inwards* (Othello 2.1)

issue 1 NOUN the issue of a marriage are the children ❑ *To thine and Albany's issues,/Be this perpetual* (King Lear 1.1) 2 NOUN in this context issue means outcome or result ❑ *I am to pray you, not to strain my speech,/To grosser issues* (Othello)

kind NOUN kind here means situation or case ❑ *But in this kind, wanting your father's voice,/The other must be held the worthier.* (A Midsummer Night's Dream 1.1)

knave NOUN a knave was a common word for scoundrel ❑ *How absolute the knave is!* (Hamlet 5.1)

league NOUN A distance. A league was the distance a person could walk in one hour ❑ *From Athens is her house remote seven leagues* (A Midsummer Night's Dream 1.1)

lief, had as ADJ I had as lief means I should like just as much ❑ *I had as lief the town crier spoke my lines* (Hamlet 1.2)

livery NOUN livery was a costume, outfit, uniform usually worn by a servant ❑ *You can endure the livery of a nun* (A Midsummer Night's Dream 1.1)

loam NOUN loam is soil containing decayed vegetable matter and therefore good for growing crops and plants ❑ *and let him have some plaster, or some loam, or some rough-cast about him, to signify wall* (A Midsummer Night's Dream 3.1)

lusty ADJ lusty meant strong ❑ *and oared/Himself with his good arms in lusty stroke/To th' shore* (The Tempest 2.1)

maidenhead NOUN maidenhead means chastity or virginity ❏ *What I am, and what I would, are as secret as maidenhead* (*Twelfth Night 1.5*)

mark VERB mark means to note or pay attention to ❏ *Where sighs and groans,/ Are made not marked* (*Macbeth 4.3*)

marvellous ADJ very or extremely ❏ *here's a marvellous convenient place for our rehearsal* (*A Midsummer Night's Dream 3.1*)

meet ADJ right or proper ❏ *tis most meet you should* (*Macbeth 5.1*)

merely ADV completely or entirely ❏ *Love is merely a madness* (*As You Like It 3.2*)

misgraffed ADJ misgraffed is an old word for mismatched or unequal ❏ *Or else misgraffed in respect of years* (*A Midsummer Night's Dream 1.1*)

misprision NOUN a misprision meant an error or mistake ❏ *Misprision in the highest degree!* (*Twelfth Night 1.5*)

mollification NOUN mollification is appeasement or a way of preventing someone getting angry ❏ *I am to hull here a little longer. Some mollification for your giant* (*Twelfth Night 1.5*)

mouth, cold in the PHRASE a well-known saying of the time which meant to be dead ❏ *What, must our mouths be cold?* (*The Tempest 1.1*)

murmur NOUN murmur was another word for rumour or hearsay ❏ *and then 'twas fresh in murmur* (*Twelfth Night 1.2*)

murrain NOUN murrain was another word for plague, pestilence ❏ *A murrain on your monster, and the devil take your fingers!* (*The Tempest 3.2*)

neaf NOUN neaf meant fist ❏ *Give me your neaf, Monsieur Mustardseed* (*A Midsummer Night's Dream 4.1*)

nice 1 ADJ nice had a number of meanings here it means fussy or particular ❏ *An therefore, goaded with most sharp occasions,/ Which lay nice manners by, I put you to/ The use of your own virtues* (*All's Well That Ends Well 5.1*) 2 ADJ nice here means critical or delicate ❏ *We're good... To set so rich a man/ On the nice hazard of one doubtful hour?* (*Henry IV part 1*) 3 ADJ nice in this context means carefully accurate, fastidious ❏ *O relation/ Too nice and yet too true!* (*Macbeth 4.3*) 4 ADJ trivial, unimportant ❏ *Romeo .. Bid him bethink/ How nice the quarrel was* (*Romeo and Juliet 3.1*)

nonpareil NOUN if you are nonpareil you are without equal, peerless ❏ *though you were crown'd/ The nonpareil of beauty!* (*Twelfth Night 1.5*)

office NOUN office here means business or work ❏ *Speak your office* (*Twelfth Night 1.5*)

outsport VERB outsport meant to overdo ❏ *Let's teach ourselves that honorable stop,/ Not to outsport discretion.* (*Othello 2.2*)

owe VERB owe meant own, possess ❏ *Lend less than thou owest* (*King Lear 1.4*)

paragon 1 VERB to paragon was to surpass or excede ❏ *he hath achieved a maid/ That paragons description and wild fame* (*Othello 2.1*) 2 VERB to paragon could also mean to compare with ❏ *I will give thee* bloody teeth If thou with Caesar paragon again/My man of men (*Anthony and Cleopatra 1.5*)

pate NOUN pate is another word for head ❑ *Back, slave, or I will break thy pate across* (*The Comedy of Errors 2.1*)

paunch VERB to paunch someone is to stab (usually in the stomach). Paunch is still a common word for a stomach ❑ *Batter his skull, or paunch him with a stake* (*The Tempest 3.2*)

peevish ADJ if you are peevish you are irritable or easily angered ❑ *Run after that same peevish messenger* (*Twelfth Night 1.5*)

peradventure ADV perhaps or maybe ❑ *Peradventure this is not Fortune's work* (*As You Like It 1.2*)

perforce 1 ADV by force or violently ❑ *my rights and royalties,/Plucked from my arms perforce* (*Richard II 2.3*) 2 ADV necessarily ❑ *The hearts of men, they must perforce have melted* (*Richard II 5.2*)

personage NOUN personage meant your appearance ❑ *Of what personage and years is he?* (*Twelfth Night 1.5*)

pestilence NOUN pestilence was a common word for plague or disease ❑ *Methought she purg'd the air of pestilence!* (*Twelfth Night 1.1*)

physic NOUN physic was medicine or a treatment ❑ *tis a physic/That's bitter to sweet end* (*Measure for Measure 4.6*)

place NOUN place means a person's position or rank ❑ *Sons, kinsmen, thanes,/And you whose places are the nearest* (*Macbeth 1.4*)

post NOUN here a post means a messenger ❑ *there are twenty weak and wearied posts/Come from the north* (*Henry IV part II 2.4*)

pox NOUN pox was a word for any disease during which the victim had blisters on the skin. It was also a curse, a swear word ❑ *The pox of such antic, lisping, affecting phantasims* (*Romeo and Juliet 2.4*)

prate VERB to prate means to chatter ❑ *if thou prate of mountains* (*Hamlet 5.1*)

prattle VERB to prattle is to chatter or talk without purpose ❑ *I prattle out of fashion, and I dote In mine own comforts* (*Othello 2.1*)

precept NOUN a precept was an order or command ❑ *and my father's precepts I therein do forget.* (*The Tempest 3.1*)

present ADJ present here means immediate ❑ *We'll put the matter to the present push* (*Hamlet 5.1*)

prithee EXCLAM prithee is the equivalent of please or may I ask – a polite request ❑ *I prithee, and I'll pay thee bounteously* (*Twelfth Night 1.2*)

prodigal NOUN a prodigal is someone who wastes or squanders money ❑ *he's a very fool, and a prodigal* (*Twelfth Night 1.3*)

purpose NOUN purpose is used here to mean intention ❑ *understand my purposes aright* (*King Lear 1.4*)

quaff VERB quaff was a common word which meant to drink heavily or take a big drink ❑ *That quaffing and drinking will undo you* (*Twelfth Night 1.3*)

quaint 1 ADJ clever, ingenious ❑ *with a quaint device* (*The Tempest 3.3*) 2 ADJ cunning ❑ *I'll... tell quaint lies* (*Merchant of Venice 3.4*) 3 ADJ pretty, attractive ❑ *The clamorous owl, that nightly hoots and wonders/At our quaint spirit* (*A Midsummer Night's Dream 2.2*)

quoth VERB an old word which means say ❑ *'Tis dinner time.' quoth I* (*The Comedy of Errors 2.1*)

rack NOUN a rack described clouds or a cloud formation ❑ *And, like this insubstantial pageant faded,/ Leave not a rack behind* (*The Tempest 4.1*)

rail VERB to rant or swear at. It is still used occasionally today ❑ *Why do I rail on thee* (*Richard II 5.5*)

rate NOUN rate meant estimate, opinion ❑ *My son is lost, and, in my rate, she too* (*The Tempest 2.1*)

recreant NOUN recreant is an old word which means coward ❑ *Come, recreant, come, thou child* (*A Midsummer Night's Dream 3.2*)

remembrance NOUN remembrance is used here to mean memory or recollection ❑ *our remembrances of days foregone* (*All's Well That Ends Well 1.3*)

resolute ADJ firm or not going to change your mind ❑ *You are resolute, then?* (*Twelfth Night 1.5*)

revels NOUN revels means celebrations or a party ❑ *Our revels now are ended* (*The Tempest 4.1*)

rough-cast NOUN a mixture of lime and gravel (sometimes shells too) for use on an outer wall ❑ *and let him have some plaster, or some loam, or some rough-cast about him, to signify wall* (*A Midsummer Night's Dream 3.1*)

sack NOUN sack was another word for wine ❑ *My man-monster hath drowned his tongue in sack.* (*The Tempest 3.2*)

sad ADJ in this context sad means serious, grave ❑ *comes me the Prince and Claudio... in sad conference* (*Much Ado About Nothing 1.3*)

sampler NOUN a piece of embroidery, which often showed the family tree ❑ *Both on one sampler, sitting on one cushion* (*A Midsummer Night's Dream 3.2*)

saucy ADJ saucy means rude ❑ *I heard you were saucy at my gates* (*Twelfth Night 1.5*)

schooling NOUN schooling means advice ❑ *I have some private schooling for you both.* (*A Midsummer Night's Dream 1.1*)

seething ADJ seething in this case means boiling – we now use seething when we are very angry ❑ *Lovers and madmen have such seething brains* (*A Midsummer Night's Dream 5.1*)

semblative ADJ semblative means resembling or looking like ❑ *And all is semblative a woman's part.* (*Twelfth Night 1.4*)

several ADJ several here means separate or different ❑ *twenty several messengers* (*Anthony and Cleopatra 1.5*)

shrew NOUN An annoying person or someone who makes you cross ❑ *Bless you, fair shrew.* (*Twelfth Night 1.3*)

shroud VERB to shroud is to hide or shelter ❏ *I will here, shroud till the dregs of the storm be past* (*The Tempest 2.2*)

sickleman NOUN a sickleman was someone who used a sickle to harvest crops ❏ *You sunburnt sicklemen, of August weary* (*The Tempest 4.1*)

soft ADV soft here means wait a moment or stop ❏ *But, soft, what nymphs are these* (*A Midsummer Night's Dream 4.1*)

something ADV something here means somewhat or rather ❏ *Be something scanter of your maiden presence* (*Hamlet 1.3*)

sooth NOUN truly ❏ *Yes, sooth; and so do you* (*A Midsummer Night's Dream 3.2*)

spleen NOUN spleen means fury or anger ❏ *That, in a spleen, unfolds both heaven and earth* (*A Midsummer Night's Dream 1.1*)

sport NOUN sport means recreation or entertainment ❏ *I see our wars/ Will turn unto a peaceful comic sport* (*Henry VI part I 2.2*)

strain NOUN a strain is a tune or a musical phrase ❏ *and so die/ That strain again! it had a dying fall* (*Twelfth Night 1.1*)

suffer VERB in this context suffer means perish or die ❏ *but an islander that hath lately suffered by a thunderbolt.* (*The Tempest 2.2*)

suit NOUN a suit is a petition, request or proposal (marriage) ❏ *Because she will admit no kind of suit* (*Twelfth Night 1.2*)

sup VERB to sup is to have supper ❏ *Go know of Cassio where he supped tonight* (*Othello 5.1*)

surfeit NOUN a surfeit is an amount which is too large ❏ *If music be the food of love, play on;/ Give me excess of it, that, surfeiting,/ The appetite may sicken* (*Twelfth Night 1.1*)

swain NOUN a swain is a suitor or person who wants to marry ❏ *take this transformed scalp/ From off the head of this Athenian swain* (*A Midsummer Night's Dream 4.1*)

thereto ADV thereto meant also ❏ *If she be black, and thereto have a wit* (*Othello 2.1*)

throstle NOUN a throstle was a name for a song-bird ❏ *The throstle with his note so true* (*A Midsummer Night's Dream 3.1*)

tidings NOUN tidings meant news ❏ *that upon certain tidings now arrived, importing the mere perdition of the Turkish fleet* (*Othello 2.2*)

transgress VERB if you transgress you break a moral law or rule of behaviour ❏ *Virtue that transgresses is but patched with sin* (*Twelfth Night 1.5*)

troth, by my PHRASE this phrase means I swear or in truth or on my word ❏ *By my troth, Sir Toby, you must come in earlier o' nights* (*Twelfth Night 1.3*)

trumpery NOUN trumpery means things that look expensive but are worth nothing (often clothing) ❏ *The trumpery in my house, go bring it hither/ For stale catch these thieves* (*The Tempest 4.1*)

twink NOUN In the wink of an eye or no time at all ❏ *Ay, with a twink* (*The Tempest 4.1*)

undone ADJ if something or someone is undone they are ruined, destroyed, brought down ❏ *You have undone a man of fourscore three* (*The Winter's Tale 4.4*)

varlets NOUN varlets were villains or ruffians ❏ *Say again: where didst thou leave these varlets?* (*The Tempest 4.1*)

vaward NOUN the vaward is an old word for the vanguard, front part or earliest ❏ *And since we have the vaward of the day* (*A Midsummer Night's Dream 4.1*)

visage NOUN face ❏ *when Phoebe doth behold/ Her silver visage in the watery glass* (*A Midsummer Night's Dream 1.1*)

voice NOUN voice means vote ❏ *He has our voices* (*Coriolanus 2.3*)

waggish ADJ waggish means playful ❏ *As waggish boys in game themselves forswear* (*A Midsummer Night's Dream 1.1*)

wane VERB to wane is to vanish, go down or get slighter. It is most often used to describe a phase of the moon ❏ *but, O, methinks, how slow/ This old moon wanes* (*A Midsummer Night's Dream 1.1*)

want VERB to want means to lack or to be without ❏ *a beast that wants discourse of reason/ Would have mourned longer* (*Hamlet 1.2*)

warrant VERB to assure, promise, guarantee ❏ *I warrant your grace* (*As You Like It 1.2*)

welkin NOUN welkin is an old word for the sky or the heavens ❏ *The starry welkin cover thou anon/ With drooping fog as black as Acheron* (*A Midsummer Night's Dream 3.2*)

wench NOUN wench is an old word for a girl ❏ *Well demanded, wench* (*The Tempest 1.2*)

whence ADV from where ❏ *Whence came you, sir?* (*Twelfth Night 1.5*)

wherefore ADV why ❏ *Wherefore, sweetheart? what's your metaphor?* (*Twelfth Night 1.3*)

wide-chopped ADJ if you were wide-chopped you were big-mouthed ❏ *This wide-chopped rascal* (*The Tempest 1.1*)

wight NOUN wight is an old word for person or human being ❏ *She was a wight, if ever such wight were* (*Othello 2.1*)

wit NOUN wit means intelligence or wisdom ❏ *thou didst conclude hairy men plain dealers, without wit* (*The Comedy of Errors 2.2*)

wits NOUN wits mean mental sharpness ❏ *we that have good wits have much to answer for* (*As You Like It 4.1*)

wont ADJ to wont is to be in the habit of doing something regularly ❏ *When were you wont to use my sister thus?* (*The Comedy of Errors 2.2*)

wooer NOUN a wooer is a suitor, someone who is hoping to marry ❏ *and of a foolish knight that you brought in one night here to be her wooer* (*Twelfth Night 1.3*)

wot VERB wot is an old word which means know or learn ❏ *for well I wot/ Thou runnest before me* (*A Midsummer Night's Dream 3.2*)